ADIN ELIJAH
And the Medallion of Destiny

Adin Elijah and the Medallion of Destiny
Copyright © 2019 by A.V. King

This book is a work of fiction. Names, characters, businesses, organizations, places, events and incidents either are the product of the author's imagination or are used fictitiously. Any resemblance to actual persons, living or dead, events, or locales is entirely coincidental.

E-BOOK ISBN: 978-1-7324195-6-8
PRINT BOOK ISBN: 978-1-7324195-7-5

Library of Congress # 2019917767
Cover and Interior Design: Sandra Sch • www.SSWDesign.com

CEDRIC D. FISHER & COMPANY
PUBLISHERS
WWW.CEDRICDFISHER.COM

ADIN ELIJAH
And the Medallion of Destiny

A.V. KING

DEDICATION

To Elizabeth, I promised I would write this book during all those nights in the hospital and to my wife for always believing there was magic in my writing.

ACKNOWLEDGMENTS

Thanks to Mr. Cedric Fisher and his excellent publishing team for their passion, time, and professional assistance in making this book available to all the world.

CONTENTS

CHAPTER ONE

THE SON OF DESTINY

4:30 a.m. he awoke with a shocking jolt, staring at the ceiling, he laid there, his heart fluttering; the hair on the back of his neck on end. He had the same recurring dream of the lady in white again. She wasn't a nightmare or some ghastly horror – nothing of that sort, but he absolutely hated when she would touch her hand to his heart. Every time she did, he would get yanked back into the waking world no matter how deep in sleep he was. When he was younger the dream would be sporadic, but this past month he had been having it nightly. He blinked his eyes trying to get them adjusted to the darkness, the lavatory night-light flickered on-again-and-off-again, its random flashes of fluorescent illumination hooked his attention; it reminded him of the crown of radiant light she always wore in his dream. He turned his gaze to the old wall clock; the alarm would soon sound announcing a new day has come, filled with the same conventional struggles he'd grown accustomed to. He rolled over burying the side of his face in the flat pillow, forcing himself to fall back asleep; hoping to recapture the last peaceful hours of the remaining night amid the fifteen-bed dormitory.

Adin has been an orphan living at the Guardian Angel Home for Kids for twelve years now, it's the only place he has ever known. Sister Lizzie brought him here back when she was Mercy Hospital's liaison for disenfranchised children. She's cared for him ever since that tragic day at the hospital sealed his angelic fate. No one could have imagined a dreadful day like that would set into motion, a destiny of celestial

1

inheritance; linking him back to the beginning of creation. The home has been a residence for the orphaned, abused, impoverished, abandoned, and neglected children stemming from all different walks of life; its location bordered the outskirts of the quaint little city of Helotes in the great state of Texas. The home was a pleasant Victorian style mansion built of solid stone, making it unique among all the nation's orphanages. Surrounding the property was an ten-foot-tall privacy wall secluding the grounds from the outside world, at first glance the grounds would have given an impression it was more of a fortress than an orphanage except for the elaborate designs carved into the aged stone and the walls draped in climbing vines helped give it more of a historical look. A few years after Adin's arrival to the orphanage, the state ruled private orphanages would no longer provide residential assistance to new orphans in custody to the state, due to newly enacted child laws that immediately placed the unfortunate children with pre-selected government funded foster parents. The home's devoted staff care for the children until they reach their 18th birthday. Sister Lizzie – as she is still called, is the home's founder; she retired her vows shortly after the incident at Mercy Hospital. She uses an 18th century monarchical governing style overseeing the full-time affairs of the orphanage, ensuring the home remains staffed and fully funded despite the dwindling financial times.

Adin has grown from an infant to a shy adolescent while at the home, he is much shorter and skinnier than his fellow orphans. His complexion is fair with medium straight brown hair and piercing gray eyes. He is an unusually quiet boy, but he possesses an inner confidence that is captured in his eyes. He leads an uneventful but rather irritating life, he is teased and bullied at any opportunity because he can't explain who his parents are or much less where he comes from. The kids refer to him as the gray-eyed-freak, taking great pleasure in gossiping ear shot of him; ridiculing his mysterious life so loud at times he can hear their taunting during lunch or in passing. Sometimes he's had no choice but to just endure the hurtful rumors and hateful words. Despite the staff's efforts to discourage, prevent, and punish bullying it still remained a thriving viral plague within the orphanage as much as it was in the public-school systems.

August 20, 2016, a day before the anniversary of that terrible day that changed his life has come once again. This time it would be different, this day would mark the beginning of an adventure that he would have never imagined. The Saturday morning started out as usual, 7 a.m. the dormitory's alarm sounded its annoying chime. He rolled over annoyed the alarm woke him after he finally fell back into a deep sleep, the morning's sunlight filled the room made it difficult to ignore. The lady in white was still on his mind, he laid in his bed for a few more minutes reflecting back on it. He dreamt he was sitting beside her on a beach with talcum powder sand; she was talking to him, but he couldn't hear her, and he couldn't see her face. Even the sound of the waves crashing to the shore were silent. It always ended when she stood up, reaching her hand out to his heart. He gave up trying to go back to sleep, peeling the covers off of him. He figured enough time had gone by for him to grab a sink all to himself, a luxury he rarely enjoyed. He rolled out of his bed like all the other boys, dragging his feet like a zombie, slowly making his way to the lavatory to brush his teeth next to all the other boys already scrabbling to brush theirs. He managed to get a sink all to himself, he reached for the faucet handle to turn on the hot water – as he had done a million times before. Only this time no hot water came out, "Ugg," he sighed irritated; he turned the cold-water handle. Again nothing, no water flowing from either handle, he reached over to the hot-water handle once more and turned it again, still no water! Adin was fully awake and fully aggravated now, he grabbed hold of the hot-water handle for a final time, rotating it clockwise until the handle

3

snapped completely off. He stood there holding the broken stainless-steel handle in total disbelief, he was frozen, his eyes as wide as basketballs. The amount of trouble he was going to be in would be huge! *There's no way I'm strong enough to do that*, he tried to rationalize in his mind. His eyes darting quickly to the left and to the right to see if anyone had caught on to the damage he had just made. "Hurry up weirdo!" Kristof said while shoving him away from the sink knocking him into Jorge; a plump orphan with spectacular wit. Kristof being of rather low intellect, made up for it with his bullying, he was also taller than any of the other orphans and very strong for a boy his age; which made several children question his true age. "Ah great! You broke it dummy!" he sneered, pushing him again. His temper building, he then resorted to shoving Jorge out from in front of his sink to take it over. "You know Kristof, all the brushing in the world won't make those teeth and breath of yours any more pleasant to see and smell!" Jorge said pinching his nose – his insult was his only defense from being shoved. "Don't worry fatso! You and the gray-eyed-freak won't have any teeth to brush by the end of the day!" he said with a mouth full of toothpaste iced over his yellow teeth, staring menacingly into the sink mirror at Jorge and Adin's reflection. All the boys dressed for breakfast and headed to the cafeteria. Adin had his usual boring breakfast: bowl of oatmeal, two hard boiled eggs, and a glass of frosty chocolate milk. Today was Saturday, no chores, no school, and no home-work! His first order of business for the day was to check out the pond after breakfast, then who knows? He swigged the last of his chocolate milk, throwing his trash from his tray away, he headed for the main hall to get to the courtyard. The main hall was the heart of the home, where ever you wanted to go you had to first use the main hall. The courtyard was a favorite of the students, mostly because there was a huge pond filled with large koi fish and a garden with an old cherry blossom tree. What really else did the students have to do? None of

4

them had cell phones. What they did have were only books in a decent sized library, old DVDs for old tube TVs, aged ping pong tables, and AM/FM radios in the common rooms from charity donations. What they did have ample supply of was the most common outdoor sports equipment for fans of: football, baseball, basketball, and dodgeball. The dial up internet even took forever, sometimes the kids would leave it loading overnight only to find the page was still loading the next day. Sister Lizzie was negotiating with electricians and cable/internet vendors on rewiring the old mansion to get the kids plugged in to the 21st century as well as giving the staff the ability to use their cell phones – they routinely complained to her of never having any signal. The renovations were expensive, fiber-optic cable would have to be laid through and around the foundation. All the engineers that surveyed the grounds found strange underground anomalies from their ultrasound and sonar mapping reports that discouraged contract talks.

Walking through the archway, he felt the sun warm his face, the koi fishpond looked magical and seductive against the glistening rays of the morning sunlight. He knelt at the edge of the pond, wiggling his fingers playfully in the pond water while the other kids were throwing pieces of their breakfast biscuit for the fish to gobble up or maybe at him – the thought did cross his mind. Then something strange happened, the infamous Ms. Gorda, the largest orange-white koi fish in the pond started to swim to the surface from the depths, enticed by his skinny fingers; perhaps thinking them a bundle of juicy worms. Every student heard of the legendary fish, capable of swallowing biscuits the size of softballs! All the kids gathered to catch a glimpse of the infamous fish. He continued to wiggle his fingers in the pond to keep her enticed. As she swam closer, he changed his tactic by slowly dipping his fingers in and out of the water, it was working; she was now just a few feet away and hungry. She was just inches from her breakfast, she began to open her large-mouth ready to snack on his skinny fingers.

He knew he just had to wiggle his fingers in the pond one last time, his plan was to be the first one to touch the legendary fish, only his plan this would mark the second strange event of the day for him. She came just under the surface, her mouth ready to swallow his skinny finger whole when she suddenly stopped for no reason at all. The problem was Adin's finger would not go back into the water! TAP, TAP, TAP; his finger tapped against what can only be described as an invisible floor with every attempt to place his finger back in the water. The water would quickly become liquid as soon as he lifted his finger up then this invisible barrier when he tried to touch it. All the kids began to take notice of this marvelous event, but Adin didn't think it was marvelous. In fact, it scared him as he continued to desperately place his finger back in the water. His face was now growing increasingly concerned, "Come on, what's going on?" he said to himself under his breath over and over, until one of the orphans in the growing group of kids blurted out, "Adin knows magic!" another commented, "I wonder if he could walk on it?" The crowd of kids began to attract more kids. Everyone was itching to see what all the fuss was about until one kid, Charlie, decided it would be super funny to push him in the pond. Charlie squirmed his way through the mob until he came upon his target, the-gray-eyed-freak. He gave Adin just enough of a nudge to unbalance him, causing him to fall forward; he reacted like anyone else would have – he threw his arms out to catch himself. "Oops, sorry," Charlie said half-heartedly as all the kids erupted in laughter, then it was cut short into silence. THUMP! He opened his eyes, he was face to face with Ms. Gorda, his nose just inches away from her! He looked to his hands in disbelief, they were resting on top of the water! With both his arms bracing his weight, he looked upside down at the crowd behind him, their faces in awe. Charlie's voice broke the silence, "What the…!". If they had cell phones, pictures and video would have most definitely been taken. He remained still staring back at Ms.

Gorda; who looked just as dumbfounded, expecting for his body to plunge in the water at any moment. Poor, Ms. Gorda, she was trying to peck at his fingers from under the water, but she could not breakthrough to the surface. His mind raced trying to process what was happening when a loud voice echoed, "Whatcha doin' freak!'. He knew this voice all too well, Kristof! "Ah, just great! This is all I need now!" he grunted. He quickly pushed himself back onto his knees and jolted up to make his escape; he was able to push pass the large crowd of kids all buzzing about what they had just witnessed until he unwittingly slammed face first right into Kristof's chest. If he hadn't been looking down as he was making his grand escape, he would have seen the bulky chest of the behemoth. Kristof effortlessly shoved him backwards, he stood as a wall of defiance with his ridiculous flat-top haircut, large upper body supported by skinny peg legs, and a sickly pale complexion. Adin stumbled back landing on his bottom, he sat there staring up at the hulking kid. His mind worked out a million escape plans trying to figure out which one would be the most successful. "Way to go freak! Looks like you need to watch where you're going! Maybe you need your eyes checked out, by my fist! Time for you to pay for your friend's little comment!" he threatened grabbing him up by his shirt collar and tie with one hand; yanking him up to his feet. He raised a clenched fist with his other hand, curling his fingers so tight his knuckles turned white. Adin squeezed his eyes shut, grit his teeth, and tensed his whole body for the impending beating he was about to receive. "FIGHT, FIGHT, FIGHT!" the other children chanted.

"Break it up! Now!" Sister Lizzie said walking up to the crowd of chanting kids. *Whew*, he thought opening one eye in the direction of her voice, he let out a grateful sigh. Kristof lowered his fist and pulled him close, growling through his teeth, "It ain't over freak!" he promised by pushing him backwards with one powerful shove just before Sister Lizzie was upon them. Kristof always made it a point to display his alpha dominance in front of the all the kids. Adin stumbled backwards into Charlie, the back of his head slamming into his nose. The kids laughed harder at Charlie now than they did at Adin. Infuriated, Charlie pushed him off back towards the bully, surprisingly it helped him regain his balance. Charlie's eyes watered and his nose throbbed in pain. "Kristof! Go find something to do, other than being a royal pain! If you wish to be a brute, there are places where brutes may spend the rest of their life, do you understand?" she said. "Yes, Sister Lizzie!" he said through his yellow teeth. "Adin, to your dorm now, where you will be out of trouble's way," she ordered. "Yes, Ma'am," he said hurrying past her trying not to make eye contact with Kristof. He didn't need to be told a second time, Sister Lizzie had a habit of always rescuing him, sometimes she was a few seconds too late but nonetheless she was there for him every single time he needed her. "Charlie!" she said, "Let's talk about how you're supposed to treat others as you would like to be treated; while you scrub all the toilets this weekend!" she said with a stern look. He didn't know she saw what he did to Adin, there was no use in arguing – her word was law! Adin followed the flagstone pathway that led back to the main hall's rear archway entrance, where he passed Jorge on the way in. As he passed through the stone archway, the sound of the choir and band practicing for the Sunday recital filled the hall with saintly voices. He had tried being part of the choir one time but found he just couldn't hold a note and he wasn't fond of the classical music the band teacher was so in love with. He was more into cinematic themed music, like the 1978 Superman movie. He paused for a sneak preview at which songs they would be performing, after the first few minutes nothing he heard pleased him, so he continued down the main hallway. The main hallway led to a dead end that split to the boys' and girls' dormitories. Just before turning into his dormitory, he stopped to admire a large painting that hung in the center of the wall. It was a painting that had hung on the wall ever since he could remember, depicting a warrior angel dressed in gold knights' armor with large outstretched wings swooping down in midair. The angel was holding two swords with gold colored lightning bolts wrapped around the blades. This painting always intrigued him, he often thought of what the artist was imagining. *Did the artist know what an angel really looked like or did the artist really believe angels existed?* He was lost in thought, when his ears caught the haunting voice of Kristof down the hall behind him. "I'm gonna beat the gray out of that freak for getting me in trouble!" he sneered. "Yeah!" a voice cheered, "Man! This is gonna be epic!" another voice boasted.

He turned quickly and ran into the dormitory, bursting through the door so fast it slammed against the wall as it was flung open. The sound of the door slamming, alerted Kristof. "You can run but you can't hide freak!" he taunted from down the hallway. He quickly glanced around looking for a place to hide and eyed the lavatory. He ran in with such blazing speed he had to reach out and grab hold of the doorway's threshold to keep from smashing into a toilet stall door. He looked around the lavatory in vain, the only exit was a stained-glass window vent, its flap propped open to let the humidity out. It was way too high but maybe he could fit through it. Underneath the vent was a rutty wooden table with three stacks of white towels in three columns. He climbed on top of the table, knocking over one of the towel columns. He strained his reach for the vent with both hands, his fingers not even close to the opening. "It's too high, I can't reach", he said to himself defeated. The dormitory door slammed open, Kristof stood in the entry with two of his minions, "Come out, come out wherever you are freak!" he taunted; stepping into the room like a lion closing in on his prey. "You to the left and you to the right, don't let him get away or you two will get the same beating as him!" he threatened his minions; pounding his fist into his palm as he barked his orders. Adin could barely see the roof's chimney terrace on the adjacent side of the mansion. *On that terrace is the safest place for me*, he thought to himself trying to stay as quiet as a mouse. The trio of terror were hunting for him, the minions looked under beds and inside wall lockers while Kristof stood guard. He wished he was taller and tinier so he could fit through the vent, he knew he was trapped, with the thought of hope fleeting away; he hopped off the table ready to meet his fate. Once his feet hit the floor, he found himself standing in the middle of the roof's chimney terrace he was just thinking about! He placed both hands on either side of his head. "What just happened?" he said to himself out loud. "How did I-what just happened? Am I going crazy?!" His headache trying to figure out the impossible, he began to pace back and forth, "First the faucet handle, then the pond, and now I'm up here! I must be going crazy!" his brain still unable to comprehend what had just happened. He knew he was safe, but he also knew if he didn't find a way back down quickly, he would be in bigger trouble and Kristof would have his day with him. He sat for hours unable to get down, no key to the terrace door. He tried calling for help but his voice won't carry all the way down to the ground for some strange reason. He figured the gusts of fluctuating wind was responsible, he also tried jumping up and down waving his arms to get someone's attention but that didn't work either. He slinked down against the terrace retaining wall knowing he was going to be in loads of trouble, worst yet how could he explain this? He rested his head on his knees, "I can't believe this is happening on the day before my birthday", he whimpered. He sat there for hours until night came, the sound of keys turning the rusty old lock and the screechy creek of the rusted hinges of the terrace door caught his attention. The dim yellow orb of a flashlight turning the corner spotlighted him, he shielded his eyes from the light, "Hi", he said in a sheepish voice is all he could say. A soft and gentle voice answered back, "Adin, my poor boy! There you are!" Sister Lizzie sighed, "How on earth did you get up here? Did Kristof do this to you?" she demanded hugging him tight. "No, Ma! I… uh…I don't quite know how I- ", she cut him off, "Enough! This will be discussed in the morning", she was in no mood to investigate as to why he was on the terrace or how he got there, the point is he was safe. "But tomorrow's my birthday", he said in mild protest hoping to delay his interrogation. She sighed again, "Perhaps we can explore the reason why you are not where you should be after your birthday I suppose. Let's go!" she stomped. Relieved his interrogation would be postponed, he gave her a big hug. "Alright, alright", she said losing her ability to stay mad at him. They both left climbing down the old roof ladder down to the narrow stairwell leading back to the third story. Locking the door behind her, he gloated, "You know, the balcony really shows you the beauty of the grounds' ', he said smiling. "Adin! Your attempt at charming your way out of this is admirable but ill advised", she warned placing the bundle of keys in her black tunic pocket. As they reached the ground floor, Sister Lizzie gave him the flashlight, "Now off to bed!" she said shooing him away with her hands. He looked at her funny, he was worried that she would not be able to move about in the dark safely. Reading the concerned look on his face, she said, "I've got eyes like a cat dearie, plus I've been walking these grounds in the dark before you were born, I know every inch of this place! How do you think I found you? I'll be fine, now off to bed now", she said again shooing him away. She gave him a quick peck on his forehead, she watched him shine the beam of light to find his way until it was almost gone, his shadow grew smaller and smaller as he navigated his way down the staircases to the second-floor landing. He turned around just before he reached the second story level, "Ma, in the boy's lavatory, I accidently broke the faucet handle, I'm really sorry," he said trying to keep his voice down. "I will generate a work order for the maintenance technician to replace it in the morning, thank you, now off to bed!" She watched him disappear from the second level to the first-floor landing then down to the main hall, she whispered to herself, "You are going to be great one day my son, I hope you know that!"

The flashlight's batteries died as soon as he got to the dormitory door, he quietly opened it, taking great care not to let it slam behind him or cause the sound of the latch unlocking to give away his presence. The moonlight's illuminance revealed the fresh wax on the tile floor giving him just enough reflective light to tiptoe between the fourteen beds full of sleeping boys. Kristof's beast-like snoring is all that can be heard helping mask any sound he might inadvertently make. He successfully snuck past all the boys to the lavatory. The lavatory light was buzzing, it was constantly going out because of the old mansion's out of date electrical wiring, so Sister Lizzie allowed candles to be used but only on an as needed basis. He found the safety lighter next to a large candle, lighting it, he stood in front of the sink with the broken faucet, staring at his reflection; recapping all the events of the day. His face painted an orange hue was all that was visible in the darkness, he loosened his tie knot and unbuttoned the first button of his shirt, lifting out his rosary-like necklace with the winged lion medallion at the end; pondering for a few moments what to make of the day's strange events. "Today has been just insane!" he whispered staring at his reflection. Still he did manage to escape a beating, chalking this day to win by all accounts, he decided it's time to go to bed and put this crazy day to rest. He tucked the medallion back in his shirt and licked the pads of his thumb and index fingers to avoid burning them, so he could put out the tiny candle flame. As soon as his fingers touched the candle flame, the small flame extinguished with a hiss. Right when he opened his fingers, the tiny flame reappeared between his thumb and index fingers! He freaked out and swiped his hand like a crazy man against his shirt as if he was swatting at hundreds of bugs, only the flame grew larger with each pass against his shirt. Soon his whole hand was engulfed in flames! He was now in complete panic mode, he grabbed the handle of the sink faucet next to him and turned it on, sticking his flaming hand underneath the cool stream of gushing water. The flame extinguished leaving a fizzling sound as a thin layer of steam rose and quickly evaporated. The lavatory light flicked on, he examined his hand, "No burns, no blistering, no pain whatsoever, nothing!" he whispered to himself. "I didn't know you sleep walk, Adin", a groggy Jorge yawned. Adin nearly jumped out of his skin knocking the candle holder off the shelf, it made a racket as it hit the floor and slide into a stall wall. "Uh, I had to use the toilet is all", he said startled picking up the candle holder. "Right, me too", Jorge yawned again as he opened a stall door. "Night", Jorge said behind the stall door still half asleep. "Ah, right! goodnight Jorge," he said taking this opportunity to excuse himself and tiptoed to the safety of his bed. He reached his bunk, lifting the thin white sheet under the green wool top blanket only to find a large pile of dirt. He knew it had to be Kristof! He thought about folding the sheet of dirt up and pouring it on Kristof but he remembered the words of Sister Lizzie, forgiveness is strength of heart she would always say. He pulled off the wool blanket, giving it a quick shake. He folded the four ends of the white sheet together, trapping all the dirt, then he stuffed it under his bunk. He fluffed his pillow and flopped on his mattress, feeling it sag. He laid there struggling to make sense of the day, his mind was exhausted; he had no trouble falling into a deep sleep tonight.

Sunday morning, his 12th birthday; the annoying alarm sounded as usual. He sat up, his mind wondering if yesterday was just a vivid hallucination. The usual teeth brushing commenced with Kristof pushing around some helpless boy in his usual fashion. No faucet handle breaking this time, all is normal; or so he thought. He grabbed his breakfast tray consisting of the same oatmeal, boiled eggs, and chocolate milk. "Happy Birthday Adin ", Jorge said as he passed by with his tray. "Shut up loser!" Kristof bellowed out before Adin could thank Jorge. "Thank you, Jorge," he managed to get out of his mouth. "Attention children! The choir will be performing a special service in the grand room after breakfast, all are required to attend", Ms. Laura's screechy voice electronically squealed out of the old wall speaker. He didn't look forward to his birthday being announced before the program since it was on the same day. It wasn't a matter of embarrassment; it was a matter of kids being jerks to him when the news of his birthday broke to everyone. He made sure he was the last to finish his breakfast, "Two minutes' children! Report to the grand hall immediately!" her voice squawked giving her last and final warning. He gulped down his chocolate milk and hurried over to dump the trash from his tray. He tossed his tray in the tray bin and ran out of the cafeteria to the main hall. As he passed the main hall's courtyard entrance, he noticed the door was wide open. *The door is never open like that,* he thought as he stopped to investigate. Out in the garden he saw a man standing in front of the giant cherry blossom tree. The man looked very refined, he was tall and lean, dressed in a fine gray suit, and holding a very expensive looking cane from what he could see at the doorway. The man was touching a low laying branch running his fingers gently over the leaves. His curiosity was peaked, this was one of his orphan rescue fantasies, he had always hoped that his long-lost father would find him. That was probably every orphan's rescue fantasy, to have one of their parents find them. But for him his fantasy would never be a reality, he figured this man probably worked for a charity or had something to do with donations. He figured he'd ask if he needed any help, besides it would give him a legitimate excuse for being late, saving him from having to listen to the boring choir and spare him from the usual jerks. He gathered his courage to approach him, walking along the flagstone pathway as he had a thousand times before, he felt odd for some strange reason. A sense came over him, like he knew the man or met him somehow, but he had never seen nor met a man quite like this before. Standing there he thought for sure the man would turn around, so he waited. After a few moments, he felt a little foolish just standing there behind him, he finally said, "Sir, may I help you?" The man stopped what he was doing, his head tilted over his shoulder as if he was listening to something he recognized. His heart began to race, *maybe this is my father*, he thought, as the same fantasy popped into his head again. He repeated himself louder this time, "Excuse me, Sir, did you need any help?" The man didn't move, "Hello Adin, it's good to see you again", he said turning around, the light beamed all around his silhouette like the lady in white. Adin never experienced sunlight this bright, he had to shield his eyes. Before he knew it, the man had knelt down; his face was now in full view. He had deep blue eyes, jet black shoulder length hair that was slicked back, and clean shaven. He blurted out, "Are you my-," the man spoke over him, "Guardian", he said smiling. "I mean you no harm, my name is Artorius," he said extending his hand. Adin shook his hand back with reluctance, he could tell this man was very strong from the firmness of his handshake. "Do you still have the Lion-Heart medallion?" he asked. "How do you know my name! Who are you?" he said confused, fear starting to build in him. "I left the medallion with you the night you were born. It's the key to your past, present, and future. To your destiny!" he said. Adin's fear subsided, he lifted out the necklace from inside his shirt pulling it off over his head, "You mean this?" he said handing the medallion to him. Artorius examined the medallion in his palm, "There's much to tell you Adin, I'm afraid there isn't much time", he said looking up at the sky like he was interpreting unseen omens. "There's a choice you must make, one that may change your life forever", he said placing the necklace back over his head. "Perhaps there is a more private venue we could talk", he said standing up looking around the courtyard. "The only private place, I know is on that", Adin said pointing to the roof's chimney terrace. "Trust me getting there is a whole nother story!" he said, folding his arms. "Very well Master Adin, the terrace it is!" he said with a grin. He placed his hand on Adin's shoulder, instantly they were teleported to the top of the terrace on the mansion's roof. "Woah! How did you do that? Are you some kind of telepathic government experiment from the 80's or a real-life superhero?" he said freaking out. Artorius chuckled, "How do you suppose mankind came up with those stories of beings with superhuman strength, or that can fly, or rule lightning? Do not think the idea of it all is solely under the power of their imaginations! Those beings of legend and myth, all the ones they write about or make movies about are misguided imitations of Guardians", he said. "Okay, this is a crazy and nice trick, I did it myself yesterday without even trying so if you excuse me, I've got to get going", Adin said backing away from him until he bumped into the terrace roof door. He tried jiggling the handle, hoping Sister Lizzie hadn't fully locked it all the way. "I imagine several things happened to you yesterday, they were signs. Signs that you are not like everyone else, signs that you are of a celestial origin", traces of lightning in his eyes sparked as he spoke. Adin stood there mesmerized, "What are you?" he said curious. Artorius had his attention now, "I have come to present you with the birthright your mother left you, the Guardian birthright to train at the Temple of Aurora", he said. "Wait! You knew my mother?" he said walking towards him. "Yes, I served with her in the First Knights order", he said. "She died having me", he insisted. "She was murdered on the night you were born by a Fallen.", he said resting his hands on the terrace retaining wall, a look of sadness fell upon him. "A Fallen? What are you talking about! They told me she died for having me!" he said shocked and confused. "She didn't die having you, she died protecting you from a Fallen Guardian, sent to murder you under orders from Dagon", he said. "Why would they tell me that, why would they lie!" his anger swelling to tears in his eyes. "It was decided that would be your story, to protect you from future threats, to keep you concealed until the appointed time", he said. "What do you mean!" Adin said in frustration. "You're a Nephilim! Half mortal half Guardian, the only Nephilim in all creation," he said placing his hands on his shoulders. "There's no such thing!" he asserted. "All the things that happened to you yesterday represented the four universal elements: earth, water, wind, and fire. Can you find any of those elements in anything you experienced?" he questioned. Adin thought for a moment, counting each incident on his hand, *the water was the pond, for the wind the roof, the fire was the candle*, but he couldn't figure out what the earth element was. "I can explain three of them just not the earth one", he said holding up three fingers. "The earth element would have been your very first experience, a combination of all three elements," he said. Adin thought back, "The only thing that happened to me in the morning was me breaking off the old metal faucet handle in the bathroom, but that has nothing to do with the earth", he said doubtful. "What kind of metal was it, " Artorius asked him "Stainless steel, I think", Adin said unsure. "That was it then", he said convinced. It suddenly all made sense to Adin, everything that happened to him. There was no denying what Artorius said, he had to acknowledge that everything he was raised to believe in was not all that there was out in the vastness of the universes. Then his father came to mind; where was he, what happened to him. "What about my father, do you know what happened to him?" he said with anticipation. His anticipation was cut short, he knew by the expression on Artorius' face that tragedy befell him, `Dagon," he said. His hope was stung with heartbreak, he knew his mother was gone but the thought of his father kept his hope alive all these years. He was grateful that Artorius didn't try to sugarcoat it, that he gave it to him in one simple word. His time in the orphanage with all the counselors and volunteers exposed him and the other kids to a lot of sugar-coating explanations from all the adults. He never understood why adults choose to talk to him like a kid in kid terms when everything he'd been through wasn't kid friendly at all. Adin's heart broke hearing the truth about his mother and father. "I'm sorry," Artorius said, kneeling down to face him. "So, my mom was an angel?" he said downcast with a lump in his throat. "She was more, she was a First Knight!" he said trying to lift his spirits. "She was a brave, noble, and mighty warrior! She was my friend and I miss her very much", he said lifting his chin to face him. "There's nothing for me then, no one for me", he looked away with watery eyes. "You have a temple, you have a destiny, you have a choice!" Artorius said. He quickly wiped his eyes to hide his grief before bringing his eyes back to Artorius. What he beheld was a picture of myth and legend, his eyes widened; Artorius stood in his true form: his armor outlined in a white aura, his eyes in full blaze glowed electric blue, his snow-white silver tipped wings fully outstretched blocked the sun, his cloak flapping by unsourced wind made him a symbol of strength, love, and hope. "What say you, Adin Elijah!" he said with lightning sparking in his eyes. "I chose the temple!" Adin declared. Artorius stepped towards him transforming back into the ordinary man he first met, "Shall we?" he said extending his hand. "I need to say goodbye to my ma…Sister Lizzie first and I need to pack my things before we go", he pleaded. Artorius looked down at him and smiled, "Of course, I understand, but you won't need any of your human possessions anymore after this day", he said placing his hand on his shoulder. Instantly they were teleported back in front of the cherry blossom tree, Sister Lizzie was standing there. With her beautiful smile she greeted both of them, "Well my little bear, I see you have met Lord Artorius," she said passing her fingers through his hair. "Lord?" he said, surprised giving a puzzled look to her, *how does she know him*, he thought. Grabbing hold of her hands he broke the news, "My father is never coming for me, so the only thing left for me is the temple! I've decided to go with Artor…I mean, Lord Artorius, if that's okay. Is it okay, Ma?" he said asking for her blessing. She looked down at him with loving eyes, "Of course my little bear, there are so many wonderful things for you to behold, things other children only dream about, beautiful and magical things', she said tears building in her aged eyes. "Never forget you are part of this world too, my little bear", she said fighting back her sobs. "I won't Ma!" he promised her with the biggest hug he could give. Holding him in her arms, she looked to Artorius, "Watch over him, Captain!" she said fighting back tears that began to trickle down her cheeks. Artorius nodded his head, "Go now, your destiny awaits you my son", she whispered in his ear before letting him go. "I trust the required documentation will not impede or stir curiosity in his absence?" he said helping her move past her grief to answer him. "No, dear Captain, I am not bound by the political sway of the state.", she said gathering herself. "I trust the mystery surrounding his absence will remain undisclosed to any who inquire?" he asked her the same thing again in a different way. "Yes of course my Lord, his sacred identity will be protected at all costs", she assured him. "Very well, I will send for his personal affects in three days' time, please ensure nothing is left behind!" he said. "As you wish my Lord!" she said bowing her head again. "The children will be out soon my Lord", she said to remind him. "Thank you for all you've done!" he nodded his head.

Artorius and Adin both stood in front of the cherry blossom tree, he placed his hand on Adin's shoulder. He looked over to her one final time before leaving, "You've done a lovely job with the sakura," he said, then he shifted his eyes to Adin, "And a brilliant job with him!" saying goodbye in his own way. The traditional way humans say goodbye has never been a Guardian norm, like many inhabitants of the realms, Guardians do not believe in saying goodbye. She smiled through her tears, the sounds of children whooping and hollering in the hallway echoed in the distance, alerting them only a few seconds remained until the flood of kids would swamp the courtyard. Right when the tide of children emerged, Artorius and Adin teleported; leaving behind a gentle breeze that caught her hair lifting, it slightly; blowing her tears across her cheeks. She wiped her wet cheeks with one swift motion of her soft hands before anyone could notice, "May your heart guide you, always, my little bear!" she whispered. Soon she was surrounded by groups of kids all around the garden while she struggled to contain her heartache for her little bear. "Sister Lizzie! Adin wasn't at the recital, he's unaccounted for!" Ms. Laura said tapping her clipboard with her pen. "Yes, he was finally adopted!" she said. "By who?" Ms. Laura probed. "A very well off distant relative of his", she smiled touching a low hanging branch on the tree. "Wow, that's really odd, I didn't know he had any living family!" she said; her internal suspicions' radar began to beep – she's always been a very nosy suspicious type of woman. Sister Lizzie excused herself, patting Ms. Laura on the back as she passed her on the way to the main building. "Do you need any help with his belongings or the paperwork?" Ms. Laura called out hoping for a chance to snoop into Adin's case folder. "No dear, I'll handle it, thank you!" she said walking back.

CHAPTER TWO

ERINDOL

Artorius and Adin appeared at the top of Mt. Hebron, an interconnected mountain range that surrounds the beautiful grand village of Erindol in the Valley of Igan. The village borders the cliffs of the Raquia Abyss where the caiman blue waters of the Vitae river pour out. Erindol is home to the Sidhe, Dwarcadians, and Alfarians; they all live in harmony with each other and consider themselves loyal Erindolians.

The Sidhe – commonly called Fairies or fairy, are peaceful farmers that supply the majority of the village's fresh produce, chai-teas, starbrew, fire-water, pastries, and tailoring. They appear as timeless teen youth in stature closely resembling their Terra Firmian cousins in skin tones and weight except for their trade mark pointy ears and translucent wings. The cells in their bodies are comprised of primarily organic prana that allow them to manipulate the four elements, enabling them to cast aether spells at will. Their talents for potion making makes them very popular in the healing and love arts.

The Dwarcadians – commonly referred to as Dwarves or dwarf, are naturally rambunctious, their temperamental personalities make them well suited for the rigors of mining and stone work. Their skills in stone architecture, engineering, and artistry make them highly sought after in all the realms. Dwarves are much shorter than their Terra Firmian cousins, varying closely in size and shape to their fairy neighbors. They have stocky builds with different shades of hair and skin tones.

Some have long beards and long hair like their traditional ancestors and yet others are clean shaven with short hair inspired by the popular human influence of Terra Firma. Still, nearly all dwarves have thick muscular arms, necks, and backs making them formidable combatants if angered.

The Alfarians – commonly referred to as Elven or elf, are a proud people closest in stature to Guardians and mankind. They appear in life stages equal to Guardians and mankind except when they reach adulthood, they age ten times slower than mankind and five times slower than a Guardian. They are similar in skin tone and weight with their Terra Firmian cousins. They also share the Sidhe trade mark of pointy ears. The majority of the populace employed at the temple, village shop owners, and beast caretakers are Elven. Their talents and skills in the pranical arts, metal shaping, wood working, and beast-care make them well respected among their cosmic peers in all the realms.

"Is that it?" Adin asked pointing to the Temple in the background. "Yes, it is," Artorius smiled. "Amazing! And down there?" he pointed. "This whole valley is called Igan and down there is Erindol, a village where fairies, dwarves, and elves live together. This place is beyond the borders of Terra Firma", he said. "Are you serious? Fairies, dwarves and elves really exist too!" he said eager to go to the village. "Come, we have to go down to the fora for your uniform and armor sizing as well as all the necessary supplies before the day is out", he said placing his hand on his shoulder. They arrived at the village entrance where the village life became alive with the clinging and clanging of metal work; aromas of delicious pastries, sweet perfumes, incense, and starbrew by peddlers pushing their carts in and out of the vibrant village. The entrance to Erindol was very unique, it was a huge stone mantel standing over a red Japanese style Torii. Walking through the gate, they came upon three young dwarf children playing hide and seek. One of them recognized Artorius from a picture scroll, "Are you him?" she said curious, circling around to look him over. "It is you! Captain of the First Knights!" she gasped. "And this has to be…are you him?" she asked Adin. "I…uh… I'm sorry I don't know what you mean", he said not sure what she is trying to ask him. "Is he him, my Lord?" she looked at Artorius for validation. "Perhaps, now please run along, tell Elder Valerian I am here with, The One," he said. "At once, oh great Prince of the Air!" she ran as fast as her short legs could take her, followed by her two friends. The smell of sweet aromas filled the air and Adin's nose was on hyper sense as he passed through the gates coming to the mouth of the River of Vitae. "Hey, this looks similar to a place I visited called the Riverwalk back home when the orphanage took us to visit downtown San Antonio!" he said. "Ah, Tejas!" Artorius took a moment to reminisce. "The best place on earth!" Adin said. "You will find there are many similar things here in Erindol that can be found in Terra Firma", he said. Adin was caught off guard by this, but he lost his focus due to all the fairies, dwarves, elves, and other kids like him in the market browsing, selling, and shopping. They passed by a fairy wearing a short straw hat with a red twin tail coat and a blue bow tie standing in front a shop called The Wing Locker.

"Step right up, step right up Folks!" he said with charismatic charm. "You've heard of healing potions – a small potion bottle appeared in the palm of his hand in a poof of gray smoke, and you've heard of love potions – in a poof of red smoke a second potion bottle appeared in his palm. "But!" he said pointing his finger to the sky then to the small crowd of kids. "Have you heard of study potions!" he said as a third bottle appeared in his palm in a poof of white smoke. "I know what you're thinking", he pointed to an unsuspecting boy. "No! this will not let you cheat on your tests – for some reason its frowned upon here he said out of the corner of his mouth. "This will help you stay focused reading all the blah, blah, blah scrolls", he said. He waited for a reaction from his potential buyers, "So, how many can I put you down for?" he said pulling out a folded note book and broken pencil. None of the kids took the bait and left shaking their heads. "If ya change your minds, I'll be right here!" he said hoping to make a future sale. They continued to walk passing dwarf vendors selling arrays of eloquent stone earrings. Elven shops selling custom made clothes like The Crooked Arrow. They passed by a fairy pastry shop called Munchkin' Donuts across from there was an outdoor café called Starbrew. All around he saw the villagers dressed in robes, some in cloaks, some with a mixture of robes and cloaks and different pieces of armor. Everyone was cheerful and inquisitive, sampling pastries, listening to pitches for armor mending devices, fairy artists painting portraits, kids probing over scroll satchels with fancy brass, gold, and silver toggles at the Alufuitton – a five realms shop known for expensive satchels.

On one side of the riverwalk there were fairy cart peddlers selling fairy perfumes, incense, and potions. Fairy farmers were selling different flavored colored fruits, fairy chai-tea sommeliers giving away free samples, fairy winter creamers giving away small scoops of frozen delight, and fairy firewater distillers giving out their latest flavors. On the other side were specialty shops selling scroll writing supplies, saddles, armor polish, hair parlor services, gowns, battle paint cosmetics; there was even a stable for visiting merchants to house their animals. There were temple specific shops with huge signs resembling the symbols of the temple's five orders: Thunder-Horse, Spirit-Wolf, Lion-Heart, Fire-Hawk, and Iron-Bear. Adin pointed to the Lion-Heart order, "That's just like my necklace!" he said. "That is your pre-destined order. The temple has five orders and all first years, are called 'fledglings', they are organized into their perspective orders by their medallions until they complete their training", Artorius said. "Wow, I can't believe this is real, that this is actually happening", he said with the biggest grin on his face, "There's no way anyone back home would ever believe me; I can hardly believe it myself!" he said spinning around to glance at everything. Artorius smiled, "I'm glad you approve, we have to get all your supplies before the day is out. There will be plenty of time to browse and explore everything Erindol has to offer a young fledgling such as yourself", he said. Suddenly Adin spotted something with giant wings flapping in the light blue sky coming from the temple in the far distance.

He pointed to the sky at the direction of the object, "Is it a giant bird?" he said. Artorius looked in the direction he was fixated on, "That would be Elder Valerian, the Chief Elder of the Temple. From the looks of it, that would be Lexicon with him", he said. Valerian and Lexicon flew closer into view, Adin could see that he was riding a solid white Pegasus! "Ateh!" Valerian shouted commanding Lexicon to stop, she immediately obeyed by rearing up her front legs with a final flap of her wings. She touched down gracefully on the paved cobblestone street. Valerian was dressed in a long sleeve gray mid length tunic top with a silver colored imperial design around the collar that came to the center of his chest. He wore matching gray pants with gray riding boots. His aqua-teal colored eyes were vibrant against his ebony skin. Around his shoulder was a brown leather sling attached to a scroll encased in bronze. He swung his leg over and hopped off Lexicon. "It's been a long time Lord Artorius! You must be the young Master Adin-Elijah!" he said. Adin could immediately tell he was an important authoritative and powerful figure. "Gotehyo my brother!" Artorius said extending his right arm, "Gotehyo my Brother," Valerian said back, both grasping each other's right forearms. This is the customary symbol of respect and proper greeting followed by a brief embrace among Guardians. Lexicon folded her wings back against her body, lowering her head for Adin to pet, she looked like she was straight out of a book; beautiful and elegant. "Your amazing!" he said to her as she playfully nuzzled his face. "Adin, this is Elder Valerian, the Chief Elder of the Temple. He is also a skilled and mighty warrior, he was my Elder a long time ago," Artorius said introducing him. "Pleasure to meet you Elder Valerian", Adin said extending his hand. Valerian smiled shaking his hand, "The pleasure is all mine, young Lion-Heart!" "He will take great care for you", Artorius said. "Trini informed me of your arrival, and I saw only one scroll left, knowing it could only be for you, Master Adin", he said as he unslung the scroll, handing it to him. "Thank you, Sir", he said taking hold of the scroll. "Thank you Elder, but we have much to do and little time before the temple gate opens", Artorius said. "Very right you are, I will leave you and Master Adin to it, I will see both of you at dawn's first light", he said excusing himself stepping into the stirrup. "You might want to consider staying", he said to Artorius adjusting himself into his saddle. Lexicon reared up and extended her powerful wings, she gave one giant flap and lifting herself into the air, she gave several short powerful flaps until she was well above the village. He clicked his tongue three times, "Hiyah!" she reared up into a mighty flap that propelled her like a rocket towards the temple. "Open the scroll," Artorius said. "How do I do that, there isn't a latch or anything?" Adin said checking the scroll in every which way. "To open any scroll requires certain key-words that must be spoken, depending on how vital the scroll is will depend how difficult the key-word will be. Now you must recite the name of your order in the first script, Latium, or Latin as it is spoken on Terra Firma. It will only open when the words are spoken", he said. Adin gazed at the scroll rotating it length wise just as he was instructed. "I don't know how to speak Latin", he said dismayed. Artorius chuckled, "I expected as much. Repeat after me, Leo-Cor", he said. He began to the repeat the words as best he could, "Leo-Cor." The scroll illuminated, uncapping itself; the papyrus paper unraveled into his hands. "You're gonna have to translate all of this", he said looking up at Artorius, suddenly the scroll began to read the text within it itself out loud:

'Welcome to the Temple of Aroura, young Adin Elijah. It is with the greatest honor and privilege that you are recognized and assigned to the Lion-Heart order. The Lion-Heart order is among the most distinguished orders in the Temple's history, producing some of the greatest Guardian's history as every recorded. A complete history of the Lion-Heart order can be found in the Temple's library. During your training, you will need ample supplies to reflect the following:

1. Gray temple approved tunic w/ mandarin collar – Please ensure you acquire training tunics that will match the weather. Tunics must be long sleeved in mid length configuration with the order's crest embroidered on the left breast pocket.
2. White temple approved undershirt – All undershirts must be long sleeved.
3. Gray temple approved trousers – Trousers (belt loops optional) must not be overly tight and allow enough flexibility as to not prohibit activities such as: running, climbing, kicking, aerial combatives, and horse riding. All trousers must be gray in color with a one-inch single-color stripe along the outer seam reflecting the defining color in each order's crest. Note: As of 2015, all female trainees may now wear as an option the traditional gown for classroom instruction or trousers by recognition of Elder Valerian.
4. Black temple approved gloves – Gloves must be dragonite lined, wrist or forearm length; suitable for riding, gripping, climbing, aerial combatives, and horse riding. Note: As of 2015 Kraken and hydra hides are now approved by recognition of Elder Valerian.
5. Gray temple approved cloak (Fledgling only) – Cloaks must be fitted to the proper height with a single hood and reflect the crest of the assigned order on the back.
6. Temple approved boots – All trainees must have two sets

of boots. One set with soles suitable for running, climbing, kicking, aerial combatives, and horse riding. A second set for garrison inspection and classroom instruction. All boots must be gray in color.

7. Temple approved panoplian greaves – Greaves must be fitted to cover the ankle to the knee.

8. Temple approved panoplian forearm bracers – Bracers must be fitted to cover the wrist to the elbow.

9. Hair – Each trainee is responsible for the care and style of their own hair. Note: Erindol now has a hair parlor that can create the desired look of your choosing.

10. Temple approved training uniforms – All training uniforms will reflect the defining color in each order's crest. The student's birth symbol will be embroidered on the front and back of the training top.

Please consult your Regent for any questions regarding temple uniform standard or for any other concerns you may have. Have a great year and train hard!'

The scroll finished its instruction, then rolled itself up, both end caps securing itself; it lingered in the air until Adin grabbed it. "Come, we must get your currency to obtain your temple supplies", Artorius said. "I don't have any money or even a credit card!" he said pulling out his pockets. "We have to go to Erindol Treasury to meet with Finnobar, The Stonebreaker", he said pointing to the top of a stone roof encased in the side of the Hebron mountains. "Who's Finnobar?" he asked walking alongside him. "Finnobar is the chief accountant for the village, he is master of the currency we use here. I know you are used to Terra Firmian currency of dollar bills, coins, and credit cards. Here in this realm we use the first currency, the currency of our deeds that brings forth precious gems called praxeis petres also known as deed-stones. At one time mankind used the deed-stones as currency because their deeds where honorable and true but as mankind's heart grew wicked, the value of his deeds were traded for the fruit of the land: cotton, oil, gold, silver, copper, and so on. No longer did mankind desire his deeds be honorable so his heart grew darker. That is why humans feel wonderful and happy with diamonds, rubies, emeralds because it is the virtue of love and sacrifice that radiates from the deeds that formed the gem, not the actual gem itself; after all its just a mineral", he said. Adin pondered all that he heard for a moment, but his thoughts were interrupted by a disembodied voice. "Hello, there!" Selah greeted them in her fairy light orb form. He looked around, thinking he mistakenly heard a voice, until he took notice of the orb of light buzzing in zig zag motions all around him, he heard the voice again, "Hello Sir!" "H-e-l-l-o", he said feeling quite silly talking to a buzzing light. "My Fair-Lady, perhaps your true fairy form would be more accommodating for him?" Artorius said. In a poof of gold glitter, Selah appeared in her true fairy form, she has the appearance of a young teenage girl around sixteen or seventeen years old. Her straight platinum colored hair is cut and styled in the traditional pixie cut of her ancestors that proudly revealed one of the trade mark of all fairies, pointy ears. In her hair, gleaming in the sunlight, was a golden head band attached to a large golden flower petal. She was dressed in a white Roman style dress with a golden braided belt adorned with golden leaves. Around her neck was a two-inch-thick form fitted golden choker, on both her wrists she wore thick golden bracelets. On her feet were gold colored Roman styled sandals that wrapped neatly all the way up to her knees. Her face was a marvel, he couldn't help but notice how naturally beautiful she looked with smooth skin that was painted with splashes of golden glitter. Her eyes were deep brown and warm, he had never seen such a beautiful sight. "Can it be? Lord Artorius? Oh, my is he the-" she gasped. "Yes, he is the only son of a First Knight", he said. "It's an honor to offer the Captain of the First Knights and the son of a First Knight the very best drum cake! Won't you please try a piece?" she said pulling out a freshly baked cake from her cart. Adin was still captivated by the fact he was actually with a real-life fairy with wings and all! He almost didn't notice she was holding a piece of drum cake and immediately he felt a little embarrassed. Seeing him blush, she giggled, "You honor me by trying it, I'm excited this will be your first piece of drum cake or food for that matter in our world that you will try this day", she said offering the cupcake size snack to him. "Go ahead," Artorius said. In Erindol it is only proper that whenever a stranger offers you something to eat or drink you must accept. "Thank you, Ma'am", he said taking the warm piece of drum cake. He could smell the cinnamon and brown sugar crust on top of lemon scented yellow cake. "Please call me Selah, Master Adin", she bowed, the sunlight gleaming through her translucent wings making them shimmer with vibrant colors. "So, fairies really do have wings too!" he said. She giggled again, "Yes Master Adin, we fairies are quite fond of our wings and do treasure all the compliments we are given from handsome young fledglings". "This is fantastic", he said tearing away small pieces of drum cake. His taste buds were flooded with vanilla, cinnamon, and lemon. She cooed with delight, "I'm glad you like it, Master Adin!" "Forgive me Selah, but we must be going, the treasury is our next visit before the day is out", Artorius said excusing both of them. "But of course, my Lord!" she said with a nod of her head. "It was such a pleasure meeting you Master Adin, I hope to see you again soon!" she smiled. "I would like that very much! Thank you for the cake!" he said waving goodbye. "Oh, Master Adin, you must try starbrew with my drum cake!" she managed to holler out to him, hoping he would hear her. To her joy he turned and nodded his head smiling. He and Artorius continued their trek along the cobblestone street to the treasury.

They finally arrived at the Erindol Treasury, many other students were leaving the treasury, eager to make their purchases. The treasury was built into the side of the Hebron mountains. The Hebron mountains are commonly referred to as deed-stone mountains, the front of the treasury reminded Adin of an ancient place called Petra in Terra Firma. Embedded in the triangular shaped stone sub roof's top fascia were fourteen of the largest gems he had ever seen. Each gem was trillion in shape spaced evenly all along the fascia's border. He counted as many gems as he could remember, emerald, ruby, turquoise, pearl, and sapphire. Then there were diamonds in different colors of red, blue, pink, green, purple, black, and yellow. He had never seen or read of any discovery of gems this size as well some he had never even known existed! The steps to the treasury was a gradual incline up to the entrance. The stone doors were tall, thick and heavy, reaching an amazing height of one hundred feet. They neared the top of the stone stairway, "Geez, was this place made for giants?" Adin said. As students passed by them, he could their hear low whispers, "That's Lord Artorius, Captain of The First Knights!". "He's the one that defeated Lord Dagon!". "Who is that with him?" "Rumor has it, he has never mentored anyone and would only mentor, The One". This type of passive gossip was all too familiar with Adin, he glanced up every now and then to search for any sign of expression from Artorius amid the whispers. Every time he felt Adin's stare, he would simply look down and smile. They entered the top of the stairway into a large sunlit foyer. It seemed odd to him that there were no longer any other students or villagers inside the foyer despite seeing all the village inhabitants walking in and out. He noticed the ceiling was domed shaped with a stone painted mural depicting the cosmos being illuminated by a giant sun. The doors opened revealing a cavern like room with two staircases on either side of a large stone door on the ground floor. One stairway curved to the left and one to the right that split into a 'Y' shape that wrapped all the way around the sides of the chamber. Each staircase led to seven doors with a single gem embedded in the middle of each door similar to the ones he had seen outside on the fascia. The room was empty of any patrons except for a large rectangular altar guarded by two heavily armored dwarves standing on either side of it. Both dwarves held a massive shield with a hefty golden spear. The altar had two stone Guardians kneeling on either side, their wings folded forward with the tips touching together. Artorius suddenly announced, "Finnobar, The Stonebreaker! We require an audience!" his voice echoing around the room. As soon the echo fell silent, the two dwarf guards both lifted their spears and tapped the bottom of their spears twice on the stone ground, with each tap sparks ignited. Neither dwarf spoke a word, "Finnobar will be along shortly", Artorius said. Adin couldn't help his curiosity with the altar, the angel statues caught his attention. "May I?" he asked looking up. "It is for the altar protectors to decide, if you may", he said motioning for him to ask one of them. The dwarves looked very, very intimidating. "Sir, sorry to bother you, may I look at the statues? I've never seen anything like it!" he said. Both dwarves remained silent, they spoke only with an action, they each took two steps backwards simultaneously to allow him room to gaze upon the detail of the angel statues. He could see intricate designs chiseled into different patterns in the Guardian armor, a true testament to the dwarf skills with stone. Each Guardian held a shield with a sword sheathed behind it. Both Guardian's heads were bowed in submission, their cloaks lifted and twisted in frozen stone animation. In between the winged warriors were two hand impressions chiseled in the stone, his curiosity peaked, he began to place his hands in the impressions. "Adin!" Artorius yelled grabbing him by the shoulders pulling him back, both dwarf guardians advanced; striking the ground repeatedly with the bottom of their spears as they stepped aggressively towards the altar. Adin was sure they would attack, "I'm so sorry, my apologies!" he said raising his hands in front of him for them to stop. "No need to apologize laddie, first time fledglings are always so curious; I would be remiss to admit that its very amusing at times to witness the fright!" Finnobar said from behind him. He was so focused on the dwarves that he hadn't noticed Finnobar standing directly behind him. He pulled back the hood of his cloak, revealing a plump stoic face with fiery long red hair with a matching long beard parted in the middle that was tied with two golden strings on the ends. His hands were large and muscular, as the result of hard use in mining. "My dear friend, may I present to you Master Adin!" Artorius said. "My old friend, there is no need for formal introductions, I am told the sacred scrolls speak of his unique bloodline, it is my absolute honor to meet you Master Adin!" he said giving a formal bow; folding his left hand behind his back and his right hand in front. "Pleasure to meet you Sir!" Adin said extending his hand. "Oh, a common human greeting! How wonderful!" he chuckled, shaking his hand. "It has been too long my old friend!" he said to Artorius with welcoming arms. They both gave each other the customary forearm shake followed with the greeting embrace. "Please dear friend, you mustn't call me that! You're like a brother to me Finn!" he said. "As you are to me, brother! Now how may I be of service?" his purple cloak dragged weightlessly on the floor as he walked over to the front of the altar. Adin could see his cloak was trimmed with copper colored threading. Once he was situated in front of the altar, he requested to see Adin's necklace. "Your birthright laddie?" he said holding his hand out. Adin reached inside his shirt and pulled out his necklace for him to inspect. "Ah, Lion-Heart you are, aye? Think you have what it takes to live up to the legend of the Lion-Heart order?" he asked with a wink of his eye. Adin smiled, "I hope so!". "Do not think you will Master Adin, know you will!" he said placing the medallion back in Adin's hands cupping his hands around them. "Yes Sir!" he said placing the necklace back on. "Excellent!" he gave one celebratory clap, "Now my boy, over to the back of the altar". Adin was cautious this time, remembering what had just happened to him moments before with the dwarf guards. "Now place both of your hands in the impressions, don't be troubled my boy, nothing will hurt you", he said to reassure him. His hands still trembled, he glanced back at Artorius before he slowly placed them inside the impressions. "Now laddie just hold still, all the deeds of your heart will be weighed, measured, and judged. Your deeds will decide what treasure you have stored up for yourself!" he said stroking his long beard. The stone impressions began to glow under his hand, the light started to trace around his fingers, along the outside of his palms; steadily growing brighter and brighter. The light grew so bright that he was sure the whole room would be lit, he instinctively shut his eyes in reaction to the light. He peeked with one eye, then both, he was surprised his eyes weren't strained by the intensity of the light; in fact, no one there was shielding their eyes. He cracked a smile at his ability to manage the light, thoughts of other powers he possessed were stirred in his mind. The energy within the light began to build, he could feel his hands being lifted off the impressions. His hands began to glow, then bursts of light streamed out from his hands into fourteen arcs of light, each in a different color, shooting towards each of door's gems on the second floor. The colored arcs of light struck into each corresponding gem by color, energizing them, causing each one to brighten for a few seconds then fade to its resting state. The room returned back to its natural ambient lighting; the sound of a heavy door being unlocked echoed. "Now Master Adin, your deeds have been judged, The Collector has been summoned; he will now gather your currency. Bear in mind that your deed-stones can never be stolen or used for evil!" he said. "Yes Sir!" he said nodding. "The currency of evil is all that exists in your realm and what a pity; perhaps one day the deeds of mankind will become honorable again", he said as he pondered this hope. The sound of a giant boulder rolling away behind the center door made a deep rumbling sound, the creaking of metal hinges opening signaled The Collector was on his way. A cloaked figure the size of a dwarf appeared,

"Behold! The Collector!" he said. The Collector held a crystal chest with gold trimmed edges, the click and clank of all fourteen gem doors unlocking sounded like giant dominos falling against each other. Fourteen cloaked dwarves emerged at the threshold of each door, they stepped out in unison, all turned towards the top of the staircase. They marched in perfect concert making their way down each staircase to meet The Collector. When they reached the bottom floor, they began to form a circle, seven on the right and seven on the left with The Collector at the head. The Collector opened the chest, prompting the first dwarf to deposit his gems, followed by the second, third; until all fourteen had deposited their treasure. The gems sounded like ice being filled into a glass cup as each was dropped into the chest. Adin could see some were holding a large gem or two, while some held only a small hand full. Once each had deposited every last deed-stone, they returned back to their circular formation. All the deed-stones piled above the lip of the chest. Adin didn't think the lid would be able to close, the Collector shut the lid with no trouble, *must have been an optical illusion*, he thought. All the dwarves marched back up the stairs, walking back through each of their doors. The Collector approached the altar, "Thank you, Collector", Finnobar said. The Collector bowed in response and returned back to the middle door, locking it behind him just as the mining dwarves had done at the completion of their task. Finnobar placed the glass chest on the altar, "Now Master Adin, it is imperative that you understand how our currency works in this realm; so please allow me to explain", he said patting the chest. Adin struggled to pay attention, he was memorized by all the deed-stones in the chest, there was at least one of each of the fourteen deed-stones he had counted in various shapes and sizes. "All this is from my deeds? That can't be! I'm no one special, I haven't done anything great or saved anyone!" he said in disbelief. "The deed-stones are judged by virtues of patience, mercy, and tolerance to say the least", he said opening the chest. "You see this gem?" he said picking up a tennis ball size red diamond. "The virtue of forgiveness is represented in a red diamond, of which, this is one of the largest I have seen in a very long time!" he said with raised eyebrows. Adin couldn't help but think of all the times Kristof had mocked, threatened, or embarrassed him; but somehow, he always ended up letting go of his anger and thoughts of revenge; finding himself forgiving Kristof. Triggered by this thought, the full words of Sister Lizzie rang in his ears, *"The power of forgiveness can change the world many times over depending on the strength of one's heart"*. He never really understood what she meant by that statement but now it made complete sense. Finnobar smiled reading his face, pleased that a human boy was beginning to understand the importance of his deeds. "In our realm deed-stones are divided into two categories, shekels and argorots. Shekels are gems such as rubies, emeralds, pearls, jade, turquoise, and sapphire", he said picking up an example of each one then placing them in a small gray leather pouch with embroidered silver trim. "Argorots are only diamonds, they come in any color or size. Depending on the purchase value will depend on the whether the seller requires a shekel or agorot". "Thank you, Sir, but I will only really need enough to purchase my supplies. I don't need all this money; I mean currency. Maybe I can donate the rest", he said picking up a small yellow diamond. Finnobar chuckled, "Don't thank me my boy, all this is because of the measure of your heart, the heart is all that can be weighed, besides how will you be able to experience all that Erindol has to offer without proper currency?" he said. "True Sir, I just don't want to seem greedy", he said dropping the diamond back in the chest. "I truly understand my boy", Finnobar said patting him on the head. "My Lord, will you be making any withdrawals?" he inquired of Artorius. "No dear friend, I have all I need but much to give", he said. Finnobar gave him a puzzled look for a moment, "Here we go laddie", he said pouring the rest of the deed-stones from the chest into the leather pouch, he pulled the draw strings ends together tying them before handing the pouch to Adin. Holding the pouch, Adin knew its size couldn't possibly hold all the deed-stones that were in the chest, he examined the bag over and over wondering how its size was not proportionate to its contents. "Very well my Lord! Master Adin, it was a pleasure to meet you, train hard. You have one of the very finest Guardians I know as a mentor!" Finnobar said bowing in respect. "Yes Sir, thank you again, it was a pleasure to meet you as well!" Adin said waving goodbye. "Tomorrow you will start the journey of a lifetime, the journey to your destiny!" he shouted watching them leave. Stroking his beard, "Much to give, aye?" he said to himself recalling Artorius' cryptic words.

Walking down the long stone stairs Adin could see the busy foot traffic of all the populace again. "This place is so cool! I can't believe this is actually happening! This is actually real!" he said looking down at his pouch. "There are so many wonders in the realms. Mankind has very little understanding of dimensions or other worlds, but you will. In time you may be able to see them all", he said. "See them all! This just gets better by the minute!" Adin cooed. "Where are we headed to first?" he said ready to spend his currency. There's so many shops, cafes, and street vendors! So many interesting things for sale", he said looking around. "To the Agora, to purchase your uniforms and supplies. Afterwards we can have a nice dinner and you can rest for the night", he said. Crossing over the cobblestone foot bridge, they arrived at The Agora. "Here, one will find the finest handcrafted armor and the finest uniforms ever to be donned by a Guardian!" Artorius said. "Woah! This place is enormous!" he was awe struck at the gigantic three-story Roman styled structure with towering columns separating each story. Flying inside and out was a host of buzzing fairies carrying packages, delivering completed orders from the fairy tailors, cobblers, and armor workers to the temple. "Shall we?" Artorius said before they entered. "Yes!" Adin blurted out so loud it caught everyone's attention. Instantly his cheeks turned rosy red as the faces of his fellow students and fairy workers peered out from behind stone columns to investigate the source of the riveting yell. Artorius grinned, "Well that's certainly an attention-grabbing entrance! Is it a common practice in the earth realm?" he said. "Ah No! It's just as embarrassing over there too! You know, maybe its best if we come back, like before they close, that way I don't feel like a total loser the whole time I'm here!" Adin said feeling awkward. "Nonsense, we have a mission to fulfill but for the sake of continuity perhaps you should continue to announce 'yes' in a resounding manner everywhere we go?" he teased. "Ha-Ha, very funny, do all Guardians have a sense of humor? Because that's just the funniest thing I've ever heard!" he said under his breath. "Forgive me, the earth realm's cultural sarcasm has rubbed off on me", Artorius grinned.

As they walked up the stone stairway, hints of the rustling atmosphere inside became more evident followed by voices of passersby once again whispering, "Is that Lord Artorius, the former First Knight Captain?" "Who is that with him?" "No one has ever seen a First Knight endorse a fledgling!". "I thought The First Knights were no more but a failed legend in antiquity", one said. The weight of a thousand eyes unnerved Adin as each step he took on the blue stained stone brought him closer to the entrance of a marbled foyer. After each comment he would check to see if Artorius was affected, looking for some hint in his eyes or expression. Artorius gave no hint or expression that he was bothered at all, Adin marveled at his resiliency and confidence ignoring the comments. As a former Terra Firma Guardian, Artorius knew human children are extremely affected by their peers at that age, he knew that he had to be an example of strength. Too many kids are transformed by hurtful words, Adin would more than likely be dealing with this in the temple, so a steadfast example must be set. After all, he expected his fair share of comments as the prodigal Guardian returning to the temple. In the foyer Adin gazed upon a beautiful roman mosaic tiled floor with the inscription written in the ancient Enochian language in platinum white gold. "What does it say?" Adin said out loud. "To defend what was and the dream of what could be, my dear!" a feminine voice bellowed out. "Oh, my word! Could it be?" the voice said excited. Adin looked up to see a beautiful fairy dressed in a lavender-pink gown walking towards them. "My Lord", she said bowing before Artorius. "My Fair-Lady", he said bowing back in respect. "And you must be Master Adin-Elijah!" she said delighted. "My name is Artemis, the proprietor of this magnificent edifice", she said lifting her arms in grandeur. "Please to meet you my Fair-Lady", Adin said bowing, unsure if that was what he was supposed to do. "Oh my, are all modern humans as polite as you love?" she said charmed. "Fair-Lady Artemis is a renowned fairy in the village as well as among Guardians, she is also one of my dearest friends", Artorius said smiling. "Well, I heard you were back with someone special! I trust you are here for his uniforms", she said. "Are you ready to be fitted my boy?" she said clasping her hands, Adin nodded yes. "Both of you are coming to dinner tonight! Unless there is some distant interdimensional or cosmic battle that requires your immediate attention?" she teased Artorius with her hands on her hips. "No, My Fair-Lady for the moment all is well with all the realms", he said allured. "Well then, its settled! Since you are free from your Guardian charge at the present moment, we shall feast tonight! There is much I wish to inquire of my Lord in his absence", she said. "It would be an honor my Fair-Lady, we will not disappoint", he said. "Splendid, now come give me a hug!" she lunged for him, "We have all missed you", she whispered in his ear hugging him. "I've missed home just as much", he whispered back. Adin recognized this kind of hug, this kind of hug is the type that is special, it's the hug you give when your heart is empty and can only be filled by a special friend. Wiping forming tears from her eyes, she gathered herself, "Now, Master Adin how may I be of service?" "I needed to get my uniforms listed on this", he said handing her his scroll. "Very well, please follow me", she said. Adin looked back at Artorius for approval, Artorius nodded his head, "You are in excellent hands", he said reassuring him. This was the first time Adin would be in this new world without Artorius by his side. "Come, there is much to do before your big day tomorrow my dear! So how are you liking Erindol? This must be so much for a wee lad like you to take in all at once!" she said trying to make him feel more at ease. "It's very different but I like it", he said. "Okay my dear, first things first, we must get you properly measured for your uniform; now what order are we dearie?" He reached in his shirt collar to pull out his medallion, "Lion-Heart, Ma'am!" he said. "Oh my, a Lion-Heart! The Lion-Heart order is my favorite! But please don't let the other students know, I would feel terrible if they felt any less appreciated!" she said with a wink. Adin smiled and nodded his head in silent agreement. With three claps of her hands, she summoned three fairy fitters. Instantly in poofs of glitter three fairies appeared, "Yes Madam?" they greeted in unison. The first was dressed in a long flowing white dress with a baby-blue tunic. The second was wearing in a brown leather apron over a yellow dress. The third was wearing a red dress under a panoplian breastplate with matching forearm bracers and greaves. "This young fledgling is the chosen one of Lord Artorius, descendent of the Lion-Heart order and predecessor of a First Knight. See to it that he is prepared with great care and attention! I want him to look as noble as any Lion-Heart that has ever left these ancient walls!" she commanded. "As you wish My Lady!" all three said again in unison. "Go with them, love. There is much I must speak with Lord Artorius concerning the age. My couturiers, cordwainers, and armigers will see to all your needs!" she said.

CHAPTER THREE

THREE GOLDEN TAPE MEASURES

All three fairies introduced themselves, "It's such a pleasure to meet you, Master Adin! My name is Saria, I will be your Couturier". "Greetings Master Adin, my name is Nike, I will be your Cordwainer". "Good evening Master Adin, my name is Navi and I will be your Armiger". "It is always an honor to serve a member of the Lion-Heart order!" all three said bowing. "Thank you, I'm a bit nervous, I usually get old donated clothes where I'm from", he said. "Oh, no Master Adin! You will be suited in only the finest garments this side of the cosmos! Please follow me", Saria said. She led him through the foyer to a long hallway. Following, he could see the stone walls of the hallway had hieroglyphics of different events depicting Guardians fighting ferocious beasts throughout the realms. He slowed his pace to better watch the eye-catching battles, he came upon one scene showing a Guardian fighting a Leviathan. It came alive reenacting the theatrical moments of an ancient history that he was not familiar with. "How is it that they come alive on solid rock?" he said intrigued. "Prana, an over simplification could be described in one word that Terra Firmians call magic. Here magic is much, much more than just a forced change in reality, here it is energy that is harnessed, shaped, and commanded at levels no human being can wield. I believe in Terra Firma, wizards and witches are the appropriate terms of any absurd human being that stupidly tries their hands at the magical arts in such an archaic manner dabbling with foolish wands and ratty brooms. Have you

41

ever heard them with spells? They sound like imbeciles! And don't get me started on how they properly bugger up the simplest of potions!". She quickly caught herself, fearing she may have just insulted him. "Forgive me J, if I have offended you.", she said looking up to nowhere. "No, no, not at all. Please continue!" Adin said thinking that was weird, but really weird she apologized to someone who wasn't there. "I would love to converse more on this with you Master Adin, but we are here". He hadn't noticed that they were now at the entrance of a large room filled with a dozen fairies ushering about attending to other students. "That was a short hallway", he said certain they had only taken a few steps. "Yes, it is quite efficient", she said. Now, if you would, please stand on the discobolus", she said pointing to a floating copper disc. In his mind he didn't think it could possibly hold his weight as he cautiously stepped on. "Ah, there we are!" Saria said, with a snap of her fingers, a thin shimmery golden tape measure leapt off her shoulders as if it was alive with a conscience of its own, "Off to work you go!" she said. It swam through the air like a serpent to him, "Please Master Adin, extend your arms out to the sides". It began to measure his sleeve length from the middle of his upper back then down his right arm, then it leapt off of him back to Saria to could record the measurement on her obsidian rock tablet. "Ah, thirty-three inches, thank you!" she said scribbling the number with a firebird quill. Whenever a firebird quill is used on any object, whatever is written will be burned into it. The tape measure then wrapped itself around his chest, then leaped off again to give the measurement. This continued for Adin's neck and waist, causing brief tickling sensations that he struggled to keep in; he kept grinning and giggling each time the tape measure would give a measurement. "Okay Master Adin, all your measurements have been recorded", at that, the tape measure settled back on her shoulders to resume its slumber as if it had just finished a long day's work. "Amazing!" he said. Saria couldn't help but laugh a little at his comment.

"Now that tape measure has to be magical, right?" he said. "Yes, but it's more of an elemental enchantment", she said. "Oh", he said not really understanding what that was. "Not to worry my dear Lion-Heart, you will be all too familiar with enchantments very soon once you enter the great temple. This was a pleasure but unfortunately our time is near an end and your boot fitting is at hand. Nike will take your charge from here, good luck Master Adin!" she said bowing.

"Master Adin, pleasure to see you once more, please follow me to boot fitting", she said directing him to a second story stone staircase with a runner made of dragon hide from a forest knucker. "I wear a size seven in men's, if that helps", he said walking up the staircase. She laughed, "Master Adin, I don't believe a size seven will quite do for you here. It's a rather large boot, you'll see", she said. "Your named after the basketball shoe, right?" he said with confidence. She gave him a sideways look, "I'm afraid like the Greek god, Master Adin", she said not quite understanding what reference he was referring to. Instantly embarrassed, his cheeks grew bright red, "Oh, Master Adin, please don't feel bad, Fair-Lady Artemis once lived in ancient Greece, she suggested to my parents the name Nike. My family was once the imperial cordwainers of Mount Olympus", she said with pride. "You mean the mythical Mount Olympus", he said not believing it was real. "What you call mythology was as real as you and I at one time. Those legends faded from your history like the Greek gods and monsters of old when the Guardians expelled them", she said. "So, all of the Greek heroes and monsters were real?" he said. "Yes, but as their power grew, their hearts grew wicked and the Guardians were forced to arrest that power so that all inhabitants of Terra Firma and all the realms would be safe from tyranny". Adin's mind raced with all the books he had read about Greek mythology; he couldn't believe it was all real. "Now, beset your eyes on the masterful boot craft that has served the Guardians since the foundations of the Temple of Aurora were laid!" she said on the second story landing. Inside were fairies tirelessly working on boots: fire proofing, threading soles, shaping heels, dying leathers, and embroidering designs on exotic hides. One fairy brought a pair of boots for her to inspect. "Yes, these will do, prepare it for delivery", she said. "Here we shall find you the perfect pair of boots worthy of a Guardian! We have all manner of cloud-hoppers, turf-stompers, and wavbrogans to accommodate your time at the temple. Allow me to show you the excellent selection of hides we have for your choosing. We have Scylla, Leviathan, various dragonite, Charybdis, Chimera, Hydra, and Kraken to say the least", she said thumbing through her hide inventory. Is there any specific preference?" Hearing the inventory of hides, his stomach started to knot, it sounded like these creatures were killed for their hides; he had to ask, "Were these creatures killed just for their hides?" he said worried that his assumption was right. "Oh, heavens no! These creatures were evil! They are the defeated foes of Guardians that wreaked havoc in all the realms. All these creatures served a Dark One, The Great Deceiver, whom unleashed these creatures upon your realm long ago. Guardians were able to expel them from Terra Firma almost three thousand years ago," she said. "Some of those creatures are still talked about to this day in books and movies", he said. "I'm afraid, I really don't know you mean by movies, is it like the theater?" she said. "Kind of, like a mini theater in a box that you watch with other people that-", the more he tried to explain the more she looked at him with a puzzled look. "Never mind, I think I will go with the Leviathan hide." It was the first creature he read about from his studies. "Ah, excellent choice Master Adin! Off to work you go!" she said to her lifeless tape measure draped across her shoulders. Instantly the enchanted tape measure sluggishly lifted itself and shriveled as if it's trying to wake itself to full attention. The tape measure leapt off her shoulders coiling itself around Adin's leg like a sneaky constrictor. "That's a little too tight", he said. It loosened up a little, "That's better". Then it wrapped itself around his calf, holding its measurement to wait for his approval. "Got, it!" Nike said, it then lengthened itself alongside his knee to his ankle pausing with the exact measurement. "You sure? Last time you were one etzba off with the last fledgling!" she said teasing. The tape measure remeasured with the same measurement, "Never doubted you for a second!" she laughed. Lastly, it tried to squeeze under Adin's foot for the final measurement. "This is the oddest shoe fitting ever!" he said. The tape measure started to tap on the top his foot. "Lift your foot dearie", she said with a motion of her finger. "Oh, sorry", he said to the tape measure. "No worries, love", she said as the tape measure gave its final measurement. "That's the last measurement I needed! You see, you are a size one, a size seven looks like this", she grabbed what looked like a human size 10 boot off the shelf, the boot was almost four times as big as Adin's foot. "A size seven is definitely out of the question", he said laughing. "These boots will be like none you have ever had!" she said gratified. "I've never had new shoes before", he said ashamed. "Then it is my honor to be the first fairy to construct the very first boots for your temple training!" she said bowing. This made him feel really appreciated, knowing that someone would be taking great pride in constructing something for him that he had never had new before, he bowed back in respect, "Thank you my Fair-Lady!" he said feeling honored. "Oh, goodness! Lord Artorius certainly has picked a charmer like himself!" she said flustered, fanning herself. "Can I ask you a question?" he said. "Sure dearie". "What kind of p-r-a-n-, sorry I don't think I'm saying it right, what kind of magic did you use?" he said. "The same kind you use to help someone in need, I wouldn't worry about pronouncing anything just yet, you will become all too familiar with the terminology very soon. The temple will teach you everything you need to know about", she smiled. "Sounds like a lot, I hope I don't let anyone down!" he said.

She could sense he was feeling a bit overwhelmed, she leaned down, "Master Adin, I believe you will fair very well!". Navi arrived to escort him to the armory. "I have truly enjoyed our time together Master Adin but I'm afraid our time is now up for now". "Thank you so much for all the help and the conversation!" he said waving goodbye. "It's always a pleasure to assist a Lion-Heart!" she said waving back.

"Hello, Master Adin, pleasure to see you again. "Hello, my Fair-Lady", his formal greeting made her blush, "Thank you but Navi is perfectly fine". "What is an Armiger if I may ask?" he had never heard of the term armiger. "An armiger is an architect of armor", she said knocking on her breastplate. "Oh, like an armor bearer?" he said self-assured. "Close but not quite, I'm afraid. Will you please follow me to the armory? We must get your order in a timely manner!" she said directing him to the third story stone staircase where the armory was located. "Master Adin, how do you like Erindol?" she said making small talk as they scaled the steps. "It's amazing! I still can't believe I'm here seeing a world that up until today I would have just believed was just nonsense made up in fantasy or mythical books". "Interesting", she said stopping to turn around, "So, one book asks the reader to believe in a place they cannot see and the other book asks the reader to believe that no such place exists; except of course in one's imagination I presume? How perplexing it must be for those disenfranchised souls trapped in the middle of two ideologies!" she then turned back around to continue their journey. "I never thought of it like that, I suppose it is rather confusing", he said following closely behind her. The walls around the staircase had depictions of the cosmos in magnificent shades of purple, blue, yellow, and red with white twinkling stars. The depictions would then change into another cosmos only in green, purple, pink, and orange shades with red sparkling stars. Once at the top of the stairs he saw an impressive ordinated stage curtain. Navi waved her hand, the main valiance opened. Inside the show room were several complete suits of armor suspended in midair lining all the walls in display cases. They were organized by style, metal, and color. Some of the suits had cloaks that were flailing and flapping by an unseen wind. The midday sunlight streaming in from the arch shaped windows reflected off the armor's designs, giving them a faint glow. In the back were work stations for: armor polishing, cutting, grinding, welding, and shaping the panoplian. Adin could see in the back was a mid-size kennel for something large but he couldn't see what was in it. "It's like Halloween only, this stuff is real!" he said knocking on a chest plate. Running his fingers over the illuminated patterns in the armor was fun, like he was tracing with light. Navi waited patiently until Adin had his fill of armor browsing, allowing him to inspect each set like a seasoned shopper. After studying almost every set of armor, he ran up to her ready to place his order. "Okay, it was difficult, but I think I found the armor I want!" he said anxious. "Well Master Adin, that is good but unfortunately the scroll of reception only allows you forearm bracers and greaves", she said trying not disappoint him too much. "Yesica, Lina!" she called out to two fairies polishing and cleaning all the armor. At once Yesica and Lina reported, "Yesica, Lina this is Master Adin-Elijah; a Lionheart, son of a First Knight". Both Yesica and Lina looked on Adin in astonishment, "I have heard the legend but never thought the legend would live again!" Yesica said almost too excited to stand still. "I never thought I would service a descendent of a First Knight in all my time!" Lina said fixing her uniform. "Pleasure to meet you both, all the armor looks amazing!" he said. Both Yesica and Lina bowed together, "We are honored by your compliment Master Adin". "Now Yesica, please bring the first year's assortment of forearm bracers, Lina the greaves if you will", Navi said. Both Yesica and Lina split up to opposite sides of the room, grabbing the first year's forearm and greave selections. They emerged after a short time, each holding a wooden box lined in plush velvet with several sets of bracelets along with matching sets of strap buckles. "Master Adin, your wrists if you will", she said. He extended his arms not sure what to expect but excited for the most part. "Now close your eyes and speak the first word that comes to you". At first, he felt a little silly wondering if the word would just pop in his head or if he would actually hear a word, then he said without thought, "Riothamus!". The decorative etching of a set of bracelets and strap-buckles began to illuminate, all the pieces lifted then floated towards him. The bracelets opened and place themselves on each of his wrists followed by the strap buckles latching on to each ankle, the armor extended the length of his forearms and shins. "Duty calls!" she said to her tape measure. It vanished then appeared along his fore-arm to measure. It then burned a measuring mark in the met-al for her to cut and trim to size, it did the same for his greaves. All the measuring done, the armor positioned in proper place on his wrists and ankles, Navi instructed him to tap his medal-lion. He did as she instructed, the illuminative light dissipated marking the unification. With a single celebratory clap, the tape measure vanished again, appearing around her neck. She was pleased that he had now become one with his new armor. "Well done Master Adin! Your armor will only respond to you and to you alone. No other creature or Guardian for that mat-ter, can take that which has been commanded by you", she said pleased with a job well done. "I can't believe how easy that was! That was the quickest fitting I've had so far!" he said admiring his new purchase. "Perhaps Master Adin, the armor has been destined for you!" she said. "You think so?" he couldn't help but smile. "The armor is a unique blend of aether prana and panoplian called Achillean-steel; indestruc-tible to all manner of spells, enchantments, incantations, and any weapons other than another Guardian's. Only a Guard-ian can defeat a Guardian", she said making sure everything fit just right. "Why would a Guardian want to hurt another

Guardian?" he asked. "The Regents of the temple are better suited to answer those type of questions Master Adin, it is not my place to speak of such things", she said still examining his bracers. "The bracers will need a bit of polishing but fear not, they will be ready along with all your uniforms by dawn's first light!". He slid off the bracelets and strap-buckles, handing them to her. "Lord Artorius is awaiting you in the foyer, I shall escort you", she said. Entering the foyer, they can hear the voices of Artorius and Artemis talking and laughing amid the smell of sweet starbrew. "It has been a most pleasing experience to serve you Master Adin, I look forward to serving you again during your time at the temple in preparing all your armor needs as they arise", she said bowing. "Ah, my dear Master Adin! How were your fittings, love? I trust you were treated well and all was to your satisfaction?" Artemis said. "Yes, my Fair-Lady, everyone was very helpful and nice. Thank you for everything. Is that coffee, I smell?" he said. "My, my, you are very observable! Well then that leaves me with a story to tell you at dinner tonight", she said. "We must be going Artemis; we still have to meet with Davalin before the temple indoctrination tomorrow", Artorius said standing up. "Oh, yes indeed, you better get a move on! I don't want either of you late for dinner tonight!" she said as a hint. Artorius thanked her by taking hold of her hand and gently kissing it before departing.

"Our final destination is The Nineveh to meet with Davalin, 'Chronicler of the Five Orders'. It's imperative that you understand the history of who you are as well as the history you are now a significant part of", he said. Walking down to the riverwalk, Adin's stomach growled with all the sweet-smelling pastries, steaming starbrew, and the unmistakable fizzle of firewater. He had to ask, "Do Guardians need to eat to survive?" "No, but it's a cultural and societal normality in many realms, to include this one. It is an opportunity for a Guardian to culturally diverse one's self in the nation or society we are sworn to protect", he said. "One more question, when we first got here, we teleported, how come we just don't teleport to The Nineveh?" Adin asked. "Never forsake the journey Adin, much can be learned through the perils of a journey, besides the interdimensional journey that brought us here, would have taken us an eon walking, hence we teleported!" he said. "Duly noted", Adin said with a grateful look on his face. They passed the stables, "That reminds me", Artorius said. "Huh?" Adin responded. "An old friend I need to pick up", he said. They walked a short way more coming in view of a courtyard with statues, benches, and Jacarandas trees. There beyond the courtyard was a grand building resembling a luxurious palace with stone staircases that went out to the left and right over a massive middle door. The staircases continued back to the center meeting together at a bronze statue of a Guardian on a Pegasus. Behind the statue was a final staircase that led to a second story entrance with tall stone pillars. On the building's roof on each corner stood bronze statues of two dwarves and two fairies in battle armor. Adin gazed upon a massive building resembling a huge palace. "In those walls inhabits the history of the five orders and Erindol, much like Terra Firma's museums. Anyone may come here to learn the purpose of the five orders and honor those brave souls; dwarf, elf, fairy, and Guardian alike that gave their lives; in The Great Fall". A sense of deep pride permeated the atmosphere, as he felt drawn to this monumental place. There were students like him getting their portrait painted with the Nineveh in the background, others examining the detailed statues on the grounds, groups of others reading giant bronze scrolls. His focus was inside this captivating building, his mind raced with infinite possibilities of the ancient knowledge he would learn. Each step his heart pounded with the excitement of uncertainty mixed with curiosity. As he and Artorius walked past several statues, again comments carried by different voices were heard. "Is that the great 'Noble Wolf?" "Who is that young boy?" "Not anyone from around here!". Suddenly a loud overbearing deriding voice yelled out, "Is this the legend-ary, Noble Wolf'? Has he returned with a pup?" Adin paused in mid-step as if he was caught doing something wrong, Arto-rius detected his mounting uneasiness overtaking his excite-ment, he tried to put him at ease, "Pay no attention but I must apologize. Much of the attention that you have encountered, which I sense brings you much anxiety; is because of me I'm afraid. I have been away from the temple for a long time and my absence has left many with suspicion", he said. "I'm used to it, I guess it's just a little different than what I've dealt with back home. I pretty much knew everyone that talked about me but here among all these strangers it's a little weird", Adin said. "The Noble Wolf of the Lupus Spiritus Order, what an exciting moment this is!" the voice hollered out in the deep scornful tone now. "With a foolish gloating voice like that, you must be Davalin!" Artorius said annoyed refusing to turn around. Adin could see Davalin standing a few feet behind him, dressed in a long blue robe that dragged on the ground. His hair was long and gray braided on each side with a well-manicured gray beard. "Right you are my Lord, you have been astray for such a time, I've contemplated placing a statue of you here! That would have drawn a great many to gaze upon a prodigal Guardian", he said. "Pity you didn't, I would have been most bereaved to have caused such a colossal blow to your wily ambition", he said with tempered calm. "Then may I suggest a duel of shield-spell-sword?" Davalin chal-lenged. "I accept but I must caution you, the Nineveh will need a new Chronicler after this duel!" Artorius said turning to meet Davalin face to face. "And if I win?" Davalin said. "You may record that you have beaten The Noble Wolf in a duel of shield-spell-sword for as long as The Five Orders stand!" he proclaimed. Adin was panicked, his heart was pounding, was he was about to witness a duel that was to the death! Artorius and Davalin faced each other, neither break-ing eye contact. A crowd began to form increasing the tension in the atmosphere. Both extended their right hands and ball up their fist as they assume fighting stances. "Stand back!" Artorius ordered him. He didn't know what to make of the situation, he had seen many school-yard fights but this was different, this was a duel between two beings that some people didn't believe existed. Davalin counted off, "On the count of three: One...two...three", instantly Artorius turned up his palm, making a chopping gesture with the other. Davalin up-turned his palm and slammed it with his other hand that was balled up into a fist. "Looks like spell covers shield! Oh, Chronicler of The Five Orders!" Artorius said cracking a smile. Davalin erupted in a roar of laughter throwing up both arms, both he and Artorius greeted each other with the Guardian greeting. "I've got to stop using shield!" he said shaking his head. "Why do you think I never use the shield!" Artorius said. Adin shook his head in disbelief, "Did you two just play rock-paper-scissors?" they both looked at him like he said something out of this world. "No, it's shield-spell-sword, everyone knows that!" Artorius said. "My friend, meet Adin Elijah, he is-", before Artorius could finish introducing Adin, Davalin finished his sentence, "A Lion-Heart, only descendent of a First Knight!" he said enthralled. "How did you know?" Adin said. "By your eyes my dear boy, every Guardian has different colored eyes. You have gray eyes; the color gray represents an in between. You were born of two worlds, of two hearts; one of a First Knight and one of a mortal. How fascinating to possess all the powers of a Guardian fueled by the fragility of a human heart, to bridge all the realms! You have the look of your mother", he said looking at Adin as if he was some kind of celebrity. "You and your superstitions, Davalin!" Artorius said. "Please come inside". Davalin led ahead of them, stopping in front of the Nineveh's great granite doors. Adin marveled at the granite door's massive size and weight as they opened creating a grinding crunching sound. Entering the structure was exhilarating, he felt he was getting closer to knowing himself. Walking through the threshold he couldn't help but think what the temple would be like. "To your right is the food court, where you will find the realm's most exotic starbrew and pastries", Davalin said. Adin could see several students, fairies, dwarves, and elves seated eating, drinking, sharing each other's company. "To your left is the Relics shop, where all manner of relics can be found for purchase, but you mustn't ever take any of the relics outside of this realm! You see, Master Adin, the Nineveh is a living museum of sorts, ever changing with time as creation changes. It was built to chronicle the history of the Guardians and Erindolians", he said with great pride. "This is a fascinating museum Sir!" Adin said walking the halls, glimpsing at every artifact, stone statues of mythical monsters, and pieces of ancient weaponry. The walls were filled with what could only be described as holographic scenes of guardians in ancient battles, until he came to a large room with five halls. He gasped as he saw each arch shaped hall adorned with each of the Five Order's Crests above the archways. "Ah, this is the Warrior's Grand Room! The Warrior's Grand Room holds each order's unique origins", Davalin said. Adin stood in front of the Lion-Heart crest; the winged Panthera, became alive leaping from the crest with a thunderous roar. The Thunder-horse symbol became a charging horned Pegacorn. It reared up giving a loud neigh before vanishing. The Fire-Hawk became a soaring Haast, it gave an echoing cackle as it burst into flames flying straight at him, then circled back to its crest above the archway. For the Spirit-Wolf, a haunting howl followed by a dense mist of fog seeped from the crest; two blue luminescent wolf eyes glared. The fog parted unveiling an Amarok that sprang with outstretched wings before dissipating. The Iron-Bear symbol jumped out as a huge Arctodus bear with wings charging forward, then suddenly stopping to stand on its two hind legs; towering in height it gave a mighty growl. The presentations left Adin supremely impressed. "What's this?" Adin pointed to a stone scroll in the middle of the Warrior's Grand Room. "This is a replica of the Sovereign's riddle from the ancient of times. Young fledglings such as yourself come here in hopes of solving the riddle. Legend has it that whoever can solve the riddle will be given The Sword of Power, isn't that right my Lord?" he said to Artorius. "Again, with the superstitions, Davalin? An honorable Dwarf such as yourself shouldn't repeat such foolish things", he said. "Pay no attention to him Master Adin, I must tell you rumor that your mother solved the riddle proved deadly, that tragically was not the case as you may well know my poor boy. My sincere condolences.", he said with heartache. "Thank you, so no one has ever solved it?" Adin said focused on the inscribed words to halt the forming lump in his throat upon being reminded of his mother's death. The riddle was etched into a cobalt skystone, the words were inscribed within the tablet magnified by the crystal stone face, he was able to read its riddle aloud:

'Before the dawn of time I was there, alighting the realms from the air
The blood of kings I have inside, endowing a power from which all evil hides!
Tragedy befalls the path I stride; the sacrifice great, only one shall survive!
Whom among you will hearten this burden only to suffer it deep inside?
None have prevailed, but few have tried!
Will you fail? Let death decide!'

"Time has escaped us; we are due shortly for our dinner appointment with Artemis." Artorius said reminding Adin. "Trust that you will have all the time to explore the Five Orders both in the temple and here at the Nineveh. Davalin, please excuse us but we must be going. I promised Fair-Lady Artemis we would have dinner with her tonight before Adin's temple indoctrination", he said. "But of course, my Lord, it was a pleasure meeting you Master Adin; I do look forward to seeing you during your liberty from the temple", he said shaking Adin's hand. "The pleasure is mine, Sir, thank you for the intriguing tour!" he said delighted. Artorius grabbed hold of Adin's shoulder, "Shall we?" Adin nodded his head, instantly they vanished with a loud flap of unseen wings.

It was dark now, they appeared in the front of the Agora, it was illuminated by blue flamed torches crackling from large pillars around the building, creating a very different ambiance about the building. "It doesn't look like anyone is home", Adin said. "Up here love!" Artemis hollered from the roof top, waving her arm. "We shall be there presently!" Artorius answered back. "Before we go up, I know you have questions lingering in the back of your mind and today's events have been very distracting for you, I'm sure. I wanted to wait until you have the opportunity to rest and ask your questions with my undivided attention, I hope you understand?" he said. "It's no problem at all", Adin said understanding. Artorius grabbed hold of him once more by his shoulder and instantly they both appeared on the roof top of the Agora where Artemis had a round feasting table being set with various pastries. "I excused the help this evening, I hope neither you mind terribly", she said welcoming them with a hug and a quick kiss on their cheeks. Her blue gown sparkling in soft vibrant shimmers reflected by the blue flame torches gave her an angelic look as the embers crackled and popped in the night air. "No, not at all", Artorius answered for both of them. "I hope you two are hungry, I've sent for only the best! We have alfajor, aloo pie, blisterwell pudding, chorle cake, mooncake, and well; every pastry and best starbrew I could find in the bazaar, please help yourselves!" she said inviting them to sit. Adin could smell each sweet, mouth-watering scent mixing together. Three chairs suddenly pulled out from the table unassisted, this took him by surprise. "It's okay dearie, please make yourself comfortable", she said. All three took their seats, porcelain plates and cups floated towards them, hovering just in front of each of them. Adin was baffled, he was expecting the plate to float gently down in front of him so he could fill his plate. "Just say what you want on your plate, dearie and it will be so", she said stirring her chai-tea. "I'm afraid I'm not too familiar with the food here", he said bashful. "Not to worry, just fixate your mind on a flavor or pastry you wish to have; perhaps vanilla or chocolate pie or cake", she said. He thought for a second, there were lots of flavors he liked, he thought he'd play it safe and thought of vanilla and cinnamon, instantly a mooncake lifted off a pile behind the aloo pies and glided over to his plate. The mooncake settled down on the plate, the plate then sat itself down in front of him. "That's not something you see every day!" he said looking at Artorius and Artemis. Amused, they couldn't help but laugh before taking a sip of their chai-tea. He filled himself to his heart's content, washing it all down with the best starbrew. Still sipping on his chai-tea, Artorius excused himself from the table, "When you are finished please join me at the gazebo", he said. He nodded while finishing the last of his starbrew. He was getting his questions ready about his mother, throughout the whole day he had been given hints about her, about magic, about Guardian history but he had not heard anything from the one person who was with her. His chair slid out, instinctively sensing his desire to stand up, he wiped his mouth and took a deep breath.

He found Artorius and Artemis lounging in the front of a fairy statue water fountain inside the gazebo just as Artorius said they would be. "Please, Master Adin, join us", she said, waving her hand, a third lounging chair slid over to him. He sat down, in front of him was the most spectacular view of the temple. "Wow, so that's it!" he said sitting down. "Yes love, it is the best part of my day, to sit here and gaze upon the majestic beauty of the temple", she glowed. Flying in the night sky he could see winged horses patrolling the perimeter; flapping their wings, neighing, gliding in and out of puffy clouds mixed with soft hues of green, blue, and red. At this moment, he felt it was time to ask the questions that have been burning in his mind and heart since he could remember. "I would like to talk about the questions I have", he said. "My Fair-Lady, would you be so kind to excuse us?" Artorius asked standing up, he reached out his hand to help Artemis up like a proper gentleman. "Yes of course, please excuse me, I must see to the crockery", she said excusing herself from the duo.

Under the hue of blue flame light, Artorius looked different, "Your father's name was Arthur Elijah, he was a law enforcer; sworn to protect the people. Your mother's Guardian name was Tessla, which means 'Harmony in Balance'. She fought in The Great Fall, forced to fight against her brothers and sisters; this troubled her heart greatly for the years to come. We were hunting the last of the zoon on Terra Firma, when she met your father. She fell deeply in love with him and in doing so; gave up her wings – her oath. She severed all ties from her Guardian life, she concealed her true identity using warding spells; renaming herself Mary. This was necessary to ensure that she and your father would be safe from any harm. You see, once a Guardian gives up their wings, they become human-like, they become what we call a Ronin; which means 'one who is in service to no one'. Once a Ronin, one stands greatly to be stalked by all the evil that was once fought. One becomes vulnerable to everything mankind suffers; sickness, hunger, and death", he said. "And love", Adin whispered to himself. "Yes, especially love", he agreed. The full impact of his mother's death became disturbingly foreign to him. He had grieved for his mother many times during his life, but this pain was different, he could not understand the meaning of it. Feeling a growing lump in his throat became difficult to manage. "There is no greater power than love", he said sensing his mounting sorrow. "You mentioned earlier my mother was the last of the First Knights", he said hoping the question would force a change in mood. "Your mother was a strong, gifted warrior. She, Dagon, Kairah, Sidion, and I all served together in the First Knights. Only the best Guardian from each order was chosen to be a First Knight. The First Knights were an answer birthed out of necessity to combat the ever-growing power of the zoon that was secretly unleashed in the realms by Dagon before his treason was discovered by your mother. We all were the closest of friends, family really; until Dagon betrayed himself", he said dispirited. Now Adin could sense in his voice an old pain he had shut away, breaking through. "If you were all friends, family; then why did he murder my mother!" Adin said with anger swelling in his eyes. "Dagon was seduced by the corruptive knowledge of the second in creation. In his madness the rumor of her solving the riddle gave him absolution, she was hunted for The Power. The Power, endows its vessel with omnificence that we call, The Axion, the power of limitless creation – 'the soul of all the worlds'. It was said she constrained it and locked it away in a medallion…a medallion Dagon lusted for. She had surrendered her medallions when she gave up her wings. Dagon lost in his lust for power believed she constrained it within herself. When I got to you that night, I failed in protecting her", his words were heavy in sorrow. "He murdered my mother for nothing!" Adin said with fury. "Forgive me", he said his eyes filled with distraught. The magical realm he found himself in didn't seem not so magical anymore. "You have a birthright Adin. A right to choose your destiny, a right to become something greater than yourself!" Artorius said standing to his feet. "You see that!" he said pointing to the Temple, "That is destiny calling you, beckoning you, pleading with you to take your place among the ranks of a Guardian! To behold the power and abilities that only mortals dream about!" he said with vigor. These words lifted Adin's spirit and strengthened his heart, "I won't let you down mother, I won't let you down father!" he professed in his heart. "I'm glad you were there for us that night!" Adin said. "Forgive the intrusion my Lord but will you and Master Adin be overnight guests?" Artemis said returning from the crockery. "Yes, my Fair-Lady, there is a matter I must see to before the dawn's light. Go with Artemis, she will escort you to your quarters. I will see you in the morning, sleep well",

A.V. King

he said vanishing with a flap of his wings. "Come now dear, you must be exhausted from interdimensional travel", Artemis said leading him down to the guest quarters. "You know this kind of feels like back home, you see I was stuck on the chimney terrace this one time and Sister Lizzie had to come get me late at night. The staircase we had to walk down was kind of like this to, it was dark, but not this kind of dark", he said his voice drowning slowly out as they descended down the stone staircase. "Oh my, you have much experience on roof tops do you", she said chortled.

59

CHAPTER FOUR

THE TEMPLE AURORA

The sweet smell of cinnamon starbrew woke Adin, the bright soft glow of sunlight gently warmed his cheeks. "Good Morning Dear!" Artemis greeted. "Morning Ma'am, I mean, my Fair-Lady", he replied. He was still groggy, stammering to sit up, covering his mouth to mask his morning breath. "I believe you will find that some of the aliments in Terra Firma do not affect you here, Master Adin", she said to ease his morning breath anxiety. "Oh!" he said. Well up we go dear! Lord Artorius is waiting for you on the rooftop. Here is your first day's uniform", she said presenting a mahogany valet stand. His temple uniform was pressed, hung neatly, with his Leviathan hide boots shined to a mirror polish. He rubbed his eyes and jumped out of bed, dashing over to the valet stand. On the left side of the valet stand sat a plush velvet pillow with both of his forearm bracelets, on the right side was his greaves strap buckles. His uniform matched his eyes as he examined it. "I trust you will find the fit to your liking", she said smiling with pride, "I'll leave you to it love". "Thank you so much for everything!" he said. "It was an absolute pleasure love!" she bowed with a smile. "I will see you on the rooftop!" she said. Adin checked his morning breath just in case, "Nope, nothing, just as she said". This was a life changing moment for him; first he had brand-new custom-tailored clothes for his first day and second he was finally going to the temple that he has heard so much about. He put on his uniform, it fit perfect just as Artemis said it would. On his outer jacket, on the left side, the embroidered Lion-Heart order crest left him with a tremendous sense of pride. The gold and white crest had a sheen that would gleam with deep crimson and gold depending on the amount of sunlight cast upon it. He draped his gray cloak over himself, affixing it on his right side, admiring his Lion-Heart crest stitched on the back in the mirror. There's was no guessing which order he belonged to from afar, his reflection in his boots was uncanny; they fit and felt as if he was wearing nothing at all. He placed both his bracelets on, his greaves, and finally his medallion. Fully dressed, he had a new feeling of purpose and value radiating deep inside him. He stepped in front of the mirror pleased at his new look, he thought of his forearm bracers, "Riothamus!" he commanded. His forearm bracelets and greave strap-buckles reconstructed into their battle form, stretching out along his forearms and shins. "Too Cool! But this bed hair!" he said taking notice in the mirror. He tried patting it down on either side but his hair just wasn't cooperating. "Oh well", he said giving up, "Riothamus", his forearm and greave armor returned to their dormant disguised state of decorative bracelets and strap buckles. He rushed to the roof top to meet Artorius.

The sun was bright, the blue-teal sky was splashed with streaks of red against the back drop of the temple, it looked like it was taken right out of a page of a fantasy book. The Moirai bridge, outstretched, came into radiant view from the temple to the cliffs of the Raquia Abyss. The bridge's stone pathway laid outstretched in bleached white limestone. The pillars connecting the bridge had large angelic statues standing at attention with their swords drawn on either side' creating a sword arch. The beats of a drum sounded long and deep, "Ah, there you are! How handsome you look Master Adin! But we must do something about that hair!" Artemis said paying her complements; with a clap of her hands a trio of fairy servants appeared wearing barber aprons with scissors, combs, bottles, and trinkets. "Yes, my Fair-Lady?" they greeted. "We must do something about Master Adin's hair! We have but a few moments, time is of the essence!". The fairy servants convened for a brief moment and began their work, they moved so fast that Adin could not keep track of their physical movements. Once finished, they beckoned Artemis for approval, presenting Adin. "Now that's more like it! He looks proper now!" she said pinching his cheek. The fairy trio bowed and vanished. "What's the drumming for?" Adin said. "It's the drum ceremony just before the trumpet reception", she said looking to the bridge. "And Artorius?" he wondered. "I am here Adin", Artorius answered on top of a white horse. "Woah!" Adin exclaimed. Artorius dismounted his horse, "This is Ajax!". "Hello Ajax!" Adin said stroking his mane. "Ajax was my steed when I was at the temple, he's yours now!" he said handing him the reigns. "No way! For real? How much do I owe you? What will be an acceptable payment for him?". "No payment is necessary, he's my gift to you! He's been here alone on the temple grounds, its time he goes with a young Guardian that can give him new purpose. I must warn you, he is a hot blood, so choose your rides wisely!" Artorius said helping Adin into the saddle. "Absolutely! Thank you so much! I don't know what to say!". "Swear you will take better care of him than I have and swear that you will never leave him as I have", Artorius said. "I won't, I swear, as a future Guardian; I swear to take good care of him.", Adin declared. "Come its time now. My Fair-Lady, it has been a pleasure! Thank you for all the kind hospitality and friendship!" Artorius said kissing her hand. "My Lord, it is always a pleasure to see you and to exercise my fondness of a dear friend. I'm glad to have met my new-found friend", Artemis said smiling. "Thank you very much my Fair-Lady!" Adin beamed holding on to the reigns. She smiled and waved her good-bye. "Ready?" Artorius said to him. "Wait! What? You're going to teleport the horse too?" Adin stammered holding tight to the reigns.

The young Lion-Heart found himself at the base of

the Moirai Bridge surrounded by all the temple students on horses waiting to enter. All 199 students were aligned in a perfect column and rank; except for Adin. Every new student glanced in all directions, searching around at the sea of youthful faces, some searching for friends. Some were anxious, some were excited, yet others didn't know what to think or what lay ahead. Adin was the last to arrive at the back of the formation, all the attention now fell on him, "Are you okay?" Artorius wondered while gathering together Ajax's reins. "I don't quite know, everyone is staring at me", Adin said out of the corner of his mouth, looking around at his future order mates. "Don't let fear lead you, it is fear that changes the direction of one's journey. It is fear that corrupts the heart!" Artorius stressed patting Ajax. A trumpet blew strong and loud from the temple, "Its time?" Artorius said. "Here goes", Adin said building his courage. Artorius walked Ajax by his reigns as the formation started up the Moirai Bridge. "Where are all their Guardians?" Adin said looking around. "They don't have any, all their parents were Guardians that gave up their wings for love, passing their Guardian powers to their children". He felt really out of place now, he was clearly the only one with a Guardian, one that was not even his parent, still; he felt grateful that Artorius was there. "I'm glad you're here, I don't think I could have done this without your help but am I interfering with your Guardian duties?" he inquired. "Not at all, I am on a different path", Artorius said. As soon as Ajax broke the threshold of the Moirai Bridge, the bridge began to fall away behind them, Adin could hear the stone beginning to shift and crack as pieces fell. This startled him, he gave a look of distress to Artorius, "Fear not, the bridge has been enchanted to fall away as a defense measure against any whom attempt to access the temple without permission after we have safely passed", he said reassuring him. "That's comforting", he said with a sigh. The hoof beats in tandem with the rhythmic beating of the drums sounded like something out of a Lord of the Rings movie. He peered to his left and right as they passed by the giant statues of winged Guardians dressed in full armor with stone swords pointed overhead forming an exquisite sword arch that looked magnificent. Interestingly enough, there were no shadows from any of the statues on the bridge, no matter how much sunlight shone between each massive stone figure. Looking out beyond the bridge was the colossal abyss that protected the temple. The layer of puffy clouds that looked like an ocean of white as far as the eye could see. Adin thought they must be at an impossible height, a look of dread washed over his face. "Control your fear, don't let your heart become infected with it", Artorius asserted seeing the look on his face. "I can see your first obstacle will not be your studies or the games, but overcoming the restrictions in your mind. You have been conditioned to certain limits in Terra Firma, this programming has confined your true potential and abilities", Artorius surmised. "I'm sorry, it's just very difficult to adjust. Only yesterday, I was in the garden back home, I was raised that none of this existed and angels; sorry –Guardians are only in heaven", he confided. "I understand, would it strike you odd that I feel the same way of your earth realm at times?" Artorius asked. "I don't know why, for me; back home was only tolerable because of mother. You know, someone that gives you the strength to endure the difficult?" Adin said reflecting. "Yes, I most certainly know what you speak of", he agreed. The temple now in full view in all its splendor, was the most captivating sight he had ever laid eyes on. The temple with its silver-plated roof, glimmered profoundly, shimmering with the piercing rays of the sun. "The temple's illumination is charged by the sun; you see it must remain a beacon in the darkest of times as an eternal symbol that Guardians will never ease in their charge to protect the realms". They reached closer to the temple's entrance, a flash of fiery purple flame struck just in front of the great stone wall like lightning, it stood swirling as a pillar in front of the temple's thick stone archway.

Every fledging and their horse halted their advance, the crackling sounds of the flame lingered for a few moments before extinguishing into a purple fog-like mist. The purple haze of fog hung over the entrance to the temple, until a winged silhouette became visible. "*I see you still know how to make an entrance, Alina!*" Artorius thought to himself. "What is that", Adin muttered, tightening his grip on the reigns. "That, is Lord Alina; the Regent of the Lion-Heart Order!" he answered. In a powerful yet soothing voice, the winged silhouette exclaimed, "Do not be afraid young fledglings, my name is Alina, Regent of the Lion-Heart Order!". The purple haze completely disappeared following her introduction, bringing her in full view of every fledgling. She was a sight to behold, with her white silver tipped wings splashed with hues of various purple shades. Her two-toned long hair was styled with one high-arched braid down each side of her head, the tints of purple contrasting against her purple hued eyes. Her fair skin wrapped her sleek frame giving her a luminescent appearance against her split sleeve cutaway surcoat over a purple cotehardie. Her shoulder sword scabbard sheathed her ivory handled roman style gladius. Each of the female fledglings gasped at her in awe of her silent yet commanding presence. Alina scanned the sea of young faces, every fledgling matching in uniform except for their assigned order. Alina gave her silent approval of all the fledglings that stood before her, until she caught sight of Artorius and Adin in the back of the formation. Alina folded her wings, "Make way for Lord Artorius!" she commanded. Immediately, all the fledglings parted in the middle, allowing Artorius to guide Ajax and Adin directly to her. Adin spied a girl with a feather in her hair staring at him as he moved to the front of the formation. "It has been some time Artorius, I see you have brought the son of a First Knight to our great temple! Well shall see if he is up to the test", she mused. "I'm sure he will fair very well Alina, he has the strength of his mother", he praised. "Very well, my Lord", Alina bowed her head, concluding their brief exchange. "Follow me!" she ordered everyone. At once all the fledglings reassembled themselves back in formation, only this time Adin and Ajax would be the head. The grinding of heavy stone trembled, a stone bridge gate began to lift. All the fledglings entered into the temple's barbican, Alina gave the command for the stone wall to lower, "Minusteh", it lowered itself simultaneously as the last of the bridge fell away into the abyss, leaving only the pillars of angelic statues to remain. Ensuring every student was accounted for, she teleported herself into the courtyard on top of the rostrum. As all the children gathered around the rostrum, fairy stable hands aligned themselves next to each horse. "Dismount", she ordered. Each student carefully dismounted, the fairy stable hands quickly started to lead each horse to the stables for boarding. Ajax knelt down to make it easy for Adin to dismount, "Thank you Ajax, I shall see you soon I hope", he said stroking his forehead. "It was good to see you, old friend, rest assured Adin will be an excellent horseman and I trust you will help him become so", Artorius patted Ajax on his back. Alina stood before all the students, her eyes a look of pride and strength.

"This day marks your first day of temple indoctrination as you begin your lifelong purpose of protecting and serving the realms. You all have chosen to part take on a sacred right that links each of your bloodlines to the Sovereign. Each of you will be tested daily, not only in your academia, calisthenics, but also in your resolve. None of you is greater than the other despite the order in which each of you belong to. As of this very moment all of you are now kin. Your order is your clan, your tribe; any wanton illicit conduct or behavior shall be met with the swiftest of discipline and impairment to the violator's order causing severe affliction to that order's ability to secure any citational award. There are temple courtesies and respects that must be exercised under all circumstances. Your Chief Elder, Lord Valerian, will formally welcome you momentarily as we enter the Court of Lords. In his presence you will execute the customary salute in the form of a bow. You will all seat yourselves at his command after he has bowed back. You may address any Regent as such title but never the Elder. The Elder must be addressed by his title. Each boy and girl here are now a master of their purpose, be mindful to respect each other always". Her speech caused different feelings of pride, nervousness, and excitement in each student to swell within their chest. All Adin could think of was not to make a spectacle of himself or embarrass Artorius. Adin kept repeating the titles Regent and Elder over and over again, trying to memorize them so he doesn't sound so out of place when he had to say them. "All right then, look sharp and stay mindful of your ranks!" Alina cautioned. She teleported the short distance from the rostrum to the front of the formation. "We will now enter the Hall of Lords in a wedge formation!". Suddenly she expanded her wings, folding them to form a V-shape to represent a wedge formation. Each student bustled to position themselves on the left and right flanks with Alina at the head. Artorius nodded his head to the right so Adin rushed to join the right echelon. "Forward!" she ordered, the formation moved in unison, collapsing to a narrower wedge as each student entered the archway of the temple's main entrance. The entry lead to a large foyer known as the Hall of Lords, with five large floating flags depicting the Five Orders' crests. Standing at the base of each flag stood each order Regent. There were two sets of staircases to his left and right that lead to a second floor, that wrapped around the hall. At the center of the second floor was another staircase that Adin could scarcely see. Dressed in a radiant red gown with angel sleeves stood Regent Serene of the Fire-Hawk. Under the Thunder Horse was Regent Cassian dressed in a dark blue mandarin collared jacket. Regent Tiberius of the Spirit Wolf stood in a black collared jacket under a black robe, and Regent Marius of the Iron Bear in a light brown mandarin collared shirt with a mocha colored vest. Alina assumed her place at the head of her order's flag. "Line yourselves in two columns on your appropriate order, quickly now", she instructed. The students speedily lined themselves up awaiting further instructions. With all the commotion, Adin found himself in the very back of his order. Once each student was in place all the Regents turned to face the corridor leading to the Court of Lords. "LION-HEART!" Alina shouted, giving her preparatory command; all the other Regents call out each of their order's names: "FIRE-HAWK", "THUNDER-HORSE", "SPIRIT-WOLF", "IRON-BEAR", in unison. "Forward!" Alina shouted giving the command of execution to move. All the orders started to move one after the other in two columns with the Lion-Heart order leading the way into the Court of Lords. The tall double doors to the hall stood closed before all the orders. The doors begin to open out by a hand wave from two fairy temple stewards. Alina led her order into the large room with five sets of stadium styled seating surrounding a raised semi-circular stage. In the middle of the stage stood Chief Elder Valerian, arms folded behind his back as he patiently waited for all the students to fill the room. Bright sunlight streamed through the stained-glass windows that made up the ceiling. The Regents all called out the name of their order, starting with Alina. "Lion-Heart!" she yelled then bowed, all her students then followed her bow. "Thunder-Horse!" Regent Cassian yelled as he bowed followed by all his students bowing. "Spirit-Wolf!" Tiberius yelled out, taking his bow followed by all his students bowing. "Fire-Hawk!" Regent Serene yelled out bowing followed by her students bow. "Iron-Bear!" Regent Marius yelled out, as he bowed followed by his students. Adin's row was seated a few levels higher than the first row of his order. Artorius stood by the double doors out of respect to not cause a distraction. "You may take your seats", Elder Valerian commanded. Once all the students had taken their seat, he began his introductory speech, "Welcome my young fledglings to the Temple of Aurora! It is our greatest pleasure to have you here with us to train for a lifelong rewarding journey. Here you will not find more knowledgeable nor passionate Regents, dedicated to your success and growth", he proclaimed glimpsing Adin in the top row, giving him a subtle nod of his head as he continued, "This temple was commissioned for you, a stronghold. All of you hail from angelic bloodlines of varying degrees, so I must impress upon all of you to hold dear the honor of your bloodlines, to never forsake your destiny that awaits each and every one of you! Now, it is with the great pleasure I introduce to you the Regents of the Five Orders. Of the Lion-Heart order, Regent Alina", Regent Alina teleported to the stage. "Regent Alina is champion of the sword, master aerial combater, and 10th degree fire enchantress". During her introduction, she leapt into the air producing her wings, unsheathing her sword in mid-air. She executed a beautiful triple front flip as she descended in midair holding her sword with two hands now; the blade pointed down as if she is going to bury it in an invisible enemy on the ground. Her blade suddenly bursts into purple flame as she descended rapidly to the stage floor, stopping just before her blade is driven into it, landing firmly with a loud thud. She lifted her blade to her face in a customary salute before beginning her intricate sword kata, each strike and swing of her sword left streaks of purple flame vertically and horizontally. The lingering streaks of flame spelled out Lion-Heart. She raised her sword once again to her face, signaling her demonstration was over, then teleported back to her order's section. All the Lion-Heart students clapped and cheered for her, Adin barely could contain his excitement, he clapped as hard as he could. "Of the Thunder-Horse Order, Regent Cassian, expert in the art of the javelin, master aerial combat horse-rider, and 7th degree spell caster". Regent Cassian placed his fingers to his lips and whistled, he suddenly teleported out of the room only to reemerge riding a brown unicorn with large white spots in full gallop from the back of the stage. He raised his hand and his javelin sprang to it, as he caught it; the touch of his hand expanded it to its full length. He threw it up in the air, then pulled the reigns and yelled, "Ateh!" (Stop!), his unicorn reared up on her two back legs. Using the momentum, he did a backflip off, his unicorn teleporting back to the stable. He landed on the edge of the stage and recited a spell, "Noliteh Telarum!" the javelin stopped in midair, it flipped with the spear point down facing down. He knelt in a genuflection pose, the javelin just above him, he stood up catching it with one hand behind his back, then twirled it around in front of him. The rotational speed of the spin made the javelin look like it was a large shield, he began his javelin kata; twirling and swinging the long spear. He re-sheathed his javelin ending his demonstration with a bow. The Thunder-Horse students all clapped to their feet. He teleported off the stage to join his order's section. "Regent Tiberius of the Spirit-Wolf Order, master in the art of the ringed bowie and tomahawk, lightning combat instructor, and 8th degree sorcerer practitioner". Regent Tiberius teleported on stage, reciting a spell; "Armato-astra!" suddenly blue lightening began to spark and cover his whole body, he pulled his tomahawk from behind his back with one hand and his ringed handle bowie with other from his belt sheath. He began a series of weapon katas, with each simulated strike and swing from his tomahawk and ringed bowie produced blue lightning flashes that would pop and crack thunderously. As he moved around choregraphing his kata, he would vanish in and out of sight, leaving visible only the swings and strikes of blue lightening produced from his weapons. At the end of his kata, Regent Tiberius crossed both his arms still holding his tomahawk and ringed bowie, then bowed. All the Spirit-Wolf students stood to their feet cheering. "Regent Serene of the Fire-Hawk Order, archer-ace, 6th degree wind-wielder, and 12th degree incantation specialist". Regent Serene teleported on stage producing two sets of wings, flapping her wings in one swift motion that lifted her off the ground causing a great gust of wind to blow the first row of student's hair and clothing back. She grabbed at her decorative forearm bracers with three raised imprints of arrows. Only these arrows on her forearm bracers are not decorative at all! With one scoop of her hand she pulled three golden arrows from each bracer. She unslung her recurved bow then spun herself around at blinding speed, shooting all the arrows around the room. As soon as all the arrows were shot, she raced to the first arrow on her right, running on an invisible floor no one else could see. She grabbed it going into a forward roll in midair shooting the arrow in mid roll, back towards the center of the stage. For the second arrow, she ran horizontally along the side of wall, positioning her bow behind her back and wings, she plucked her second arrow from the air, somersaulting while firing it to the center of the stage from behind her back. She ran around to the third arrow, seizing it as she executes a side flip and fired it towards the center of the stage. The fourth arrow she teleported to, shooting it upside down back towards the center of the stage just as she had done with the first three. Running to the fifth arrow she recites, "Lockmore Danalora", the arrow flung itself at her, she caught it and fired it on the run at the sixth arrow in the far corner of the room. The fifth arrow struck the sixth arrow causing it to fire towards the center stage. The fifth arrow having struck the sixth, struck the side of the wall, ricocheting itself back towards the center stage. Regent Serene teleported to the stage, again a monstrous gust of wind blew past the first row as she reappeared in the middle of the stage. She slung her bow around her neck, with each arrow just micro seconds from reaching the center of the stage, she caught every single arrow in flight using various aerobatic movements. Once she captured all her arrows, she placed them back on her forearm bracers, each arrow becoming a raised imprint of itself once more on her forearm bracers, she bowed before teleporting back to her order. The stopping of feet and clapping roared from her students. Adin's whole body tensed with excitement at the spectacular demonstrations from each Regent, wondering if he will be anywhere near as good as them. "And finally, but certainly not least; Regent Marius of the Iron Bear Order, phalanx genius, maser of the mace and shield, and 9th degree water-chief". Regent Marius teleported to the stage, he deployed three sets of his massive brown-white tipped wings, he is much larger and bulkier than all the other Regents. He raised his arm, his hand clenched tight in balled up fist, a large beautiful brown and crimson ring adorned his middle finger, he flicked his wrist; instantly a large brown and white shield expanded into a full-sized shield with the Iron-Bear crest. He folded his wings around him, placing his shield in the center, creating a one-man phalanx.   His wings and shield gave him complete protection, nothing can pierce this impenetrable defense. Suddenly he flexed his wings back with tremendous force, creating a wave of wind so strong, Adin was nearly blown backwards as was all the other students. With his free hand he grabbed his mid-size star-ore mace slung across his body, he began his shield and mace kata with every strike of his mace against his shield left sparks with profound sounds of clanging that could be felt in every student's bones. Bracing himself he held tight to the edge of the wooden bleacher; he wasn't going to miss the final demonstration. Regent Marius moved at great speed for being so massive, his shield streamed through the air blocking invisible attacks, his mace striking invisible foes. Each pass of his mace, swooshed across the air rippling through the student audience. At the close of his kata, he stood completely still and yelled, 'AHO!', bowing then teleported back to his order. The Iron-Bear students yelled back 'AHO!', followed by the clapping of all the other order's students.

Elder Valerian took center stage, "These Regents along with their assistants will be your instructors in various disciplines, listen well and train hard if you are to succeed in passing with gold stars. At the end of the year, I convene with The Council of Light to determine each new year's training theme to judge each order's submission for the meritorious service award; an honor, recognizing one member of an order that distinguished themselves throughout the training cycle. There is also the Elder Order Citation that recognizes one order every year for outstanding academic, athletic, and selfless service. Each Regent is responsible to ensure the training and academic curriculum is met for each training cycle for their order to be considered".

As Elder Valerian closed his greeting, he announced, "Regents! Escort our fledglings to the dining hall if you will, I shall meet you there momentarily". "Yes, Chief Elder!" all the Regents shouted in unison. All the students exited in the orderly fashion the same way they had entered, Artorius pulled Adin aside waiting for all the students to leave the room. "This is where I leave you", he said. Adin didn't like what he heard but he knew it was inevitable, he couldn't possibly except Artorius to be with him every step of the way. "You will be fine; your Regent will look after you and your fellow classmates. I will be around now and again from time to time to help you whenever you need me most", he said trying to comfort him. Adin extended his forearm, Artorius smiled and shook his forearm, sending him off to join his order. "He's got a strong heart", Valerian marveled, standing behind Artorius. "Yes Elder, he does!" Artorius agreed turning around to meet him. "Does he know exactly how his destiny has unfolded?" Valerian said. "He knows enough to build his resolve for now", Artorius answered. "You feel it wise that he builds his resolve on filtered truth?" Valerian inquired raising his eyebrow. "The boy will make the right decision, I'm sure of it, I bet my life on it. He just needs time to adjust to our way, our world, to understand his purpose", Artorius said with great conviction. "Take caution Artorius! The council still has a bitter taste of the First

Knights corruption still fresh on their tongue, suspicion has already been cast against him because of you!" he cautioned. "With Dagon and his followers imprisoned, Tessla's execution; one would think that the First Knights' purpose has long been forgotten, much less any concern over a First Knight's offspring!" he said disgusted. "Not since it was constituted by the council to dissolve the conception of the First Knights, has there been such an extreme measure to exterminate the forsaken", Valerian elaborated. "Ah, noble efforts to extinguish not only the memory of the First Knights but now the offspring of a First Knight I see! Do you share in that intention as well Elder?" he prodded. "No, I do not! The council has good reason to fear a quickening of the First Knights, there are still four of you in existence, with Adin now five! That equates to a celestial threat that some believe must be purged for all time!" Valerian asserted. "The boy is a descendant of a First Knight, not a First Knight there is a difference! I am shocked the council with all their great wisdom cannot discern that for themselves!" he said annoyed. "Adin is safe here, Artorius. I will see to that until such a time, if such a time he no longer follows the Guardian way", he said with absolutism. "All the more reason, I must stay as close to him as possible!" he glared at him. They both knew that Artorius must be invited to stay to fall under the temple's protection, after all Artorius was now a Ronin. "I'm glad you mentioned that, in fact I am in agreement with you! Besides it would be good for you to stay here while Adin is in training, perhaps there will be an opportunity for reconciliation between you and your Regent brothers and sisters. I can employ your expertise and talents among the Regents to keep you gainfully employed", Valerian settled the matter. "The Regents, will not be at all amused by this, are you sure this is a wise decision?" With a grin Elder Valerian answered, "No more of a wise decision than the one you have made bringing the boy here", he stated. "Very well, I submit to wise counsel", Artorius conceded, bowing his head. "Now let us feast on the village's delicacies and the finest starbrew!" Valerian said. "I won't be but a moment Elder, does the skychamber still stand?" Artorius inquired. "Yes, I would not permit the destruction of the chamber after the disbanding of the First Knights, there is much that I value there; reminders of a time when all five of you were-", Artorius interrupted him, "The pinnacle of a Guardian's power!" he groaned. "No! I was going to say, the divine picture of unification", Valerian corrected, placing his on his shoulder. Valerian could sense that Artorius still has great pain for the fall of the First Knights. "Forgive, my outburst Elder", he lamented. "Nonsense, my boy! Now, can we feast? Or shall we stand here like two fools reminiscing of the old times?" Valerian said trying to sway the mood of the conversation. Artorius chuckled, "Very well, lead the way my good Elder!" as he motioned with his hand for direction. "What? You know not the way? Really? You who was never late to a feast versus your training?" Valerian teased. "Well I've been out picking up where a certain Chief Elder left off in protecting the realms", Artorius teased back. "In my day, I was able to protect the realms with no help and little to no effort!" Valerian said with pride. "Yes, Elder and back in your time I suppose they discovered starbrew I imagine", he said trying to get in the last word. "Yes, as a matter of fact they did, then a sly earth realm thief stole the starbrew bean", he said irked. "Hmmm, so how where all those realms protected but you allowed a thief to acquire starbrew beans and smuggle them back to the earth realm?" Artorius questioned stroking his chin. "Ah, you youngsters will never let us live that down!" Valerian sighed. Both burst out into a brief laugh. "Come, you can revisit the skychamber once you been introduced at the feast. I trust Master Adin will feel more comfortable seeing you there", Valerian said with his hand on Artorius' shoulder. "Again Elder, I submit to good counsel; but seriously I really don't remember the way to the dining hall".

Adin passed back through the threshold of the Court

of Lords, joining his order now in a single file line; he glanced occasionally to his left and right, taking in all the visual stimulation of décor, statues, color, and all his fellow classmates. He was relieved to see that his classmates looked like normal ordinary kids his age, only every student had the most brilliant colored eyes, some in solid green, blue, hazel, pink, and purple. Two large double arched doors stood before them, "This is the Dining Hall!" Regent Alina turned to announce. The doors automatically opened just as the Court of Lords doors had done with the same two temple stewards. Adin struggled to view the interior of the large dining hall, tip toeing; attempting to look over the shoulders of the various students in front of him that were just as curious as he was. Regent Alina led the Lion-Heart order to the left as they entered, "All the way down to the end of the grand table", she ordered. The first student followed the curvature of the enormous wooden table to the right, Adin waited patiently as he inched his way forward, the line moving then stopping in various lengths. At last he approached the opening, inside he could see a huge round table, known as the grand table. The grand table is semi-circular in shape with an opening in the middle for fairy food attendants that faced the entry, behind the grand table was another wooden semi-circular table much shorter that he assumed was the dining table for the Regents and Elder. He walked around the grand table until he came to a seat, he looked around anxiously at his fellow classmates to see if anyone would sit or stand. Glancing around he could see ceiling to floor tapestries of each order's crest hanging on the walls. Between each tapestry was a stained-glass window in vibrant colors. One window depicted a great tree, the second a vast void of eternity, the third a forested field, and the fourth of vast planets. Adin spied a dwarf on a scaffold with mortar and a trowel, he was applying the mortar in various spots humming to himself. Once all the students were positioned behind a chair, every order's Regent walked to the semicircular table known as the Regent table and stood behind a designated chair waiting just as he assumed. Elder Valerian and Artorius entered the dining hall, all the Regents except Alina were in astonishment at the sight of Artorius. "He's still here?" Regent Cassian whispered, soliciting an answer from any of the other Regents. "Apparently the Chief Elder wishes it so brother", Regent Tiberius answered. "Wasn't he one of yours?" Regent Cassian scoffed. "Yes, brother. However, he has not lost favor with the Chief Elder as we can all see", Tiberius said appeased. Regent Cassian looked at Regent Tiberius with a loathing look. "Brothers, please, control yourselves", Regent Serene urged. Adin was excited that Artorius was still here, he had thought the Court of Lords was the last time he would see him, remembering Artorius' last words. "Please everyone, take your seats", Valerian implored. Artorius stepped out to the right corner to ensure he is not a distraction for everyone as Elder Valerian addressed the students. "During your stay here, there are many important incumbents that keep the temple in order so that you may train with the highest focus, rest assured that you will display the upmost respect and honor to these incumbents. Failure to do so will not be tolerated and will be met with the swiftest of punishments. Does everyone understand?" he said. "Yes Elder!" every student shouted. "The temple employs trusted and noble fairies, dwarves, and elves; each selected by their passion and skill", he said beginning his incumbent introductions. A fairy wearing a crimson gown with a mustard yellow apron emerged from the doorway. "Please meet our most wonderful Banquet Master, Fair-Lady Elinor", she presented herself then bowed, joining Artorius. "You may have noticed our Mason Master, Solomon", Elder Valerian pointed in Solomon's direction. Hearing his name, Solomon stopped, he immediately began to turn the scaffold by pulling on the ropes. He faced the students, gulped giving a very nervous smile followed by a jittery wave of his hand. He pulled the ropes again to turn himself back around to resume his work. "You must excuse Solomon, he is very passionate about his masonry tasks about the temple, thank you Solomon!". Solomon peered over his shoulder to smile once more, giving one more quick wave of his hand before returning to his masonry work. "Our Grounds Keeper, Fair-Lady Ru. Fair-Lady Ru entered the doorway in a matte green gown with a brown leather belt holding her gardening towel, weeder, and pruners. In her hands was a small copper planting pot, she lifted it to her mouth as she whispered an incantation. Steadily a red rose started to bud to maturity from the rich soil. The rose began to lift itself out of the soil, it floated to the center of the grand table. There it began to glow bright red, replicating itself into one hundred red roses. Each rose floated gracefully to each female student. The girls were ecstatic with gleeful praises each taking hold of their roses to examine and admire it. Fair-Lady Ru again whispered another incantation, suddenly another flower emerged from the potted soil. This flower developed into a fire-wheel, a circular flower with pointy petals with an orange-red center. The fire-wheel flower floated to the center of the table just as the rose had done. Bright yellow flame began to ignite from each of its pedals, it started to spin replicating itself just as the rose had done. Each fire-wheel flower floated to each of the one hundred male students, each male student took hold of their fire-wheel, Adin's fire-wheel reminded him of the sparklers back home. "Thank you, Fair-Lady Ru, these flowers are her welcoming gifts to you. The roses and fire-wheels are yours to keep, please take good care of them and they shall take good care of you". Ru bowed then excused herself to the Regent table. "Our Sword master, Lord Hylandir!" Lord Hylandir appeared in the center of the grand table, in a black mandarin collared jacket lined in silver threading, gray trousers, black riding boots, with a black cloak lined in matching silver thread with ornamental designs. He bowed to welcome all students before he teleported to the Regent table among the other Regents. Our Stable Masters, Gouyen and Taza, keepers of the all the beasts that each of you will train with. Gouyen and Taza, are twin elven brother and sister, they entered together, Adin could see that Gouyen had on a thick buck skin tanned gown and Taza wore a thick buckskin tanned shirt with matching pants. Both had a single white solid stripe under their bottom lip that ran down to the base of their neck. They both stopped at the opening of the grand table, bowing. Gouyen and Taza both lifted their hands and began to sway them back and forth creating a mass of white swirling cloud. They both shaped the energy into a ball of swirling white mass, Gouyen held hers in the palm of her left hand, Taza held his in the palm of his right hand. She took her finger and dips it into the ball of swirling white. She began to draw a white shaped toy horse with her finger in the air, it suddenly became animated, rearing up before running to the grand table. Taza dipped his finger in his mass of swirling white, drawing another horse. The horse became animated just as Gouyen's had, then bolted for the right side of the grand table. Both horses ran on top of the table, passing each student. All the students cooed in astonishment with sounds of joy and laughter as the horses jumped over plates, silverware, and cups. Gouyen and Taza once again dipped their fingers into their swirling mass of white cloud, drawing in the air winged animals that resembled a bear, a hawk, a wolf, and finally a lion. Each drawing became animated, running or flying around the table, every student was amazed and impressed with the entertainment. After a few short minutes, all the animated creatures began to fade into streaks of white, racing back into their perspective ball of swirling white cloud. All the students clapped, Gouyen and Taza responded by bowing. "Ah, thank you so much for the entertainment Gouyen and Taza!" Valerian said while clapping. They both bowed before joining the Regent table. "Our Chief Muse, Fair-Lady Calliope, her renowned voice is highly sought after in all five realms!" Elder Valerian announced. She was dressed in a dazzling emerald green down, her auburn hair styled up with white gold hair clips. She smiled with affection, bowing. "Fair-Lady Calliope heads our poetry, music, and drama disciplines", he said, she clapped her hands and a troupe of fairies' swooshed in, wings flapping as they positioned themselves from the shortest to the tallest like a choir debut. Among the fairies was Trini, excited; she waved to Adin. Adin cracked a smile and waved nonchalantly back. Fair-Lady Calliope began to hum, initiating the fairy choir to begin their short welcoming hymn:

"We welcome you, young guardians; those with hearts for a lion will find the strength to always win. We welcome you, young guardians; those with thunder for a horse will lead the charge with no remorse. We welcome you, young guardians; those with iron for a bear will overpower those who dare. We welcome you, young guardians; those with fire for a hawk will find their mark is never off. We welcome you, young guardians; those with spirit for a wolf will always fight for what was took".

At the end of the hymn, everyone clamped, Fair-Lady Calliope smiled with pride; her fairy chorus was received very well. "Thank you, Fair-Lady Calliope, for that riveting hymn", Valerian said excusing her to the Regent table. "Our Tournament Master, Lord Gabdor!". He teleported to the front to of the grand table. He was tall and lean with manicured hair. His goatee was perfectly trimmed around his mouth and chin. "Welcome! I trust I will be seeing those of you who wish to participate and compete in the temple tournaments. Each order will have their own teams divided into the competitive arts of Glaive Star, Spell Craft, and Battle Wing; for the test of The T.R.I.A.D.S.", he said hoping to solicit recruits. "Thank you Lord Gabdor, I am sure those students wishing to compete will seek you out in no time!" Valerian said excusing him to the Regent table. "Finally, may I introduce the heart of this temple, Sindri! Sindri is the Temple Keeper, in charge to ensure the temple's needs are meet as well as assisting me in the administration of the temple", Sindri bowed as the last introduction of the day. "Now, there is a Code of Conduct scroll on the table in front of you, outlining the rules for your residency here at the temple", he said. Everyone looked down to find a scroll unraveled in front of them that was not there before with the words, 'Code of Conduct' written at the top. "Each order has living quarters with a common room suited for study and leisure. Once the day is out, every student will be confined to the boundary of your perspective common room. If you are discovered outside your common room without the permission of your Regent, positive discipline will soon befall you at the discretion of your Regent's authority. The appeal process will require a request for counsel through your Regent to me, at that time I shall appoint a time and place in which to discuss your appeal or grievance. There are Gatekeepers which patrol the temple skies and grounds for your protection, if you are caught by them, you will surely suffer a likely fate of banishment from the temple; your memory eradicated and you will be exiled to Terra Firma to live out the remainder of your life. Each of you shall treat each other with dignity, respect, and fairness; failure to exercise these virtues will most surely be granted a positive disciplinary lesson. Finally, your training shall be the focus of your desire, we are preparing you to protect and serve all the realms; that task is not one to be taken lightly. Lord Artorius will be joining us here at the temple, he has accepted my offer to assist the Regents in your training". Some of the Regents spurned the thought Artorius would not only be taking up residence at the temple but now assisting them in their personal instruction to their own orders! '*How preposterous!*', Regent Cassian, Regent Marius, and Regent Serene thought. At the end of Valerian's code of conduct speech, Artorius acknowledged the whole room with a nod of his head. Adin was relieved, although he felt like a stranger without the slightest clue, he felt assured Artorius would not let him embarrass or disgrace himself. "Now everyone, take your right thumb and place it on the scroll where there is an outline of a thumb-marker", Valerian instructed. Each student placed their thumb on the marker. "Now press down firmly and repeat, "Turandum", he said. All the students repeated the words just as he instructed. Suddenly a red flame emanated from under each student's thumb then slowly fizzled out. Adin lifted his thumb off the scroll, he saw his thumb print scorched into the scroll. The scrolls rolled themselves up and lifted off the table towards the elder. "Sindri, please secure the Code of Conduct scrolls and secure them in my living quarters, I shall review them prior to the month's end", he said. "At you wish, my Elder!" Sindri bowed opening his scroll holder for all the scrolls to float into. "Now Fair-Lady Elinor, if you would please. I do hope each of you is hungry, we have prepared a special entrée for each of you to help you feel more at home for your first day", he said taking his seat. She clapped her hands summoning twenty fairy attendants with stacks of meals floating behind them. Each attendant began pointing their hands at each student and the plates would float to each placing itself in down front of them. The drink serving attendants had pitchers of starbrew, chai-tea, and firewater. The drink attendants would point to a student's glass that was in need of refilling and the pitcher would float and pour into the cup until filled then move on to the next person in need of their beverage refilled. Fair-Lady Calliope's choir chorus began singing songs with lyres, flutes, and drums. Adin had never been so excited to eat a meal, with the music, unlimited food and drink, and surrounded by other kids like him; he couldn't think of a reason to ever want to go back home. All the students busied themselves with their food, finally feeling comfortable enough to talk to each other. The grand table reminded him of the story of King Arthur and the round table, whereas every knight was equal, this revelation brought a smile to his face.

"Will you be joining us my Lord?" Fair-Lady Elinor asked Artorius. "No, I have some business I must attend to, thank you my Fair-Lady", he said. "I understand my Lord, please call on me if you require anything from the kitchen. Oh, and please call me Elinor", she said. "Thank you, Elinor, I know where to find you if such a need arises", he left the dining hall. He teleported to the skychamber; it was once the quarters for the First Knights. The door looked the same as it did before, "I wonder?" he thought. He then began to speak the unlocking phrase once used for entry into the chamber, "Vires Quod Virtus" – 'Forces that power'. The door unlocked with a loud 'clack'; a poof of dust burst into the air. The door began to slowly creek open, he stood still taking a deep breath, it was the first time he had entered the chamber since the First Knights were disbanded. The interior torches began to alight with the undying blue flame. He entered the chamber, "It must still be here", he said, the door screeched as it slowly closed behind him.

CHAPTER FIVE

THE GIRL WITH THE SILVER FEATHER

Adin was feasting on his favorite kind of pizza, peperoni and sausage! '*How did they know what my favorite food was!?*', he thought with each bite. "Attention!" Elder Valerian bellowed out, catching every ear in the dining hall. The music stopped, the singing stopped, the clinking and clattering of silverware striking plates ceased. "I encourage everyone, once you have filled your bellies, introduce yourselves to each other; get to know your brothers and sisters. That is all", he sat back down to resume his drumcake delicacy. Adin looked around, cleaning his fingers on his napkin, his plate lifted to float back to the kitchen. He felt a tap on his shoulder, he turned only to see a girl smiling down at him. "Greetings, I'm Lozen!" she said smiling with her arm extended. She had almond colored skin with long black hair pulled back in two single braids on either side of her head that curved down to the back of her neck. In her hair she had single silver feather hanging down on the left side of her head. It was the girl staring at Adin on the Moirai bridge! "High-yah", is all he could say trying not to sound so awkward, as he stood up to shake her hand. "Not like that silly, like this", she took hold of his hand and placed it on her forearm as she grabbed for his. "Your really are new here, aren't you?" she said with a sympathetic grin. "Yeah, I am. Is it that obvious? All the customs and greetings, the bowing, it's a little overwhelming for someone like me", he said trying to explain away his shy awkwardness. "Someone, like you?" she said confused. "I'm from the earth realm", Adin exclaimed. "Ah, I see. You're what we call a '*Washi'chu*' it means, Outsider". "Outsider?" Adin huffed. "Hey Atreyu!" she called out to a boy seated on the far right of the grand table. Atreyu was talking with a blonde-haired girl named Persaeus, he glanced over looking in the direction of her voice. He saw and nodded to her asking what she wanted. Adin looked to see who she was calling, he noticed Atreyu staring at them. His long black hair was down, relaxed, with the same kind of feather woven into it. Adin continued to stare in his direction, unsure about what is going to happen next. Lozen waved him over so he stood up, his chair pulled out from behind him to give him room, he gestured for Persaeus to follow him with a small wave of his hand. Now Adin really wasn't sure what was about to happen, he started to feel a little uneasy. Back home whenever a situation like this happened, it usually meant it wasn't going to go well for him, especially since he was referred to as an outsider. Each passing second as Atreyu and Persaeus came closer to him, his heart pounded harder. "Goteyo", Atreyu greeted him with the formal forearm shake. Adin reluctantly gave the forearm shake, sensing his uneasiness, "Hey! Relax brother, we're of the same order, remember? I'm Lozen's brother, Atreyu". Adin immediately felt very foolish, "Yes of course, forgive me, I was just telling Lozen how-", he is cut off by Persaeus. "Pleasure to meet you, I heard Regent Alina say you are the son of a First Knight, is that true?" she implored. "Yes, I am", he said. "Hey, you gonna try out for any of the games? I'm going to try Glaive Star! The game in my opinion is the most challenging, you know! Having to run with a stick and ball, dodging opponents without dropping it, trying to outscore the other team!" Atreyu said mimicking the actions of the game. "I don't think I know that game", Adin said. "Well then maybe we should give you a few lessons, aye?" a deep voice suggested from behind. "Adin, meet Lucian", Lozen said introducing a herculean looking boy. Lucian was a tall boy, much taller than the four of them. He had a broad chest; his hair was styled like a warrior, the sides of his head were shaved high down to the skin, the top mass of his hair pulled back into a single thick braid that had several silver clasps in it. Adin turned to meet Lucian, he hadn't anticipated how tall or bulky he was. He looked up at the giant boy standing with his arms folded, his face stoic, "Pleasure to meet you Lucian!" he greeted nervously. Suddenly Lucian cracked a smile and chuckled, "Pleasure to meet you little brother!" giving him a powerful forearm shake. Adin began to chuckle as well, realizing his anxiety was all for nothing. "I like to call him Washi'chu!" Lozen said joking to the group. Everyone laughed together, a new bond now forming. "Hey, I heard the earth realm has the best music!" Atreyu commented. "I heard an earth realm thief stole a starbrew bean!" Lozen noted. "I heard the earth realm has the fanciest clothes and hairstyles!" Persaeus said. "I heard the earth realm has this mighty game, called football?" Lucian stated. Everyone was flooding Adin with questions about the earth realm, tying up most of the early evening. Adin couldn't believe how welcomed he felt, it struck him that although he came from a different place than all the other kids around him, he was still treated like he was part of a long-lost family, the evening was coming to a close.

"Where is Lord Artorius?" Elder Valerian asked from his place of honor at the Regent table. "He said he had business to see to, Elder, he did not stay", Fair-Lady Elinor answered as she was coordinating the cleanup with her fairy stewards. "I see, thank you Fair-Lady Elinor. Regents, I shall take my leave for the evening, see to it that your orders are taken to their chambers with instructions for tomorrow's agenda", Elder Valerian commanded before teleporting. "As you wish!" all the Regents acknowledged. At once all the Regents hollered out the names of their orders: "Lion-Heart!" "Thunder-Horse!" "Fire-Hawk!" "Spirit-Wolf!" "Iron-Bear!". Every student stopped what they were doing, the room became silent. "We are at the finality of the evening, assemble yourselves in the Hall of Lords!" Regent Alina ordered. All the students returned to their seats; they begin an orderly exit to the Hall of Lords. "They are learning quickly, this bunch!" Regent Marius noted, pleased with their quick discipline. Once all the students are assembled by their order, each of their Fairy stewards monitored the cleanup, making sure the enchanted brooms, dust pans, washing rags were all cleaning everything right. Other fairy stewards are setting chairs, upside down on the grand table with quick flicks and twirls of their hands. Outside the dining hall, all the Regents stood at the back of their orders while Regent Alina walked to the front of the assembly. "Listen well!" she cautioned. "Each order has a staircase the leads to your living chambers, separated by two towers; one for males and one for females. Every door is enchanted in this temple and will only open to those whom have permission to enter, and no! You cannot teleport inside an unauthorized chamber either, in case some of you are wondering. To open a door that has been granted by your Regent, you must have your medallion necklace on your person. Once you are in your common room, you have three options available to you to reach your personal chambers, however; only two will be of any use to you for now. The first is a staircase at the back of your common room that leads to each four-person chamber with four beds, there are five levels in each tower. Each bed has your name etched into the foot board, your belongings have already been taken up and placed in their proper place. Each level is equipped with a bathroom and shower for your personal needs. Should you require assistance outside of a Regent's charge, such as: a problem with water, broken boards, the temperature, or sleep walking; throw a pinch of zilly-wood that is located in a brown clay jar on each of your night stands into the pontifex. A temple steward will respond to you shortly, if it is an emergency, request an audience with the on-duty Regent. To my right, you will find the Spirit-Wolf and Thunder-Horse staircases. To my left, you will find the Fire-Hawk and Iron-Bear, once on the second floor, you will find the Lion-Heart staircase in the center, any questions or concerns? Good then! Off you go, a temple steward will brief you each morning of the day's syllabus via the pontifex. See to it that you do not forget your syllabus!" she ended her speech with a nod of her finger. "Goodnight, rest well!" she closed, all the students began to climb the stone staircases to their orders. Adin, Lucian, Lozen, Atreyu, and Persaeus raced each other up the stairs to see who was the fastest, Atreyu beat everyone. "Well, here it is!" Atreyu said out of breath from dashing up the stairs as fast as he did. "Well since you're the first one here, it's only proper you be the first one of us to open the door", Persaeus pressed. With a smirk, Atreyu pulled out his necklace, the door unlocked and slowly opened to nothing but darkness. He looked around at each of them unsure if he should enter. "First one to the door, gets to go through the scary darkness!" Lozen teased. "So not funny!" Atreyu scoffed. He entered, the darkness engulfing him, everyone's face was plugged into the doorway waiting to see or hear anything. The room became lit, "I can't believe it!" is all they heard Atreyu exclaim. Hearing Atreyu, the group spilled into the room, only to behold a most spectacular view of the common room. Crowded around the entry, they saw Atreyu lounging with his feet up on the sofa sectional chaise. "Isn't this place great!?" he said spreading both his arms in welcome. "The fireplace wasn't on, that's why it was so dark!" he said. "I've never seen a fireplace that big before!" Adin said. Persaeus flopped herself on the sofa, "Comfy!" she said in delight bouncing up and down on the cushion. The rest of the thirty-five Lion-Heart students started to trickle in the common room, taking a moment to explore it. "Off to our bed chambers, I suppose?" Lozen suggested. Everyone agreed, with their bellies full and the exhaustion of the first day wearing on them all. "Woah! We have to climb more stairs to our beds!" Atreyu whined. "No, you can teleport if you know how!" Lozen teased, she stated her name at the foot of the girl's tower. "Lozen", she said, instantly she vanished. "Persaeus", Persaeus said, waving bye before she too vanished. "Okay, I'm so trying that now!" Atreyu cooed. "See you on the other side!" he razzed Lucian and Adin just before he spoke his name. In a poof, he vanished. "You coming little brother?" Lucian said stepping in the space where Atreyu once stood. "Yeah, be right up!" Adin reassured. "Lucian", instantly Lucian vanished. Adin stood in front of the common room's fireplace; all the other Lion-Heart students had made their way to their chambers already, only a few used the stairs just to use them. Adin hardly noticed he was alone in the common room, his body muffled out some of the fireplace's blue candescent light as he stood in front of it. He wanted to reflect on all the excitement of his first day, "I wish Sister Lizzie could see me now, five of a kind", he said smirking with new pride at the thought of his new found friends. He walked to the spot each male student had used to teleport to their chamber.

Elder Valerian arrived at the door of the skychamber, suddenly a voice broke the silence, "My Elder!" Captain Pateon called out from the shadows, emerging from a dark corner. He rendered the customary bow. "Forgive the intrusion Elder, but there was a light coming from the skychamber, I thought it suspicious since the skychamber was sealed for all time", he explained. "Thank you, Captain, Lord Artorius has returned and will be resuming his quarters once more, please ensure all Gatekeepers are aware of our guest". "So, the rumors are true! A prodigal Captain of the First Knights has returned home, has he no shame?" he snapped. "Take caution in your tone Captain, I recognize the stigma surrounding the arrival of Lord Artorius, but I must impress; was it not he that shattered the very foundations of the Fallen's empire and was it not he that imprisoned Dagon? A corrupted Guardian that had defeated legions of orders, to include yours, before meeting his demise at the hands of Lord Artorius! You may not agree with his residency here, but rest assured he is still an unyielding celestial force that has yet to be challenged!" Elder

Valerian warned. Realizing Valerian has made his point he looked downcast in submission at his scolding. "Please forgive the delay in notifying the Gatekeepers, I was hoping to have joined Lord Artorius in entering the skychamber. As you can see, he is as impatient as he was when he was a fledgling", Elder Valerian said. "As you wish Elder, a thousand apologies for my careless comments. I shall return to my night sky duties if it pleases the Elder?" Pateon petitioned. "You may resume your duties Captain", he said dismissing him, "As you wish Elder!" taking his leave back to the citadel. Elder Valerian pondered for a moment, *"Why didn't he alert me earlier whilst I was in the dining hall of the skychamber's breach?"* "Vires Quod Virtus", he said, the door opened slowly as it did for Artorius. Before entering, he saw in the center of the dimly lit room, a darkened figure stood motionless underneath the skylight. Stepping further into the chamber the figure is someone he just mentioned, Artorius, transfixed; gazing up at the night sky in deep thought. "I had forgotten the memories of past battles and the bond we all once shared only to become an echo of our former purpose", he grieved staring out the skylight. "It is as I had said, nothing touched or changed for that matter", Valerian repeated again. "If I had known, I could have-". "Could have what? Swayed Dagon? Kairah? Or Sidion? To resist the corruption germinating within the Chronicles of Destriel? They made a choice to serve darkness, to follow darkness! The decision to cause imbalance in all the realms, to rip away the righteous purpose they swore to uphold! They betrayed their solemn oath and murdered their brothers and sisters, innocent Sidhe, Dwarcadians, and Elves! I will not allow you to distance yourself because of your fallen brethren! The son of Tessla, the son of a First Knight, stands in the fragile balance swaying to either side. I know why it pains you that it is him, you still see a part of her in him and you are selfishly trying to keep that part of her alive. But I warn you Artorius, you will have condemned that poor boy!" he said convicting

Artorius. "You had faith in me once as the last true Captain of the First Knights, have faith in me once more with the lingering trust you have for me now. I failed to destroy my brother Dagon, in my weakness seeing only my brother at the edge of my sword and not all of creation's enemy. I shall not fail Tessla! My resolve is fortified Elder, more so than it has ever been!" Artorius affirmed looking into Valerian's eyes. Valerian saw a level of emptiness he has not seen since the time of the Great Fall. "No one can know the strength it requires to destroy a brother! I am sorry it fell to you Artorius, but I fear my dear friend, fate may repeat itself and when that time comes, you will have but no choice!" he said prophesying before he took his leave. Artorius stood alone in the room, Elder Valerian's words echoing in his mind, only the flickering sounds of the room's torches could be heard. "Fate is bound by action!" he proclaimed alone in the room. He unfolded his wings and bolted out of the skyline ceiling window of the skychamber, the force of his ascension caused layered dust to scatter across the room, bedding tousled, and any loose articles blown off their stands.

Adin stood at the foot of the Lion-Heart common room staircase, "Adin", he recited. Instantly he found himself in front of the skychamber door. He looked around, "Uh, okay, pretty creepy looking door! Still, it is better than the one back home", he reasoned shrugging his shoulders. He pulled out his medallion necklace, the door unlocked, creaking open slowly; reminding him of every horror movie he had ever seen. "This is how you're going to die, stepping into a dark room that you know you looks scary!" he told himself. He peered in the room, nothing but darkness. "Atreyu? Lucian?" Lozen?" Ah stupid", he whispered to himself. No girls would be in the boy's chambers, "Hel, H-e-l-l-o?" he called out; hoping for a friendly response. He inched closer to the opening, squinting to see any discernable objects, listening for any of slightest sound of snoring. Nothing, he gathered his courage stepping through the darkness, as his foot broke the threshold of the door, the undying blue flame torches sparked to life. The wall torches all alight themselves, illuminating the room causing him quite a startle. His heart nearly burst out of his chest; he could feel his blood rushing through his body in crashing waves in between his frantic panting. He gulped, slowly he began to calm himself, inside the disheveled room he could see five beds with the names: Artorius, Tessla, Kairah, Sidion, and Dagon. Next to each bed were five complete sets of mirror polished golden armor. '*Hmm, strange, a girl would be sleeping in the same room as a boy*', he thought. Hanging above each bed were medallion necklaces, fully intrigued he walked over to his mother's bed, lifting the polished golden necklace off its hook, expecting to find one of the five orders symbols; much to his surprise no symbol of any of the five orders. The symbol on this medallion necklace was a double-edged sword with a set of wings. "I wonder what this symbol means, wait, do all of the medallions have the same symbol?" he rushed to check each headboard's hanging necklaces finding Dagon's necklace in polished gold with the same symbol, '*Murderer*' he thought to himself quickly releasing the necklace, it smacked against the wall. He stood in front of Artorius' bed, reaching for his necklace, it was polished gold as well with the same sword/wing symbol! None of them have any of the five orders but all of them have the same symbol, '*This must be the symbol of the First Knights?*' he rationed. His curiosity peaked; he began to explore the room. Finding the cascading light still to dim, he grabbed a nearby chair and placed it against the wall where a torch holder was anchored. He climbed on top of the chair, taking hold of the torch stick handle. He stepped down, motivated by his new-found light, he began to pick up strange looking objects under the torch's light expecting to find some answer to the medallion mystery. He walked over to tapestries hung around the room portraying animated scenes of five armored Guardians battling great beasts, defeating large armies of enemies, and the same five

Guardians posing together, laughing; in what he presumed to be celebratory moments. The tapestries covered every inch of stone wall, leaving no section of wall exposed. He paused briefly to watch each animated tapestry silently retelling its recorded moments. He only recognized Artorius from the tapestries, only he couldn't figure out which woman was his mother. Artorius looked different somehow, he looked more zealous he thought, he hadn't noticed until just now that Artorius was not the same Guardian he was in the tapestries. '*It must be terrible for him*', he told himself pondering his assumption. Finding nothing that would unravel the mystery of the medallion symbol, he thought it best to inspect the armor, perhaps he would find a clue hidden within the armor. He checked every set of armor, refusing to examine Dagon's. By exception, all the armor pieces were of the same style, all mirror polished gold. He looked over at his mother's golden armor, "Nothing, like the rest of the armor sets, nothing hidden that I can see" he said frustrated. He finally inspected Artorius' armor, baffled, he was beginning to give up on the mystery; when he took notice of Artorius' golden helmet suspended above the plated chest armor. The helmet appeared to be molded to Artorius' head with a full facial guard wrap around leaving only a large eye slot, it reminded him of a motorcycle helmet. A solid pearl white stripe ran from the top center of the helmet down the back, He ran his finger along the stripe, the pearl felt smooth to the touch. He could now see the stripe ran from the center of the helmet to the facial guard all of the way down in the front. On either side of the helmet were two wings erected. He couldn't resist the temptation to try on the helmet, it looked to cool! He looked around the room. '*Duh! Nobody's here*', he made fun of himself as he placed the helmet on his head. The helmet slumped down and forward on his small head, as he lifted it up, he noticed a pair of yellowish green eyes staring at him from the ceiling skylight in the armor's reflection. He almost jumped out of his skin, "What the!" he blurted out in full panic mode lifting the helmet off his head as he spun around so fast, he tripped over himself crashing to the floor. The torch flew out of his hand landing against the wall, leaving the room darker despite the other wall torches. Landing on his back with a thud, the back of his head slamming hard against solid wooden plank, his vision became foggy. He could barely see the yellowish green eyes crawling closer to the opening of the skylight. A dark animal like figure dropped down from the skylight onto the floor without making a sound, the yellowish green eyes stared at him, his vision grew narrower, now the eyes were directly over him. His vision nearly gone, all he could see was a mouth full of pointed white teeth opening, then nothing but a feeling of warm wetness against his cheek.

Adin woke up in the infirmary to an enchanted sponge lightly dabbing his cheeks. He sat up his head was pounding; he felt a bandage. He looked around the room, no clue where he was. "How are you feeling Master Adin?" a voice came from the corner of the room. He looked to the sound of the voice; his vision sharpened. He saw a man mixing an elixir, "I wasn't expecting a patient so soon, I must admit you have me a disadvantage. I've just returned from the Fields of Arau, restoring my lacsem root. I've notified a temple steward to send word to Regent Alina, that is your Regent, correct?" Lord Tadrian said to check his mental awareness. Adin looked at him unsure what to say. "Forgive my rudeness, I am Lord Tadrian, the temple physician", he said introducing himself. "Hello Lord Tadrian, how did I get here?" Adin asked still groggy holding his head. "A Gatekeeper noticed a light in the abandoned First Knights' skychamber. He went to investigate but couldn't enter so had to fetch Elder Valerian, who brought you here", he explained. "Not to worry, Regent Alina and Elder Valerian will be here shortly". A knock on the door, "Come in!" he called out. Regent Alina and Elder Valerian entered the infirmary. "Need I say anything Master Adin!" Regent Alina said enraged crossing her arms. "You have brought great dishonor upon yourself and the Lion-Heart order, you have committed a violation warranting your expulsion!" she thundered. At that moment, Artorius entered the infirmary walking with great intensity, "Forgive the absence of my knock!" he said apologizing as he passed Lord Tadrian by. "Are you alright?" he said to Adin with worry in his eyes. "No need to worry yourself Lord Artorius, Master Adin will recover just as well back in the earth realm! He has violated the Code of Conduct, therefore; it is within my power and authority to expel him! I am sorry Lord Artorius but that is my judgement!" she said exacted. "Your judgement! You haven't changed much Alina, save for your new title as Regent!" he fired back. "He violated the temple code! Or has your heart been accustomed to forsaking all codes of law!?" she questioned. "Only those codes or laws or whatever you wish to call them that condemn the innocent! Do not mistaken yourself, I will defend all who challenge Adin's innocence!" he warned all in the room. Adin felt like he was sinking in his bed, glancing back and forth from Regent Alina to Lord Artorius, fearing he has kicked himself out of the temple. "Please you two! You still fight as if you too have never been apart! The question here is how did Master Adin manage to find his way to the skychamber at all?" Valerian said with an inquisitive look. "What do you remember?" he prodded. "I'm so sorry Elder, I didn't mean to cause all this trouble", Adin pleaded. "Quite alright my boy but please tell us how you came about the skychamber? That chamber has been sealed since the time of the Great Fall, by me no less", he said alarmed. "Last night, I was the last person in the Lion-Heart common room, I went to the male tower to go to my chambers", he began, "Yes, go on", Valerian implored him. "Then I said my name, I arrived at the skychamber door thinking it was the door to my chamber. I took out my medallion and the door opened, the blue flamed torches lit, and I looked around the room", he admitted. "Go on", Valerian said sensing there was more to the story. "Then, I noticed the five beds with armor next to them and medallion necklaces hanging above each headboard. I couldn't see much so I used a chair to grab a torch. I saw Lord Artorius' armor and I tried on his helmet, that's when". "Yes, yes, go on!" he said encouraging Adin, Regent Alina and Artorius listened intently. "Then I saw yellowish green eyes staring at me from outside the skylight through the reflection of the armor. It freaked me out and I tried to turn to run, I lost my balance and fell. Last thing I remember was a mouth full of teeth opening, then warm slobber on my cheek for some strange reason", he finished. "That would be Kofka!" Artorius reasoned. "Kofka?" Adin said puzzled. "Yes, Kofka is my totem animal, he must have caught my scent and followed it to the skychamber looking for me", Artorius surmised. "Well then the mystery is solved, Lord Tadrian is Adin fit to return to training?" Valerian said relieved. "Yes, Elder he is, I can see no reason to keep him further", Lord Tadrian said putting away his elixir to remove Adin's bandage. "Thank you, Lord Tadrian, for your expertise! Regent Alina your judgement has been overruled; Master Adin will remain here at the temple. Regent, please escort your student to his classes, he has already missed the morning's first lecture and breakfast", Elder Valerian commanded. Regent Alina not pleased at all obeyed as she has been commanded, "Yes my Elder, as you wish!" she said parting with a bow. "Thank you, Regent", he said knowing she was not happy being overruled. Touching his bandage she looked to Valerian and Artorius then to Tadrian, her eyes eager to state the obvious; how could Adin be injured? Valerian gazed at her as if to say, "Now was not the time". "Come Adin, we have little time to get you prepared for the day's agenda!" she said motioning for Adin to follow her. He hopped of the bed, "Thank you Sir", he said to Lord Tadrian on his way out. "A pleasure Master Adin", he responded with a nod of his head. Walking with Regent Alina, Adin commented, "Ah, if we teleport, it might be best if you do it, my teleporting skills are a bit fuzzy! You know I bet its quite a view of the grounds from the skychamber!" he said trying to make light of the situation. All that can be heard is Regent Alina's sarcasm, "Really? That last part sounds like an excuse you've used before!" she miffed as they walked down the corridor out of sight.

"Lord Tadrian, how is it that Adin was injured during his fall? He should have been impervious to any injury", Artorius questioned. "You are quite right, metabolically, it would appear that his angelic blood has been suspended from metamorphosizing his cells", Lord Tadrian deduced. "I don't quite understand", Tadrian said in deep thought. "Only a Therian Curse has the power to do that?" Artorius suggested, "Perhaps", Tadrian considered, "But that is a rare ancient fairy curse!". "What do you suspect?" Valerian said back to Tadrian. "Possibly, if the curse was introduced before his blood metamorphosized his human cells, the question is how and when?" he said sitting down to better think. "That would explain his injury and his inability to be healed. He is now a danger to himself, a student from the earth realm cannot survive the training trials in a mortal body, he will likely be killed", Valerian said worried. "Whomever cursed him, may be unaware if it has taken effect at all, we should keep this a private matter until we can detoxify his body. I know it sounds cruel but that is the only advantage we have, if his assassin believes the plan failed then we may be able to find who's responsible! Forcing them out from the shadows", Artorius said. "Agreed", Valerian affirmed. "Lord Tadrian, please check all perishables coming into the temple to ensure, this assassin does not succeed again", he ordered. "Right away, my Elder!" he said teleporting himself to the kitchen. "Artorius, please keep the friction between you and Regent Alina at a minimum as best you can", he said hoping that there would not be another outburst in front of a student. "Aye, I'll do my part as long as she stays out of the way Elder!" he said before he teleported to the

Lion-Heart common room. "I was afraid he would say that!" Valerian said shaking his head.

Regent Alina and Adin arrived in the Lion-Heart common room. "Go on try teleporting to your chambers, once you are in your chambers you will find your uniform is already laid out for you to put on then report back here immediately", she instructed. Adin successfully teleported to his chambers on the fifth level, finding his uniform laid out on top of the bed with his name just as Regent Alina said it would be. He glanced around pleased to find that Atreyu's name etched in the bed to the right of his. The third bed had the name Lucian etched into it and fourth bed's name had Tristan, *Hmm, don't think I've met him yet, this place kind of reminds me of my old dormitory only way higher!"* he thought as he quickly changed into his uniform. Lord Artorius arrived in the Lion-Heart common room. Alina politely tried to distance herself yet remain cordial, careful not to inspire another fight. "Master Adin won't be but a moment, he is readying his uniform", she advised. "Alina", Artorius said with a soft tone, "I'm sorry for my behavior in the infirmary, please forgive my harsh words with you, I still respect you as a dear friend and Regent", he said sounding vulnerable for the first time since she has known him. "And I you, Captain", she responded back trying not to look into his eyes. "I'm no Captain, not anymore", he corrected her. "You still look like a Captain to me!" she said forgetting herself, letting her secret vulnerability for him slip from her heart. Realizing what she has said, she quickly composed herself changing the direction of the conversation, "It is a little disconcerting having you here my Lord, you are of course a First Knight! Your presence here has the other Regents feeling as if they will not measure up", she confided. "I am not a First Knight, not any more than I am still a Captain! My only reason for being here is a covenant I made with Tessla to always protect her son!" he made plain. "Interesting, as to why you are still called 'Captain of the First Knights!" she impressed upon him with an inquisitive/sarcastic expression. "Do you trust it is your word to Tessla that brings you here, or your enduring love for her?" she questioned. He studied her face, her choice of words that solidified her feelings for him never ceased. "You never stopped?" he pried. "Never!" she answered agitated. Before he had a chance to finish his question, Adin's voice interrupted the tense atmosphere, "All set!". Alina took this opportunity to change her demeanor back into a disciplined Regent, "Today Master Adin, you learn the Guardian history", she said with a somber look. "Can't wait to hear it all!" he said excited. All three teleported to the Orator Dome where all the orders were scheduled for their first history lesson. Inside the dome was a large auditorium with bench seating surrounding a center stage, Adin spied Atreyu waving him down. "Go, Master Adin, I believe Master Atreyu has secured a seat for you", she said. Adin walked briskly down to the row of seating, stepping over the sea of legs saying, "Excuse me", every five seconds until he got to the seat Atreyu saved for him. He flopped himself down, "Thanks", he said with a sigh. Lozen and Persaeus were all seated on the same row together with Adin and Atreyu. "Where were you last night?" Atreyu asked the question on everyone's mind. Leaning over he whispered to all of them, "You wouldn't believe me! I'll tell you as soon as we go to lunch. I don't want to get in any more trouble or bring any more attention to myself!" he said. They all agreed with a silent nod of their heads and brought their attention back to Regent Cassian, who was now standing in the middle of the stage.

Fair-Lady Calliope's choir began to hum while enchanted musical instruments without anyone playing them began a melody. The room darkened and the dome ceiling came to life with vibrant colors of nebulas with sounds of cosmic rumbling. Every word Regent Cassian said became animated acting out everything he spoke of the Guardian history. "In the beginning, was the Sovereign, King of Elysium. In his delight, he created from his archeus the first two of our kind: Lord Elder Valitor, The Son of Fire and his brother Lord Elder Destriel, The Son of Light', hence forth calling them 'Watchers'. The Watchers stood at the Sovereign's side, witnesses to his creation of the five realms so named: Terra Firma, Lithorah, Vesta, Noroth, and Hehleon. The Sovereign then created all the inhabitants of these realms, all creatures of every kind were created. On the final day the Sovereign rested on His throne as 'Everlasting King' of all creation. After one millennium had passed, The Son of Light inquired of The Sovereign, "Father, why do you allow such creatures to rule themselves? They have no respect for the toils of your work! They destroy the realms as easily as they destroy each other! Allow my brother and I to rule over them to ensure balance in all creation, for there is none higher than us, save you Father! The Sovereign burned with fury, *"My Son! What has become of this treachery you speak of? You mean to rule that which you did not create!"*. Viewing the growing darkness in The Son of Light's heart, the Sovereign ordered his banishment from the kingdom. The Son of Fire was tasked with expelling his own brother from the Sovereign's Court. The Son of Light was banished from the presence of the Sovereign for a millennium, hence forth renamed as the 'Lord of Eternal Darkness' and his brother the 'Lord of Fiery Light'. Within that time the Dark Lord brought his great treachery before all of creation, spreading an evil plague for all to be damned by his words on the hearts of any who would listen. The curse unleashed, turned creation against itself in twisted and wicked ways. The Sovereign dispatched the Lord of Fiery Light to bring forth his brother for judgement of his celestial crimes. The Lord of Fiery Light seized his brother, a celestial battle commenced ending with the Lord of Fiery Light the victor. His brother slayed in combat; he secured his brother's archeus. Wounded and battle worn, he returned to The Sovereign and presented his brother's archeus. To safeguard creation, The Sovereign, took his slayed son's archeus dividing it into five lesser powers never to be conjoined again. From these powers he created 'The Five Guardians' to restore balance. The Five Guardians were commanded to guard each celestial world but never interfere with the inhabitants. But the Lord of Darkness's curse had already saturated all the realm's people, rooting itself deeply in many hearts, transforming them into vile creatures obsessed with destruction. The Five Guardians unable to contain and eradicate the sweeping curse stood ready to give their lives in fulfillment of their Sovereign's commandment. Rested and healed from the battle with his brother, the Lord of Fiery Light petitioned his father to help The Five Guardians. The Sovereign agreed to his petition but only if he would be willing to sacrifice his own archeus to The Five Guardians. The Lord of Fiery Light agreed, giving each Guardian a piece of his essence, ins forth destroying himself for all time. Having the combined power of the Lord Fiery Light's archeus with their own, The Five Guardians triumphed and restored balance to all the realms. But the realm's balance would once again be threatened by their celestial hosts, for The Five Guardians' hearts had grown prideful, they descended in wantonness from their thrones of air and took wives for themselves, bringing forth offspring that was never sanctioned by The Sovereign. The union between a Guardian and a realm inhabitant birthed the Nephilim, offspring that were endowed with the celestial powers like that of their Guardian fathers. Their time brought forth an era the inhabitants called, 'The Age of Heroes', but heroes and heroines they were not; many used their power to intimidate those lesser than them into subjugation. All the inhabitants were forced to worship the Nephilim, calling them "Immortals" and "Princes of the Universes". The Sovereign's fiery anger burned bright and he summoned The Five Guardians to court. The five Guardians stood trial before The Sovereign, *"Why have you betrayed your bloodlines!"* the Sovereign charged. *Why have you given the Nephil-*

im to realms that were not made to contain their power!" he fumed. *"You will no longer be free to enter the realms under your custody; I will fashion an animal that you be your only key. The Sovereign fashioned five horses: one brown for Terra Firma, one white for Lithorah, one red for Vesta, one gray for Noroth, and one black for Hehleon. You will hence forth purify all creation from your wicked offspring. Then you shall return to me my firstborn's archeus, for you are no longer worthy to possess such a power! You shall be known as 'The Five Horseman'. Your days will become numbered, for your immortality is hence forth stripped from you for all time, you will return back the power for which you were created"*. Fear and terror gripped the hearts of The Five Guardians and they did as commanded. The realms suffered great and terrible floods, planets within the cosmos destroyed, mountains of fire engulfed all the lands. The Five Guardian's wraith against their offspring was great, for their offspring were as they were, having none above them. Alas, not all the Horsemen's offspring were wicked and they spared only the virtuous. Balance restored, The Five Guardians returned the Lord of Fiery Light's archeus to the Sovereign and built The Temple of Aurora as a stronghold to shelter the last of their offspring. It is here in this very temple they established the Five Orders: Lion-Heart, Thunder-Horse, Fire-Hawk, Spirit-Wolf, and Iron-Bear to symbolize the spirit of each celestial realm. They trained their offspring in the temple, continuingly testing the limitations of their powers; writing thousands of scrolls for their descendants to study from. Sensing the last of their days was near, they ordained Five Regents to lead each order. To Ensure their failure will never be repeated, they appointed a five-member committee with one Elder Guardian Chieftain, called The Council of Light. The Council of Light governs the Five Orders to ensure that the Guardian hierarchy remains true to their lifelong purpose of defending the realms. Before the Horsemen's time was upon them, they requested an audience with their Sovereign. Standing before Him, they returned their horses and knelt in worship. Each surrendered his archeus willingly, the Sovereign pleased with their humble sacrifice; awarded them His favor and mercy. Seeing all they had done to ensure the celestial realms would be protected by noble Guardians, he blessed their offspring making them full-blooded Guardians, hence forth sanctioning the five Guardians as 'The Ancient Ones'. It is rumored the Sovereign fashioned a sword of power to contain the Lord of Fiery Light's archeus, only to be retrieved by solving a death riddle. The Ancient Ones returned to their creator in Elysium. For two millennia the realms enjoyed peace until a plague of nightmarish creatures of great power matching that of a Guardian called The Zoon, swarmed; attacking all the realms with unquenchable blood-lust. The Zoon were no creations of the Sovereign, The Five Orders responded in full strength, halting The Zoon's plague from further advancement in the city of Arcadia. Most of the Zoon were imprisoned in He-hleon, where they await the Sovereign's judgement. The last of Zoon, the most treacherous, fled to the shadows of the realms. To eradicate the remaining threat, The Council of Light commissioned an order of elite Guardians, The First Knights. One Guardian from each of the Five orders would be chosen to enlist as a First Knight, only the greatest of the five would be commissioned as Captain of The First Knights. Lord Dagon was chosen as Captain, but he entered into trea-son along with two Knights, Lord Kairah and Lord Sidion. Lord Tessla soon discovered the treacherous plot from within their ranks. The betrayer Lord Dagon, whom had polluted himself with the teachings by the Lord of Darkness, sought for himself the soul of all the realms. Lord Dagon corrupted two-thirds of The Five Orders, assembling a mighty army unto himself. Dagon sought to enslave the realms to rule over them just as the Lord of Darkness desired, The Council of Light issued celestial warrants for all the traitors to be brought be-fore them for judgment. This duty fell to the last legitimate First Knights, Lord Artorius and Lord Tessla. Lord Artorius was chosen as Captain, he along with Lord Tessla rallied the last remaining one-third of loyal Guardians. Aided by fairy, dwarf, and elven allies he defeated Lord Dagon and his dissolute army. This battle became known as the Great Fall, leaving The Five Orders' ranks nearly decimated. Defeated, Dagon was sentenced to execution and his rebel army imprisoned for all time, hence forth known as 'The Fallen'. All were stripped of their order medallions, exiled from the temple forever, and imprisoned to the vast emptiness of the Dark realm. Lord Dagon was tried and found guilty of treason in the highest order, a final order of execution fell to the last of the First Knights', Captain Artorius. But like our ancient predecessors, he too failed in fulfilling his commandment. He failed to execute Dagon, instead imprisoning him, to suffer a separate fate away from his rebel army. Dishonored, he exiled himself from the temple, The Council scorched by betrayal; ordered the immediate dissolvement of the First Knights", Cassian said glaring at Artorius. Artorius glared back, he knew Cassian meant to insult him, a flap of his wings and he was gone. Cassian smirked, "Now you are dismissed, lunch will be served in the dining hall and in the temple courtyard", he said pleased with himself at Artorius' departure. All the students begin to exit the Oratory Dome. "Let's go!" Atreyu motioned with his hand to the group. All five of them left the Oratory Dome, walking to the dining hall. "Okay, we are all dying of suspense Adin! What happened to you last night? You never came up!" Atreyu remarked. "It's, ah, it's going to take a few minutes to explain", Adin said rubbing the throbbing pain behind his head. "Trust me, you're going to want to be sitting down for this!" he said to the group. Once in the dining hall, all five realized the noise was too loud for Adin to explain every little detail, "Perhaps outside would be better to hear what happened?" Persaeus suggested. "Right!" Atreyu agreed. They all grabbed handfuls of red apples, cheese, bananas, and bread running into the courtyard in search of a secluded comfortable spot to sit down.

"Okay, out with it!" Lozen demanded, Adin began his tale of adventure, all four listened intently, drowning out all the laughter and chatter of the other order's students enjoying lunch around the courtyard.

"The last thing I remember was the awful pain in the back of my head and seeing teeth then feeling something licking my face". "Allow me", Lozen said standing up to check the back of his head. "That can't be!" she said shocked. "Can't what? Atreyu questioned. "What's she saying?" Adin said distressed. "You have a bump alright but that's impossible! The reason that should be impossible is because, well, none of us can be hurt or become sick! It's part of what we are, practically invincible except by the hand from another of our kind. Has anyone told you of this? I mean surely Regent Alina and Lord Artorius should have told you in the infirmary?" Lozen said, her words repeating over and over in his mind. "We have to be back in a couple of minutes, if we are late, Regent Alina will never let us here the end of it!" Persaeus warned. Back at the Oratory Dome, all five ran into Artorius at the entry. "Lord Artorius, can we meet with you after dinner tonight in the courtyard?" Lozen asked on behalf of the whole group. "Certainly, I will be looking forward to it Lady Lozen", he said. All five returned to their seats for the 'Teleporting Basics' class taught by Regent Serene. "Now for some reason, unbeknownst to us, someone has teleported into the wrong place. So, we will take the remainder of the day practicing our teleporting skills until we are as proficient as the temple stewards", she said.

CHAPTER SIX

A WICKED PLOT

The dining hall was filled with sounds of laughter, chatter, and music. Most of the students were enjoying their choice entrees, visiting with each other, and yet some where already studying their scrolls whilst sipping starbrew. Adin felt he could get used to this kind of life, "Where's Lord Artorius?" he asked Atreyu scanning the room. Atreyu struggled to speak with a mouthful of frybread, he could only shrug his shoulders. "Really Atreyu! You act like you've never eaten frybread before!" Lozen scoffed rolling her eyes. "Its super embarrassing with your mouth full of food like that, father would not be pleased with such poor manners!" she heeded. Sarcastically Atreyu smiled with a mouth full of frybread showing a frybread smile. "What's frybread?" Persaeus asked. "Oh, itz dah vest!" Atreyu said chewing his frybread. "Her dry sum", he offered tearing off a hearty piece for her. Adin's plate floated to him, "Oh, we are going to eat outside", he said to his plate of food as if it was a real person. The plate began to follow him as they all headed to the courtyard. Outside was delightful, the sky was a sapphire blue with streaks of matte orange. The torches of undying flame burned bright blue, casting royal blue shadows giving the grounds a different look and feel. The grass was soft and plush just as it had been earlier in the day. They went back to their spot they had found during lunch and sat down to enjoy their dinner plates full of their favorite foods. The plates began setting themselves down, followed by glasses of each of their favorite drinks. "Am, I interrupting?" Artorius asked the group. Atreyu nearly choked on his frybread, struggling to swallow a large balled up piece in his mouth, "Lord Artorius, you really shouldn't do that, you scared the life out of me! How'd you sneak up on us so quietly?" he marveled. "Old trick your father showed me when I was young!" he said, surprising him. "You know our father!?" Lozen said in disbelief. "Yes, your father and I were in The Noble Wolf League together", he said. Snapping his fingers, Atreyu blurted out, "That's what father meant, when he would talk about The Noble Wolf!". Smiling, Artorius asked, "Lady Lozen you wished to speak to me?" "Yes, my Lord, Adin injured his head and I don't understand how that is possible", she said bewildered. Artorius knew there was no use in hiding Adin's secret amongst his new friends. With a concerned look on his face Artorius began to explain, "Tell no one of this, Adin has been cursed by something he has eaten, whoever cursed the food he ate knew exactly what he would eat and when he would eat it. The curse has stopped his cells from metamorphosizing, particularly the cells responsible for his invincibility. Forgive, me Adin for not telling you, but your assassin may not know his wicked plot worked, I have asked all involved to keep this matter private until we have discovered the perpetrator". "But that means Adin will be susceptible to anyone who harms him whether intentional or not!" Lozen appealed. "Yes, that is why I am asking you all to help look after him while I will be away, seeking answers to this treacherous plot", he said. "When will you be leaving", Adin asked worried. "Tonight. No one knows but you five, I am trusting all of you to keep this to yourselves. I don't know what other traps lay in wait for you and I don't want any of you to get hurt partaking in a task none of you are trained for, if you see something or someone suspicious notify a Regent or Gatekeeper immediately! Does everyone understand?" he said looking to everyone, they all nodded yes. "Tomorrow you start your spell defense training", he said on a lighter note. "But if I can be hurt!" Adin said troubled. "You will have your forearm bracers as your defense, Regent Serene will teach you how to protect yourself without the use of any weapons for now", Artorius assured him. "I won't let anything happen to you and from the looks of it, your new friends won't either", he said to put him at ease. "Now, trust in yourself as you did all those years in the orphanage, I know Sister Lizzie taught you to be resilient, did she not?" he said stirring him. "She did!" Adin said. "Very well, I take my leave, there's much I have to do, I shall return in three days' time", Artorius said before disappearing, leaving the sound of a mighty flap of invisible wings. "Can't wait until we can do that!" Atreyu said starstruck. "You won't be able to get off the ground brother with a belly full of frybread!" Lozen teased. "You won't be able to either with that big head of yours!" Atreyu teased back; she threw a piece of frybread at him. "Don't worry Adin, we'll get through this!" she said. Suddenly a voice emanating from the undying flame spoke from the pontifex, "Attention! All students interested in trying out for the games, please report to the dining hall. Lord Gabdor will be giving his presentation, that is all!". "Should we go?" Adin asked the group, "Couldn't hurt! Besides I think Battle Wing is pretty exciting!" Persaeus admitted.

They ventured back to the dining hall; the sounds of abundant life mixed with music was invigorating from the news of his curse. Standing in the middle of the round table Lord Gabdor began his presentation, "I imagine everyone here is interested in one of the temple's games, yes?" he said posing his question to all the students seated. "Now I must impress that your extracurricular interests must not interfere with your training! You must maintain a gold standard in each of your assigned disciplines. In the game Spell-Craft you will compete against the brightest students, matching wit against wit mixed with talent and skill in casting spells to defeat your opponent. It is truly a philosophical sport! In Glaive Star you will pit a team effort against rival teams from each order, each game may be played in any of the five realms. Your value as a team member is essential to the success of your team, hence your order. For those spirited youth that love the thrill of singular efforts, the wind rushing through your hair, the tandem hoof beats matching that of your own beating heart, can find satisfaction in Battle Wing. If you love horses, then this is most definitely for you Thunder-Horse! Every gamer will also be required to assist with Erindol's community initiatives, helping the residents to enhance their daily lives as well as foster stronger bonds between the residents of the remaining realms. These games are for the pure entertainment of the Sovereign, there is no true "winner or loser" just the journey of participation into an understanding of your true self. Oh, and the thrill and exhilaration of the game isn't bad either!" Lord Gabdor smirked as if he is reminiscing his time as a gamer. "Now who's interested!?" he said. Immediately every hand of his audience shot straight up into the air. "Now the Spell Craft sign up is here, Battle Wing over here, Glaive Star here", he said pointing to three scrolls that floated to each student.

"It looks like we will have quite a year this time!" Serene said from the Regent table with mild enthusiasm. "It appears so but only the triads will tell", Regent Marius commented. "Yes, but remember dear brother, nothing remains as it was when it first began", Regent Tiberius remarked. They all signed up for Glaive Star. Persaeus also signed up for Battle Wing. "Can we sign up for more than one game?" Lozen asked Lord Gabdor. "Of course, Lady Lozen but you will be held to the same gold standard as everyone else. Listen carefully! Glaive Star first gathering is this Saturday at ten am. Battle Wing at noon and Spell Craft at two pm. If there aren't any further questions, you are all now released to your leisure time, thank you!" he said bowing. All five returned to their spot in the courtyard amongst the students leaving to their chambers for the night, Atreyu flopped himself on the soft grass folding his arms behind his head, giving out a silent yawn. "You look how I feel!" Lucian said. "I didn't think

strong ones like yourself got tired at all", he said yawning.
"Well to keep fit for duty, requires much energy both physically and mentally and my mental stamina is expiring", he
said fatigued. "Okay brother, I get it, you're tired", he said
with the biggest yawn yet; his words almost unintelligible. "I
think we could all use some rest; tomorrow is going to be an
exhausting day!" Lozen said to the group. "Yes, she has a good
point, spell defense is the first of a series of disciplines that is
the core of a Guardian's skills!" Persaeus said excited. "You
guys go ahead, I'm not that tired, I'll be up in just a few. I
just need to sit here a moment to clear my head before I go
to bed. I don't want to be tossing and turning all night", Adin
said. "We will all stay with you brother!" Lucian said. "No,
I need to just-", before Adin could finish, Lozen spoke, "Are
you sure? We can all stay with you", she said sensing he was
is in internal turmoil. Reading his eyes, she knew he needed
some time to himself, given all he has been through. "If you
need us, just use the zilly-wood dust in the pontifex", Persaeus
said reminding him. "I will", he promised her. They left Adin
to his thoughts. "Is that a common Terra Firmian custom?"
Persaeus asked Lozen. "Yes, it is one that many Terra Firmians invoke to be left to their thoughts, when their thoughts
have clouded their minds", she answered. "Oh, how terrible
it must be to be under such weight in one's mind", Persaeus
said to herself. Now alone Adin sat down resting his forehead
on his knees. *'I don't think I can do this'* he thought to himself.
Worried that he will be in mortal danger tomorrow with Artorius away made him feel as if he was standing on unstable
ground. Up until now Artorius has been with him, reassuring
him, strengthening him, and encouraging him. The moment
Artorius was not with him, he got lost and injured himself.
The blue flame of the courtyard pontifex began to flicker and
grow brighter catching his attention. "Master Adin!" Artorius'
voice called out. He looked around until he heard Artorius
voice call out again. "Master Adin!". "Ah, right the zilly-wood

magic dust stuff!" he said to himself as he got up to go to the flame. "Ah, how do you use this thing? Do I just speak into to it?" he said in an empty courtyard. Realizing he looked foolish talking to himself, "This is Adin", he said to the flame. Artorius' face appeared in the blue flame, "I have something that belongs to you that you can use tomorrow during your spell defense training. I think you will find it of great use", he said. "Thank you, I was worried about tomorrow. This spell stuff sounds really serious and I'm definitely not like the other students, at least not now", he said discouraged. "I understand and you are right to be concerned about tomorrow, however; I am sure at the orphanage you have dealt with more challenges than what lay before you now. You survived as a fledgling without any of the powers your fellow students possess now. That makes you stronger than you will ever know, that is your strength of heart. Focus on this tomorrow and each day until you have harnessed this truth for yourself", he said to embolden him. Everything Artorius said to him was both comforting and confusing, he had never looked at his life's predicament as a symbol of strength but only of survival. "The 'mortal toil' is your first obstacle, you must harness your power to overcome it. Only you can do this, I believe in you as I always have. I must go now and you must find the peace in your spirit to rest", he said ending the conversation. Instantly the blue flame returned to its normal burning brightness and light, he took a deep breath and began his trek back to the Lion-Heart common room.

Adin found the common room empty; his presence ignited the sounds of crackling embers from the fireplace breaking the silence. Walking over to the staircase, "Adin", he recited, instantly he found himself in his chambers; Lucian and Atreyu sound asleep along with Tristan. Atreyu was laying half way on the bed, his head underneath his pillow, he quietly walked over to his bed and changed into his sleeping clothes. Folding back the plush and thick bed spread, he appreciated how comfortable it felt versus the green wool blanket he had for many years in the orphanage. Climbing into the bed, he laid his head against the softest, fluffiest pillow he had ever felt. Pulling the covers up to his chest, he began to feel at ease and relaxed thinking that tomorrow may not be so bad. The comfort of the pillow and bed spread brought a smile to his face, he glanced down by his feet only to find a pair of illuminated eyes staring at him just above the footboard. He froze in fright, slowly he looked down, he could feel one impression of a foot by his feet then another. He braced himself, stiffening his body, he thought about calling out to Lucian and Atreyu but reasoned there was no time for them to help him. He now felt the full weight of something looming on top of him and warm moist panting breath. He closed his eyes and grit his teeth, *'this is it, a monster is going to devour me'* he reasoned. Suddenly a warm wet tongue licked his face, he opened one eye only to find Kofka, Artorius' pet wolf or what he thought was a wolf. Kofka sat happily on his body, panting and licking his face. "He was waiting on your bed when we got here", Atreyu's said half asleep. "He was jumping on Lucian and licking my face until we told him to go wait under your bed", he yawned before rolling over to fall back to sleep. "Well that explains why Atreyu was hiding his face from you!" Adin chuckled while scratching behind Kofka's ear. "Listen you can sleep on the bed but by my feet, deal?" Kofka agreed by nuzzling his face against Adin's before turning around and curling himself up in ball. He noticed that Kofka had feathery wings that he wrapped and tucked around himself like a blanket. He sat up in bed, "Now, that's not something you see every day!".

The next morning, the sunlight streamed in the arched windows of the chamber, giving everything a renewed look and feel. Lucian and Atreyu were already up strapping their boots on before making their beds. Adin woke up to Kofka licking his face. "Hey! Thought we had a deal!?" he said greeting Kofka, patting his head. "We felt you needed a little extra time to rest since you were up later than us last night", Atreyu said. "How do you feel little brother?" Lucian asked. "I feel good, hungry", he said rubbing his eyes. "You guys go ahead; I'll meet you in the dining hall for breakfast. Hey where's the other kid?" he said looking over at Tristan's neatly folded bed. "Guess he's an earlier riser than all of us, see you there", Atreyu said before he and Lucian left. Adin sat up, "Well time for a shower! You want a bath?" he said to Kofka. Kofka immediately jumped off the bed and crawled underneath it. "Guess that means no", he said shrugging his shoulders. He crawled out of bed, looked around and spied a heavy looking arched shaped wooden door with three sets of large towels hanging on the wall. '*That's probably the shower*', he wondered as he walked over to the door. He grabbed a towel, the door opened without any assistance to a spacious stone rectangular room that looked like a shower area but without the normal shower plumbing or even shower heads. Adin hung his sleep clothes on a bronze hook behind the door and wrapped the towel around his waist. There was a stone table against an adjacent wall with three old looking sea shells, each filled with a purple, red, and blue crystal-like powder. Underneath the purple filled shell inscribed on a gold plate was the words, "In Odorem Bellator". The red filled shell read, "Angelus Odore", the last; the blue filled shell read, "Spiritum Bellator". Walking around the room, he took notice of drain covers on the floor. "Okay? Where are all the shower heads, where does the water come out of?" he said to himself, "Where's the soap?" he said still looking around. Walking completely around the whole room, all he could find were words etched into the stone walls. "Demisimber", he recited. Suddenly the coldest, crispest water fell from above his head. "OH MY GOD!" Adin howled leaping to the left only to have the water follow him as he began a slippery escape around the room, the water followed him in endless pursuit. Outrunning the water for a brief moment, he read the second set of words, "Feverectum!" the water then turned hot; way too hot for him. "Whoa!" he yelped as he began another slippery escape. He ran around the shower room, yelling out the words etched into each wall he came to. "Crucemos!" water blasted him horizontally from his right-side defying gravity as it splashed him. "Finitor-irrigo", the water stopped, then blasted him horizontally from his left side, once again defying gravity. "Lympscarsio", suddenly all the water stopped. Drenched, he kept turning around expecting water to come from any direction. Suddenly he realized what was about to happen, he looked down in disbelief, "You have got to be kid-", he yelled, a massive swoosh of flood of water blasted him from the ground up knocking him backwards. Just before he crashed to the stone ground that was certain to cause serious injury, Kofka was there to brace his fall, spreading his wings like a safety net; catching him. Kofka bolted to the threshold of the shower room, carrying Adin as if he was on a mobile gurney. Safe on the wooden floor of his chambers, Adin rolled off Kofka's wings, "Thanks Kofka, that was literally the most dangerous shower in the world!" he said dripping wet. Kofka shook the water from his fur coat and wings as the final touches to Adin's morning shower. Spluttering water from his mouth, "Really Kofka! Was that necessary?" he said unamused. Kofka barked back in response, giving Adin one more light sprinkle of water as he shook the remaining water off of him. Adin laughed to himself and grabbed another towel to dry off. Dressed in his training uniform, he ensured he looked presentable in the mirror, he couldn't shake the thought now of him getting hurt; he was interrupted by the pontifex. A fairy voice spoke through the chamber torch, "You will be late to class, breakfast is now over!". Terrified he would be late to class, he leaped to the staircase to teleport, "Grimoirium", he said.

Appearing at the entrance to class, he found his order. The grimoirium was a large arena with a sand pit in the center surrounded by bleachers. He saw Lozen, Persaeus, Atreyu, and Lucian waving him over. "We were beginning to worry", Persaeus said. "I had trouble with the shower", Adin responded. "Yeah, might have forgotten to tell you about that!" Atreyu said with raised eyebrows. "If it's any consolation to you, Atreyu filled the whole shower room with water, almost up to the ceiling!" Lucian laughed. "When I heard all this commotion, I checked on him and he looked like a cat in water, paddling around to each wall struggling to read the words!" Lucian laughing harder now. "I could have drowned!" Atreyu mumbled. "Hello! You can't drown dummy, you're not like", Lozen caught herself. "Not like me", Adin said finishing her comment. "I'm sorry Adin, I didn't mean it like", she said with regret. "It's okay, no big deal!" he said irritated pushing past everyone to the front of the group where Regent Serene was waiting for everyone to situate themselves. "That was so stupid of me!" Lozen said disappointed with herself. "He is under a great deal of stress, his irritation is not pointed at you", Lucian tried to console her as the group gathered around Regent Serene to receive instruction.

"In this arena you will hone your spell binding, spell bounding, and spell casting skills, this is the first discipline necessary to defend against all pranical arts", she said pacing back and forth. "I thought nothing could hurt us?" a boy named Vito from the Fire-Hawk order said out loud. Scanning each youthful face, sensing the question was on everyone's mind, she continued, "Your right! If the pranical arts are casted by anything or anyone other than a Guardian, then yes you will be unharmed; but casted by such as a Fallen; then you will be harmed if not killed. If a Fallen casts' any spell you will be most certainly affected by the very nature of the spell. Casting by any other may temporarily immobilize you for a brief moment, however; those effects depend heavily on your individual archeus. I know of several Guardians that have developed their archeus to such a degree, that they are unaffected by spells in combat by non-Guardians, one in particular; Lord Artorius. Now, everyone gather in a half circle!" she ordered. All the students formed themselves in a half circle as ordered. "During this evolution, you will receive training instruction in the formation of a half circle. Once we have covered a subject spell we will then partner up and practice on each other. Some of you will catch on more quickly than the others. I cannot stress the importance of mastering this skill, without proper technique you will most certainly loose the battle!" she cautioned. Suddenly Regent Alina appeared with the sound of wings trailing her appearance. "Forgive the intrusion, Elder Valerian requested Regent Cassian last minute and ordered me to assist in his stead", she said; Regent Serene nodded. "We were just beginning with a demonstration", she said. "Lord Artorius left this in my care for you", Alina said to Adin removing a leather envelope from her cloak. "Master Adin", she invited, he walked to meet her with every eye on him, he could hear various voices in the group, "What's in it?" "Wonder what he left him?" "What makes him so special?" "He asked me to ensure you received this", she said giving Adin the leather envelope. "What's in it?" he asked. "I did not ask and it is not my business", she answered. "I will need you as an uke", Regent Serene urged Regent Alina. She nodded and walked to the other side of the arena opposite of Serene. "Now, while training, our only goal is to familiarize ourselves with the subject spell not to harm our partner! Does everyone understand?" she forewarned. "Yes Regent!" both orders responded in unison. "Now your forearm bracers are made of star ore, capable of defending against any spell or weapon attack, however; that success is based off of the wearer's ability and skill. If a spell strikes you, you will most certainly feel a slight zap, many students describe it as a small electrical shock". All the students were growing more excited in anticipation of casting spells, some were adjusting the fit of their bracers. "Watch carefully as we begin, whenever an exhibition or demonstration takes place, it is customary to bow to your opponent as a sign of respect. Regent Serene and Regent Alina bowed to each other. Both then shifted their customary bow into fighting postures, suddenly Serene jumped into the air shouting, "Impeirmasa!" raising her hand over her head as if she is going to dunk a basketball, a ball of white electrified energy immediately manifested in her palm. With tremendous ferocity she flung the ball of white energy at Alina. Crackling through the air, the white energy ball rocketed, zigzagging its way to its target. Every student let out a sigh of uncertainty, wondering if Alina would be able to block the attack in time. Just before hitting her, she struck it with her forearm bracer, it exploded in a blast of energy. The Impeirmasa's destructive energy is absorbed in her forearm bracer, permeating along the surface of her bracers, in stringy illuminated tentacles. Regent Serene spun around to face her students, "Now that was an Impeirmasa attack, it is a form of concentrated energy that moves in erratic patterns just before it strikes the intended target to rout any potential defense. Defending against this attack will require patience and a still mind", she said turning to face Regent Alina, both bowed again and this time it was Regent Alina's turn to attack. She stomped her foot with a mighty thud on the loose sand, creating a cloud of fine particles, she extended both of her arms out in front of her with clenched fists towards Serene. Reciting the words, "Pertinculum!" the cloud of sand molded itself into three darts of compressed of sand, hovering in midair, waiting for her to send them. Opening both her hands, signaled all three of the darts to race towards Serene.

Serene sprinted to meet them, smashing two of the darts with each of her bracers, except the third that seemed to have disappeared as the other two were being destroyed. Advancing on Alina, she gave no sign of slowing down, she advanced until she was just a few feet away from reaching her. One student voiced the question on everyone's mind, 'Where is the third dart?" Serene stopped inches from Alina, her feet slid in the sand by the powerful momentum of her speed. "There it is!" Vito shrieked; the final sand dart shot straight for Regent Serene's back. She sensed it, spinning around crossing both arms in an 'X', uncrossing them just in the nick-of-time ; smashing it to pieces as it struck her forearm bracers. Teleporting back to her group of students, "Now that is a demonstration of offensive positioning into defensive positioning. This skill requires timing and control", she explained to the class. Concluding the demonstration, she arranged every student into pairs. "One of us should be with Adin at all times, help make an easy defense for him", Lozen suggested. "But if that happens, wouldn't that look at if we are always taking an easy on him?" Persaeus pointed out. "She's right!" Adin said. "If you guys are always my partner, someone is bound to notice that the spells are way too easily defended!" he said dejected. "Some of the spells we will be practicing are rather harmless for us but fatal for a mortal, little brother. Are you sure about this?" Lucian questioned. "It's not worth getting killed over this Adin, maybe you can fall ill all of a sudden!" Atreyu said attempting to change his mind. "No, if I don't go through with this, it will be obvious that something is wrong with me and that will draw unwanted attention. I'll find a way to deal with this, I have to, because I have no other choice!" he said unmoved. Lozen paired up with Persaeus while Lucian and Atreyu paired up. "As soon as you find your partner, two lines! One with Regent Alina and one with me!" Regent Serene ordered. Adin got paired up with Bestion of the Thunder-Horse order, not by choice but of consequence, everyone was too afraid to team up with Bestion and for good reason. Bestion looked monstrous compared to Adin, he was a handsome boy with cropped hair, his muscles were well defined, and the look on his face was absolute confidence. Little did Adin know Bestion has been mentored all his life to graduate at the top of his order to pursue his ambitions of solving the Sovereign's riddle, he wanted to be the greatest Guardian

119

to ever wield the Sword of Power. Adin opened the leather envelope pulling out a diamond shaped note tied at the ends. He untied it to find a gold ring in the center, he unfolded the note, it was written by Artorius. 'This was your mother's; it belongs to you now'. Adin cracked a slight smile, the ring had elaborate decorative designs in white gold. He put the ring on, the designs glowed for a brief second, "Everyone have a partner and in place?" Regent Serene called out snapping Adin out of his admiration of his ring. He quickly looked around, finding Bestion staring at him annoyed. He ran over opposite of Bestion, "Sorry", he said trying to apologize. Bestion just responded with a look that he was all too familiar with in his past dealings with Kristof. "ON GUARD!" Regent Serene and Regent Alina announced. Every student assumed their own fighting stance. "Remember! We are only learning to defend not to harm our partner!" Serene said. Adin could feel his heart thumping like it wanted to burst out of his chest, he was both excited and scared as to what would come. Bestion looked undeterred, confident, and determined to do him in, at that moment both Regents called out, "Hachimeh!" the command to 'fight'. Bestion let loose the Impeirmasa spell, Adin crossed both his arms using his bracers as Serene had done, the impact felt like an 18-wheeler had hit him. His body was thrown back several feet, he landed with a thud on the soft sand. All the students stopped at once at the sight of him flying backwards through the air until he crashed into the sand, both Regents teleported to him immediately. Lozen, Atreyu, Lucian, and Persaeus struggled to contain themselves from helping him. Adin could feel all the wind had been knocked out of his chest, his whole body felt sore. He sat himself up, peering over to his friends, reading their concerned faces; he shook his head, "no" to discourage their involvement. "Master Adin, are you okay?" Regent Serene asked helping him to his feet. "Plant your feet next time Master Adin, or you can expect the same result again and again", Regent Alina instructed with no compassion. Regent Serene looked at Regent Alina dismayed, "Alina! There's no possible way he should have been affected like that!" she said shocked. "He didn't plant his feet, Serene! A mistake he won't soon forget! Up now Master Adin, we don't want to hinder training for the rest of the students!". Adin grabbed at his chest, brushing off all the sand on him; he began his walk back to his line. "There is no walking in a training evolution Master Adin!" Alina yelled at him. He began his brief painful trek to Bestion, taking his place, assuming his fighting stance once more.

"On guard, Hachimeh!" is called out again. Bestion with no sympathy for Adin whatsoever did not withhold any of his strength, he used the Pertinculum spell, superman punching the sand beneath him. The sand particles burst up into the air forming the same three sand darts as Alina had done. With a devilish look in his eye, he flung open his fingers in Adin's direction, the darts launched at his command. Adin stepped back preparing for the impact, all three darts closing the distance in seconds, he managed to block one with his right bracer, it shattered instantly; only to suffer the strike of the last two. One dart struck him in the chest and the second struck him just above his left eye. He felt as if he was struck by a high-pitched baseball in both his chest and face as his feet lifted off the ground. The attack knocked him head over heels, he landed on the plane of his shoulders and neck, again instant pain wrecked his body. Lozen could take no more of watching her friend suffer, she rushed over to him. Kneeling down beside him, she burned with fury, she eyed Bestion out of the corner of her eye. Atreyu, Lucian, and Persaeus followed, rushing over to help Adin up. Lozen stood up, her fists clenched tight, she glared at Bestion. He stood there, unaffected with quiet pride at his performance. Lozen's eyes filled with rage as she summoned the Impeirmasa spell, the ball of bright pure energy formed in her hand. Seeing his sister's fury firsthand, Atreyu feared she would surely get into trouble, he

knew what his sister meant to do. "Lozen! Stop!" he demanded. Persaeus hopped to her feet to grab her by the arm to keep
her from lifting it against Bestion, "Lozen! Stop, please!" she
begged. Suddenly Lucian stepped in front of her, towering
over her. "Little sister, you must stop!" he said placing his hand
on her shoulder to restrain her. She was locked in on Bestion, she started to drag Persaeus, Persaeus' feet digging into
the sand left grooves as she was being pulled. Lucian felt the
strength of her forward advance, "Lozen! Attacking another
student will expel you. If you are expelled, what will your father say?" he said hoping she would come to her senses. That
was all Lozen needed to hear to snap out of her rage, her eyes
began to relax and soften. "It will be alright little sister, all of
us feel the same way. Right now, Adin needs us here for him
not expelled", he said calming her. Regent Serene and Alina
again teleported to Adin, only now he was more visibly hurt
than before. His left eye started to swell with a light trickle
of blood running down the side of his face. "I will take him
to the infirmary, please take over instruction for me", Regent
Serene said "Of course", Alina said. Upon hearing the exchange between both Regents, he blurted out, "No! I'm fine, I
can train!". He helped himself up with the assistance from all
his friends, with a stoic look on his face he stared fearlessly at
Bestion, he forced his aching muscles into his fighting stance.
"Remarkable!" Serene said in silent astonishment of his determination. "That's a Lion-Heart for you!" Alina replied with a
satisfactory smile on her face as she returned to her side of the
arena. "Back to training now", Serene commanded Lozen,
Lucian, Atreyu, and Persaeus. "On guard, Hachimeh!" Bestion used the Impeirmasa spell again only this time he used
both hands to create two balls of energy and slung them at
Adin. Adin quickly crossed his arms again waiting for the two
energy blasts. Right as they both reached him, he uncrossed
his arms with such intensity it looked as if he was breaking
free of invisible chains. The energy explosion created a thun-

der-struck where he stood, causing everyone to slam to the ground to include both Regents. The thunder-struck was followed by a blinding streak of blue fiery light that drowned him out. Regent Serene and Alina were the first to recover to their feet, fearing the worst for him. Both teleported to him just as the light subsided only to find the burnt sand beneath his feet had turned to glass reaching out in a half moon shape. He stood there; the whole ordeal felt as if he was inside a firecracker. His ears where ringing, his skin felt hot, and his body felt like it was surging with heat. His hands were still covering his eyes, holding his face. "Master Adin, are you alright?" Alina asked in a delicate tone. The blue glow slowly extinguished as he cautiously lowered his hands, he looked around as if he did not know where or who he was. "Master Adin, dear boy, are you okay?" she said now with mounting worry. She feared he was terribly injured, "I...ah...I'm fine", is all he said before he blacked out, Alina caught him before he collapsed on the sand. The students all stared in disbelief, raising themselves up, asking the incontrovertible question; "What just happened?" His vision narrowed to black as he lay in the arms of Alina, the last of his senses, his hearing; is all that is left to capture the aftermath, "The sand has melted to glass Alina!" Serene said shaken, Alina looked to the glass burned into the ground, she didn't say a word. Serene knew she had to take control of the situation, "It appears Master Adin has accidently triggered an advanced spell defense technique! Everyone back to your places, training will not be suspended for such accidents! Hachimeh!" Serene hollered quickly giving the students no time to speculate as to what just happened.

CHAPTER SEVEN

FIRE-STAR

Adin awoke back in the infirmary, the flicker of blue candle light illuminated the room. His feet felt heavy; something was laying on them. He grabbed the candle holder and propped himself up only to find Kofka curled in a ball, on top of his feet. He reached over to scratch Kofka's ear, "He's been with you the whole time Master Adin", Lord Tadrian said from a lounger. "What happened? Last thing I remember was loud, very loud thunder then blinding light when I was defending against Bestion. He used a dual attack against me and not by accident I suspect!" he chided. "Well Master Adin, I cannot comment on the particulars with your training evolution but I can tell you that you were brought here by your Regent. The injuries are minor, but you will have a bruised eye for some time, I have mixed together a treatment called 'ochir clay' that you can use until it is fully healed. It will conceal the outward appearance of the injury to others but you will still be able to see it, apply twice a day as needed. It was used in ancient times in Terra Firma for rulers, kings, and those in pretended power. It was used to conceal their injuries after battle or attempted assassination in order to solidify their false god-like status", he said handing the jar to him. "Why would a Guardian need it?" Adin said looking the jar over. "It's a fairy treatment used for the fairies and dwarves that were put under the sword during the Great Fall. Fairies and dwarves used it on their loved ones so they would look more presentable for the funeral services", he said heartbroken. "I'm sorry, I didn't mean to sound so ignorant", Adin said hoping he hadn't inadvertently opened some kind of emotional wound for him. "Not at all my boy, not at all. Well, I believe it's time I advise your Regent that you are awake, I will be releasing you back without any restrictions, unless you object?" he said. Adin shook his head 'no'. He threw some zilly-wood into the pontifex, "Regent Alina, this is Lord Tadrian", he said waiting for her to answer. "Lord Tadrian, good evening. How may I help you?" she asked. "Your young Lion-Heart has awoken; I see no need to keep him for further treatment", he said assured. "I understand, thank you for tending to his injuries Lord Tadrian. I will send for him in the morning", she said. "Very well Regent, I shall see you first thing in the morning". Adin laid back down, his eyes felt heavy and his body very tired.

He woke the next morning to the sight of all his order friends. Lozen had brought some starbrew and Atreyu had brought him some frybread. "How are you feeling little brother?" Lucian asked. "Good as I'm going to be for now", he said sitting up in his bed, pulling his feet out from under Kofka. Kofka was too lazy and comfortable to move aside. "How much training have I missed?" he yammered. "Oh, not much other than the other orders asking us what happened to you, most of all Bestion, but I don't think he had any concern for you. I think his pride was questioned more than anything", Persaeus answered. "How did you manage a level of defense like that!" Atreyu said unable to contain himself. "I mean that thunder clap and blinding light was, well something that shocked all of us, even the Regents!" he said even more excited than before. "Look! I don't know what happened or how it happened! All I remember is that Bestion did an intentional attack, he wanted to hurt me or worse. I was so angry! As soon as he cast the spell, all I could think of was to deflect the spell right back at him!" he said peeved. "Well you did more than that! You floored everyone in the arena, that's not possible from a fledgling such as ourselves!" Lozen said. "Forgive me, but that does not sound at all like a 'thunder-clap' but that of a 'thunder-struck', Tadrian chimed in. Everyone looked over at him, "A 'thunder-struck' can only be used by a Guardian who has mastered the 'thunder-clap' to harness its energy and direct it. This could not be mistakenly done! Are you sure no other Lord or Regent was present other than Regent Serene and Regent Alina?" he said now stepping out of his lounger. "When was the last time a Guardian used the 'thunder-struck'?" Adin asked. "Only in battle, that I have seen", he said; his words were stern and perplexed mixed with a look of disbelief on his face. "Well it appears Master Adin is in excellent hands", he said changing his tone and the direction of the conversation. A knock on the heavy wooden door, "Come in", he said, Elder Valerian and Regent Alina stepped into the room, "Well I see it appears that you have grown fond of visiting the infirmary Master Adin", the elder joked. "You might want to move my bed up here for the time being Elder", he said joking back. "I find this no joking matter!" Alina scoffed. "Come now Regent, making light of the matter does not imply it is without concern. Besides, this is customary in Terra Firma I am told, unless I am mistaken Master Adin?" he said soliciting Adin's support. "Yeah, he's pretty much spot on, back home there's a lot of joking that goes on at other's expense", he said sitting on the side of his bed. "Master Adin has already proven to be a remarkable fledgling despite not possessing any Guardian strengths. Wouldn't you agree Lord Tadrian?" the elder regarded. "Oh, yes Elder! Most remarkable indeed!" he said back with a bit of nerves. "Is he fit to attend Lord Hylandir's presentation?" he asked. "Yes Elder, in fact I was going to release him to the care of his order's comrades, with his Regent's permission of course". "That will be fine Lord Tadrian. There will not be any practical evolutions, just a demonstration", Alina said dismissive. "Come Adin! This will be a sight! Lord Hylandir is the undefeated champion in all five realms!" Atreyu raved as the group huddled together to leave. "Lady Lozen before the day is out, I need you for counsel", Regent Alina ordered. "Yes Regent", Lozen acknowledged. "Do you guys mind if we walk? I don't feel like my body can handle teleporting at the moment", Adin asked the group. "Of course, little brother!" Lucian said. Persaeus waved her hand to open the door for the group. "Who would have thought magic would hurt so much", Atreyu quipped. The grinding sound of wood on stone floor drowned out their voices as the infirmary doors began to close, their voices becoming faint as they walked down the corridor. "He summoned a-", Regent Alina began. "Thunder-struck", Valerian finished her sentence. "How could one so young do such a thing with no training whatsoever!" she said disturbed. "Indeed. What of his injuries Lord Tadrian?" Valerian inquired. "Other than on site loss of consciousness and a black eye, nothing of great concern to his wellbeing. He will need the time to heal but nothing that I can surmise as life threatening my Elder", he said. "So, we must assume this attack was painstakingly constructed for him. It would appear this assassin is growing bolder, more elaborate in scheme or as I feared, another assassin is afoot!" he theorized. "What news of the food vendors", he asked Tadrian. "My inquires continue further into the dispensaries in the village", he said hopeful. "Of course, please notify me with the findings once you have completed the inquires", the elder ordered. "I do hope we find this cowardly assassin!" Tadrian declared. "Any word from Lord Artorius?" Valerian asked looking at Alina. "No, my Elder, no word as of yet", she said disappointed. "Very well, I fear greatly for Adin's safety if we do not find these treacherous assassins soon!". Valerian and Alina left the infirmary. Hearing the door closed, gave Tadrian the privacy to ponder, *Another assassin? Could it be so?*.

"Are we going to be on time?" Adin asked trying to keep up. "The Gladitorium isn't far from here", Atreyu said. A fairy voice from the pontifex torches came through, "You are five minutes late!". "Ah great!" Adin said irked. "Pay no attention to silly fairies!" Atreyu said trying to ease his agitation. The journey from the infirmary to the gladitorium placed their journey deep within the temple's bowels. The sounds of striking steel, bashing shields, whistling arrows, and the exhausted labors of determined students echo in the stone corridor except for a bold voice that carried above all the battle-like sounds. "In your second term you will be introduced to the 'Protective Arts', where you will receive intense instruction in weapon forms to complement your pranical arts. A Guardian that has mastered the pranical and protective arts will open the door to the celestial arts in the years to come," the voice expounded. The group entered the gladitorium, "I thought we were missing a few students, welcome! You missed my introduction," Lord Hylandir said offering them to sit. "Forgive us Lord Hylandir, we were coming from the infirmary with Adin," Lozen said. "Master Adin, I've heard so much about you, a pleasure. Now all of you please join the others", he said. The gladitorium was a huge arena, triple the size of the grimoirium both in width and height. Adin could see students were sparring one on one and negotiating obstacle courses. Up above the ceiling were clouds, he thought he saw silhouettes of winged figures. "Now as I was saying, the protective arts are just that! To guard those whom you are sworn to protect and each other! There is no room here for fool hardy or negligent behavior, any abuse or threat of abuse will be cause for immediate expulsion! Now, my weapon of choice is the 'Ame-No-Murakomo-No-Tsurugi' meaning 'Heavenly Sword of Gathering Clouds!" he said drawing his long sword from his shoulder slung scabbard. The steel made a distinctive grinding sound as the blade is unsheathed. "The steel is star-ore, forged and shaped into the unique shape of the blade you see now, each blade is different just as each of us are different", he said admiring the sheen of the steel. The steel was embossed with an elaborate Celtic design on the blade collar with a golden circular guard. The handle was made of ruby wrapped in a diamond pattern golden fleece. "The sword is a part of me just as my arms and legs are a part of me. The sword is always pure, it can be wielded for light or dark but it in of itself cannot be tainted. The sword has the power to protect or extinguish life just as the pranical arts, therefore; the utmost respect, humility, and control must be the pillars of its master", he said twirling his sword into the sheath. "Allow me to demonstrate", suddenly five elves in armor appeared marching in a single file. The first had a sheathed long sword, the second had a bow, the third had an axe and dagger, the fourth had a lance, and the fifth had a mace and shield. They each broke off from the line and surrounded him. Suddenly each fairy readied their weapons, arming themselves for battle. All bowed to Lord Hylandir followed by his bow in return. Without warning all five attacked, Lord Hylandir exemplified the expertise of a grand swordsman, feigning off each skillful attack with unmatched technique and grace. The sounds of star-ore striking star-ore left visual pops and crackles of energy. The whooshing sounds of star-ore blades slicing through the air captivated the students. Lord Hylandir looked well aged but moved like a young Guardian. All five elves were no match for him, Adin couldn't help but wonder if Artorius was as good if not better than him. The demonstration was over all five elves were defeated; he rendered the customary bow. Each of the five elves crawled to their feet to give their bow. "There will be times as a Guardian, when you may not have the opportunity to use the pranical arts due to the number of adversaries you find yourself facing, to use either or is at your discretion, completely up to you. Now, from the protective arts you must choose your path". Five more elves then appeared each with five chests filled with wooden replicas of weapons that were used in the demonstration. All the students formed into five lines to choose their weapon of choice. Adin chose the longsword, Atreyu chose the axe and dagger, Lucian chose the mace, Lozen chose the bow, and Persaeus chose the lance. As soon as each student took their wooden weapon, it shrunk to fit each student's hand and height. This was the break Adin needed to get his mind off of everything that had happened to him so far. He looked his sword over, admiring the craftsmanship, *one day I will be able to wield this sword like Lord Hylandir* he thought. He could remember past movies of sword swinging heroes that further ignited his excitement until his attention was distracted, "Has everyone chosen their path? Good! Now we must record each path by order. We will start with the Lion-Heart order first, Master Adin step forward. Now, everyone pay attention! Master Adin step up to the table. State your name, order, and touch the papyrus with your chosen path", the sword master instructed. "Adin Elijah, Lion-Heart!" he said avid. His name and order magically inscribed on the papyrus by a white flame. Once he touched his sword to the papyrus, the name 'Malg-Ozongon' burned into the papyrus. Lord Hylandir leaned over, translating it out loud, "Fire-Star', interesting; that is the name of your path", he gave an inquisitive glance at Adin. "Next", he called out for another student. Lozen's bow's name was 'The Soul-Striker', Atreyu's axe's name was 'Hard-Lightning' and his dagger 'Wolf-Tooth', Lucian's mace was 'The Dawn-Breaker', and Persaeus' lance was 'The Slayer's-Spear'. This continued until all the students had their names, orders, and wooden training aids recorded. "Once your first term has been successfully completed, you will commission a work order to forge the weapon you will wield as a Guardian. This will take two more terms to complete by the end of your fourth term. Now it is time for break, I shall see everyone at the start of the second term. If any of you wish to practice after hours, please send a request through your perspective Regents. Learn your training aids, that is learn your path; the balance, the weight, become one. Respect your training aids for The Forger will speak to each of you to determine how each will be created", he concluded. The class dismissed for lunch to the great hall, all the students were sporting their wooden training aides. Flopping himself down on the soft grass Adin, laid back, letting out a sigh. "How are you feeling little brother?" Lucian asked. "Sore, but I'll live", he said relaxing. "I've had black eyes before and have been beaten up plenty of times back home", he said with his eyes closed. "How awful for you!" Lozen said concerned. "It must have been horrible for you there and now you are feeling the same way here", she continued. "Still though, this place is better by far. I didn't have friends like you back home but I do miss mother", he confessed, "What classes did I miss?" he said sitting up. "Well, you missed language arts and randori", Persaeus said. "Wow! Even here you have to read boring books!" he said covering his face in disgust. "What's ran-d-o-r-i?" he asked. "Language arts teaches us the languages of all the realms, so that we can communicate and to learn our own celestial language", Lozen said. "Okay now that's pretty cool!" he admitted. "And randori is unarmed hand to hand combat", she said answering the second part to his question. "Glad I missed that, my body could use the rest", he joked. "I could go for an oreo heaven with cinnamon ice cream right about now", he sighed again. "What's that?" Lozen asked. "It's probably the best dessert in all of Terra Firma!" he boasted. "Is that it?" Persaeus asked pointing to his plate. He sat up and leaned over to see his plate, in the center dripping with hot chocolate fudge was the tallest oreo heaven he had ever seen! The plump hot brownie held three large scoops of cinnamon ice cream which in turn held a mountain of fluffy white whip cream adorned with bits of oreo cookie, peanuts, and a luscious golf ball size cherry on top. Adin's eyes gleamed, seeing his face light up made Persaeus want to try it. "Oreo heaven!" she commanded. Instantly her plate was filled with a tall oreo heaven to rival Adin's. The enticement was too much for the rest of the group to resist, Lucian, Atreyu, and Lozen followed. Within moments, all five were rewarding their taste buds with sweet mouthfuls of warm soft brownie with chilled cinnamon ice cream, all groaned at the instant gratification. "And to top it all off, the finest starbrew!" Adin ordered. "What's the finest starbrew little brother?" Lucian grinned. Adin shrugged his shoulders, "I don't know but I'm about to find out!". Silence fell over the group, he took a sip, smacking his tongue against his lips he blurted out, "Now that's the finest starbrew!" he declared. The group roared to laughter as each ordered 'the finest starbrew'. "What do we have left for the day?" he asked the group. Sitting back in nostalgia, Atreyu answered, "Erindolian history, which reminds me, we should get going. Don't know if we can use you as an excuse again if we are late, Regent Tiberius may not be so understanding", he joshed getting to his feet. "Come little brother!" Lucian helped Adin to his feet.

Regent Tiberius waited patiently as his students slowly trickled in, taking their seats. Today would mark the first week of the temple's indoctrination. He was pleased that no one was late as he eyed Adin and his companions entering the room. The room was incredible, limestone walls and floors with buttresses supporting the ceiling. "In front of you is an oration scroll, it will reveal the history of Erindol, as I lecture please follow along on your scroll", he said. "Now, Erindol's history dates back to the time of The Great Fall, it was used primary as a safe haven for the sick and battle wounded to heal. The Fall left many Sidhe, Dwarcadian, and Elven families displaced, the population thereby consisted mostly of the refugeed and orphaned that were brought in. Alas, many who stood and fought were put under the sword by the Fallen without mercy. Fearing that their homes and former lives were forever gone, those that recovered, chose to stay to begin a new life here. The temple provided protection and the Sidhe along with the Dwarcadians, and Elven worked to build Erindol as you see it now", he said with a wave of his hand, the wall became transparent and the students could see the village in present time. Lozen raised her hand, "Has any human ever laid eyes on Erindol?" "Only one, back in the time of Terra Firma's fifth century. He was a remarkable human king that made the Guardian code his own". "I guess we are letting anyone come here now", Bestion commented giving Adin a disgusted look. "Those that are invited here are done so in line with their destiny Master Bestion!" Regent Tiberius snapped at him. The scroll in front of Adin showed the distraught Sidhe, Dwarcadians, and Elven pre-Erindol, his heart broke for them. He knew all too well what it is to be lost from your family to be orphaned in a strange place, to never quite feel at home. "I miss you mother", he whispered to himself. "What was that?" Bestion said pestering him, "You miss your mother!" he badgered rubbing his eyes like he was crying. Zorah, Ragnar, Marpesia, and Kylan all began to join in laughing with him. They were all from Thunder Horse order and Adin instantly knew they were aligned with Bestion, they were his supporters; hence his followers. Lozen, Lucian, Atreyu, and Persaeus stared back at them with intensity. "Enough! Save your vigor for the triads or the grimoirium, we are here to learn about the Erindolian history! If you wish to taunt like meddlesome toddlers, I shall remind you that your invitation to this temple can be revoked!" he said. The room grew silent, "Now, Erindol is home to the Sidhe, Dwarcadians, and Elven. The Sidhe can be described with the modern word of 'fairy', they are a distant cousin to humans. They served Terra Firma as the 'spirits' of the forests, deserts, and mountains. The Dwarcadians were too cousins of humans, whom served the great stones of Terra Firma. The Dwarcadians used their stone knowledge to assist humans in building the great stone structures that still stand to this very day in Terra Firma". "Like what?" Thassian of the Fire Hawk order asked. "For example, the great pyramids of Egypt, Stonehenge in England, Petra in Jordan to name a few", he said showing each place in present time. Each student's scroll revealed each of the great structures Regent Tiberius named with images of dwarves working on each structure during construction: measuring, cutting stone, mixing mortar, and polishing stone. "The Elven are the closet to humans who were masters of all creatures, teaching the languages of all beasts, fowl, and everything that crawled on land or swam in the great seas. All this co-habitation, so to speak; came to a tragic end. Humans lusted for their supernatural powers in order to become powerful like their ancient predecessors found in Terra Firma's cultural mythologies. They were subjected to barbaric persecution and fled the Terra Firmian realm forever, leaving behind traces of their former existence that was dismissed as merely mythical legend in the years to come. Erindol resembled much of Terra Firma if you haven't noticed with its sprawling apple trees, lush green glens and magnificent stone structures. Soon Erindol became a place of great interest to other realm inhabitants, commerce in deed-stones, trade, temple merchants, commodities in star-brew, pastries, armor, perfumes became highly sought after. Soon the refugees found the peace and happiness they once knew in Terra Firma, families blossomed and the past was put to rest behind a bright and peaceful future. You fledglings are here just in time for Terra Firma's weeklong festival that begins in two weeks. Your studies over the weekend, is one scroll describing what you find most interesting about Erindol. Your scrolls are due first thing come the new moon, any questions? No? Good, then, enjoy the rest of your evening. Ah, Lady Lozen, Regent Alina asked me to remind you of your counsel with her before dinner", he said dismissing the class. "Yes Regent, thank you for reminding me. I will see to it now!" she said. "You guys go ahead; I have to meet with Regent Alina for counsel". "For what?" Atreyu asked worried. "No idea, I'm sure it's nothing, I see you all at dinner", she said.

Lozen teleported to Regent Alina's staff quarters, she knocked on the door, "Come in", Regent Alina beckoned. The door opened by itself, Lozen found Regent Alina researching several scrolls scattered across her escritoire. "Ah, Lady Lozen, thank you for being so punctual. I won't take but a moment of your time. There has been a concern I have had since the incident involving Master Adin during the grimoirium training", she said still looking over a scroll. "Yes Regent", Lozen answered unsure of what Regent Alina was alluding to. "Do you remember anything of that time, in particular, just before Master Adin had his incident?" she asked. "I'm not sure what I saw Regent, I imagine I saw what everyone else saw and heard", she said still not quite sure if she was answering correctly. "Forgive me, allow me to start over. The reason I have asked you for counsel is because of the incident with Master Adin. I noticed you kept a keen eye on him during training and I believe that perhaps you may have seen something no one else might have due to your, observations", she said keen. "Regent forgive me…Adin…Master Adin is just a friend, a comrade in the order nothing more! I swear!" Lozen said frightened that Regent Alina was indirectly accusing her of an infatuation with him. Not meaning to frighten her, she placed her hand on her shoulder, "Lady Lozen, any infatuation is none of my concern, but I need to see what you saw that day. The only way I can do that is using 'the sight' but it requires your permission. If I can see through your eyes, I am certain I will find a clue that will help us find what exactly happened to Master Adin", she said tenderly. "I see", Lozen said relieved. "What must I do?" she asked her. "Come, sit. I need you to clear your mind". Lozen sat on the plush throne like chair in front of her. "Now close your eyes and think back to that day just before the incident", she said stepping in front of her. Lozen slowly closed her eyes, feeling Alina's hands cupping around her face. Alina's eyes began to glow bright purple as she is now connecting to Lozen's subconscious. Now fully engaged in her subconscious, Alina was back in the grimoirium. Boom! She witnesses the thunder-struck energy strike the ground in front of Adin, everyone crashing to the ground in micro slow motion around her, then the blinding fiery blue light erupted. Still in Lozen's subconscious mind the light is still very blinding, she partially shielded her eyes as she walked towards him. She can see him cupping his eyes with both hands as she entered the flood of the light. She skimmed the arena searching for perhaps an unseen foe, but no one other than Regent Serene and the students were present. Suddenly something caught her eye, she walked further into the light until she was just a foot away from Adin. Between his fingers were the signs of extreme heat that was creating the blinding light. She inspected his hands to get a better look at what she now realized was the source of the light, it was his eyes! Her eyes began to fade back to their normal state as she slowly removed her hands from Lozen's face. "Did you find anything Regent?" Lozen asked. Still in shock Alina mumbled, "Thank you Lady Lozen, that will be all". She sensed Alina found something she was not quite sure of, she complied and bid her a good night. Just before she left her chambers, "Lady Lozen. You know, he really is a remarkable boy!" she said in deep revelation. "I believe all Lion-Hearts are, Regent", Lozen said. Still in shock, she smiled and nodded her head. Lozen stood outside the door trying to make sense as to why she was dismissed so abruptly, it meant the obvious, Regent Alina had seen something in her subconscious that had shaken her to the core! She would have to tell Adin but only when the time was right, she teleported to the dining hall. Regent Alina thumbed through the scrolls, scattered on top of each other, "Maybe there is a scroll that explains how a human boy can do that!" she said shuffling through more scrolls.

CHAPTER EIGHT

WINGS OF STEEL

The Lionheart and Thunder Horse order assembled in the Fields of Aaru. Regent Cassian studied each youthful charismatic face, certifying each training uniform was in proper order. Behind him were eighty sets of shiny kite shaped objects, only with all the pointed corners rounded, suspended in midair with ten fairy assistants. "Today we learn the art of aerial piloting, with these", he said pointing at the shiny kites, "These are sky gliders! Truly fascinating training wings! These wonderful fairy inventions have allowed young Guardians to learn aerial piloting quicker, safer, and more efficiently than in my day. In my day once you earned your wings, you were tossed from a moonwalk. Down you fell, if you didn't master your wings during the fall in oh, let's say, fifteen minutes; then you became well acquainted with the ground", he said with blatant concern. "How long until we get our real wings?" Yusuf impatiently questioned. "A little ahead of ourselves, aren't we?" Lord Cassian ridiculed. "Each of you will be fit and issued one set of gliders that will be synced to your medallions. No medallion, no flight! Once you have finished being fitted and have left your mark, return back to formation!" he said. All the students all ran up to each fairy attendant determined to get their hands on a glider. "There are enough gliders for everyone!" he reminded the mob of students but it was no use. This was the chance to fly, like a real Guardian! To soar to the heavens! This was every kid's dream both human and Guardian alike! Adin's turn came up, he spun around while his fairy fitter placed his glider on his back. He smiled ear to ear, he was one of the last students to be fitted now but that didn't matter, "Just relax, the glider will form to you love", she instructed. The backpack felt weightless; he looked over his shoulder to make sure it was on. "Okay, that looks good! Give it a good tap!" she said admiring the fit on Adin's back. He taped the medallion with his palm, his wings expanded with a swoosh! "Those some mighty fine wings yer got there!" Atreyu said in his best Texas accent. The fairy laughed, "Now back to the lot!" she said.

"Good morning Lion-Heart and Thunder-Horse! It is my utmost pleasure to instruct you in your first day of aerial piloting! My name is Instructor Vera. Now your gliders are infused with fairy dust, this is what allows the gliders to mimic, anthropomorphically, your wings by skeletal muscular connection", she began her introduction. "Skeletal muscular connection?" Atreyu repeated looking around to see if anyone else thought that was strange. She smiled, "Yes, skeletal muscular connection is quite simply mind to muscle connection. "For instance,", she thought for a moment. "Do you play Glaive Star?" she asked Atreyu. "You bet I do!" he said. "When you swing your spear, do you have to tell all the muscles in your back, hips, and arms to move or do they just move at the thought of you swinging?" she posed this second question to him. "I just tell myself to swing", he said grasping her point. "Precisely! You physically swing with every fiber of your being, every fiber acting as one under the power of your mind! The gliders will respond to your mind in exactly the same way, it may be strange for some of you at first but you will soon be flying as natural as a dragon. It's going to be different for everyone but that is why we are here to help you!" she finished with a smile. "Any questions?" she asked both orders. Several students shot their hands up in the air, she pointed at Nevan, "How fast can you go?" he asked. "Well, the speed of your flight depends on how efficiently you communicate that to gliders, but I assure you, Lord Cassian will have a training speed that he will advise you of shortly and I with the other fairy assistants will be up there with you to make sure everyone's safe". She pointed to another student, "How high can we go?". "Well that is more of question for Lord Cassian, he will set the hard deck. Any more questions? No? Well to sum it up, just think fly!" she added. "My Lord, the glider instructions have been declared!" she reported to Lord Cassian. "Thank you, Instructor Vera! Everyone take a knee! Who here can tell me the most iconic image of a Guardian that is still prevalent today in all the realms?" he asked the group. No one could answer, Adin seized this opportunity. He knew exactly what he was talking about, all of these kids have never been to Terra Firma so they surely didn't know that a Guardian is depicted as an angel with feathery wings, like in the painting back in the orphanage. He shot his hand straight up into the air. Everyone turned to face him, even Lozen the sharpest girl he knew waited for his answer. "The most prevalent image is an angel with wings!" Adin said with total confidence. "Correct!" Regent Cassian said with mild enthusiasm, he had wanted one of his students to answer the question for Thunder-Horse's honor. "Why is it Master Adin, that angels have wings on Terra Firma?" he asked him; a near impossible question. "Because angels have wings?" Adin answered a question with a question. "Valiant try my dear boy. No! Guardians have metaphysical wings, in the ancient days we appeared as you see me now!" he demonstrated by beginning to walk on invisible steps in midair, he walked up and stood five feet off the ground then back down again. The students were beside themselves, unable to contain their astonishment! Regent Cassian enjoyed the attention, that's how Thunder-Horse's personalities were, like show ponies prancing for attention. Adin couldn't help but think that was the coolest thing he has ever seen and to think soon he would be flying! "Throughout the ages, the manifestation of wings became more symbolic of our identity among the realms and dare I say a fashion statement!" he said expanding his wings. "As more and more Guardians donned their wings the more it was realized that wings embodied much more than the concept of flight; they represented discipline, direction, dedication, and daring! Later flight become an academic skill test in the years to come. Once you are promoted from fledgling to apprentice in your third year, you will be given the chance to test for your wings", he said folding his wings. Bestion shot his hand up in the air, "Is there any way to get our wings faster?" he said. "I do love your enthusiasm Master Bestion! Yes, to answer your question but that is on a case by case basis", he answered. "Like what?" Thecla asked. "To earn your wings before the allotted promotion, you must have had to accomplish a great feat or have been summoned to war. Alas, the era of great feats is no longer upon us nor is war thankfully!" he said, the last of his answer quieting every student's tongue. "Shall we my Lord?" Vera broke the silence. "Yes, yes. The hard deck for this evolution is one tenth of a league, your altitude is twenty-eight thousand cubits, and your speed for today will be one scalar only! Break off evenly into ten columns in front of a flight assistant, I will be overseeing all flight patterns from the air! Any questions?" Every student answered by jumping into a line, Adin chose Instructor Vera's line. "Alright my young fledglings! Today we are going to have a lot of fun! We are going to cover quite a bit of Erindol, once we are off the ground, I'll be acquainting you to the rules of the air. I only have one rule, safety!" she said. "What's my only rule?" she asked her group, "Safety", they all yelled. "Wonderful, now let's begin with take-off. Now you may guess that take-off involves you running a short distance at maximum speed then leaping into the air, your wings deploying as you fly into the sunset. Am I right?" she asked grinning. Some of the students nodded their heads, she chuckled. "Well, I'm afraid that's done more for dramatic impact rather than practical application. So, when you see that, you'll know it's just for show but don't tell anyone I told you", she smiled placing her finger against her mouth in the universal hush sign. The students laughed, Adin was pleased he picked her, she made him feel comfortable, so comfortable in fact that he forgot just how dangerous this could really be for him; since he was a still a human. "If for whatever reason, you find yourself going 'ballistic', don't panic the wings will automatically compensate your speed slowing your decent all the way to the ground if need be", she attested. "What's going ballistic", Thora asked. "Glad you asked, my Lady. Going ballistic simply means that the wings, because they are made of enchanted metallurgy, are bound to the physical rules of all the realms. Kind of like the water we have here, it is bound by the gravitational rules of this realm. Let's say you climb rocketing straight up and you find the glider can no longer flap or propel, gravity will take effect and you will free fall. Once your air speed balances the wings will redeploy". Reading the growing anxiety in each student's face, "Once you earn your real wings, you won't have to worry about such limits, your wings will be a part of you; these are just training aids like your wooden weapon aides", she assured. "Is everyone ready?" she said, every student nodded their head ready to soar. "First things first, now, you! Come right here please!" she said pointing at Atreyu. "What's your name love?" she asked. "Atreyu, ma'am", he said thrilled. "This your first time flying?" she asked him. "Uh, yes, yes Fair-Lady", he answered excited. "Oh, dear, I fear for you then", she said with a grave look on her face. The look on Atreyu's face was priceless! He had a look that screamed terror, "I'm just joking Master Atreyu!" she said laughing, causing all the other students to burst out laughing, some in tears. "Oh, thank the Sovereign", he said grasping his chest. "Okay, now what I want you to do is think of the preparatory thought just before you're about to run or leap on the ground", she said in her instructor voice. Atreyu nodded his head, suddenly his wings deployed, with one flap he was five feet in the air! His wings flapped steady and gracefully. "Brilliant Master Atreyu! Now, just hover there until I have all of your order mates up in the air with you!" she called out from the ground. "Alright everyone, as a group! Think of that moment just before you jump, run, or dive!". One by one, each student was airborne, but Adin was still stuck on the ground. Frustration started to flood his face, "No worries, love, let's see here. Trying thinking about the first time you ran with all your heart, not out of fear but out of joy!" she encouraged. Adin thought back to a dream he once had about his mother. He remembered the feeling of longing to hug her, to feel her embrace. "Now, open your eyes Master Adin", Vera said. Adin was in the air! He was actually in the air like his order mates! "Well done, Master Adin, well done!" she said; he was unable to hide the huge smile across his face. He looked around at the joyous faces of each student enjoying this evolution just as much as he was. "Next we have to learn to glide, I will fly out to a certain distance, then one at a time each of you glide to me. Think of gliding through water only you are propelling yourself with your upper chest and back muscles versus your legs. Just glide, flow like water, got it?" she asked. With one flap of her fairy wings she glided out to 555,555 ells;

roughly 500 kilometers. She hovered, "Okay! Whosoever ready, come!" she yelled. Lozen smiled, her wings flapped once, she glided perfectly. "My, my, my Lady! Are you sure you don't belong in Fire-hawk with gliding like that!" she complimented her. Atreyu and Lucian couldn't wait, they looked at each other, then darted to Vera. Atreyu was in a near perfect glide like his sister, he inverted himself, looking up at the sky. He looked back at Adin, "Check this out!" he shouted. He crossed both arms behind his head and if that wasn't enough showboating, he crossed his legs, laughing all the while. Lucian laughed at Atreyu briefly but in his mind, he was already imaging he was a full-fledged Guardian, flying over the realm he was assigned to protect. The thought of this, fueled his passion to take up his place that his parents paved for him. Fujin was next, he darted towards Vera, only he decided to twirl through the glide. High-fiving Atreyu as he got to hovering group. Saanvi, Thora, and Persaeus huddled together. "We've got to show these boys we can look cool gliding too!" she said rallying them. "Uh-oh, looks like the girls are going to out do you boys!" Vera teased. Thora launched, then Saanvi and Persaeus, gliding just above Thora, she reached up and grabbed Saanvi and Persaeus' free hand, she pulled them in then flung both girls together, towards the boys. "Looks like we have aerial acrobats in our mist!" Vera said amused clasping her hands together. The boys stunned by Thora's strength. "I can toss all of you too as well, if you like!" she jabbed at the boys. All that was left was Adin, Betram, and Vilhelm. "You want to race?" Vilhelm asked Betram. "You're on! Loser has to polish the other's boots!" Betram bet. "Deal!" Vilhelm said. "Adin, can you call it?" he asked. "Yeah, sure! On your mark! Get set! Go!". Both boys rocketed to Vera, Vilhelm being the victor. Now was Adin's turn, he couldn't think of anything cool to do in the air, or even if he felt confident enough to do something like the others. "Come Master Adin! After this, we will take a tour of the temple and village!" Vera shouted to motivate him. She had heard rumors that he was having a tough time adjusting, she hoped today would be a great day for him. She was determined to do everything in her power to see that he had a safe wonderful time, she couldn't explain her fondness for him, nonetheless she felt for the young boy. 'Here goes', he coached himself. He thought of speed, speed like Artorius. Foom! within seconds, he flew a few yards past the group, knocking everyone around like bowling pins. He couldn't believe how fast he flew! He nearly tumbled over in the air at his sudden stop, his hair in disarray. Vera's eyes said it all, '*How did this boy just do that?*' she stared in disbelief. He glided to Vera, her look of shock still shone on her face, "Like that?" he asked, not sure if she upset. "Umm, yes. Goodness, what were you thinking?" she said astounded. Everyone righted themselves looking at each other, their hair in a mess just as Adin's. "I, thought of speed", he said with pride. "You thought of speed, the need for speed?" she said taken back fixing her long brunette hair. "Yeah, I suppose I felt the need for speed!" he said now quite proud of himself. There was no argument there, "Need I remind you the speed for this evolution is one scalar Master Adin! You were flying at least at three scalars!" Lord Cassian said displeased. "That was AWESOME!" Atreyu blurted out, Lord Cassian gave him a heated look. "Carry on!" he said before catching sight of Ragnar, yelling, "Head up boy, how many times must you be told!" flying his way now to address Ragnar. "Who's up for a quick tour of the temple grounds and the village before lunch?" Vera asked. Every student was now restless wanting to fly and explore more. "Okay we stay as a group, no wondering off, we will fly in a wedge formation. This is a test question, so you may be asked this again", she said with a wink of her eye. She positioned herself in the front of the group, "Okay, whenever you see, the lead-wing extend both arms like this in a 'V' shape that means-", she was cut off. "A wing formation!" Atreyu spouted out unable to control his eagerness. "Okay, I see we have experienced fledglings, I take it there is no need to explain the wedge formation", she said pleased. "We had to do it with our horses on the first day", Atreyu spouted out again. "I see, well off we go then, try and keep up!" her voice trailing off as she shot forward, every student shooting forward to catch up.

The view of the temple from the air was amazing! On the ground you couldn't tell just how enormous it really was but from the air, it was a sight! Adin could see all the stable Pegasus grazing outside the temple walls. Some on duty Gatekeepers waved as the group flew by, they circled back around. Adin flew closer to Vera, "My Fair-Lady what's that?" he pointed to a solitary tower just outside the northern temple walls. "Oh, that! That's the Suratrat! A place to hold temple lawbreakers! Don't worry you'll never see the inside of that dungeon", she said turning her attention to another student's question. Down below Adin saw the river Vitae glistering like deep blue tinsel, the villagers were busy with their everyday routine: cleaning their outdoor cafes, serving patrons, walking and talking without a care in the world. They even passed by the Agora, Fair-Lady Artemis was on her rooftop lounging.

She gave a spirited wave as the group passed by, "Hi Artemis!" Adin called out from the heights as he flew overhead, she continued her wave until all had passed. He looked over at Vera, "That's my friend Artemis!" he said with a huge smile on his face. "My, my! Aren't we the popular one!" she said winking at him, his smile grew wider. They came upon the snowcapped Hebron mountain range, some of them scooping up snow as they glided arm's length from the peaks. Every thought was the same, snowball fight! They began throwing soft slushy ice at each other. Adin was having such a blast, for a brief moment he had forgotten all about his injuries, the plot against him, and his assassin. The wind gusting against his face in roller coaster currents made him feel free, strong, and full of hope, he felt a lot like his favorite superhero, Superman! "Okay, let's take it down to the courtyard! Go easy, watch the glide slope! Easy now, there you go!" Vera said pleased with all the student's performance. They touched down in the courtyard without any trouble, the rest of fairy assistants and their order students began arriving too. "Alright, its lunch time! We'll meet back here for the next aerial evolution", she released her students. "Instructor Vera, I'm really not that hungry, can I practice until lunch is over?" Adin asked her. "Certainly, but stay around the temple grounds, safety first! Right?" she said winking her eye. "Right!" Adin said nodding his head. Adin lifted into the air, looking up until he was well over the courtyard. He enjoyed being in the air until a voice behind him broke his solitude. "Saw what you did back there, pretty fast. Think you can beat me in a race?" Adin turned around to see Bestion with his Glaive star team. "Thought I beat you in the grimoirium," Adin answered back dismissing him. Bestion's face turned to pure anger, you think that freak accident will save you this time!" he fumed. Atreyu, Lucian, Persaeus, and Lozen flew up to see what all the commotion was about. "Everything okay, little brother?" Lucian asked Adin staring down Bestion. "Really, you call him little brother? That's cute!" Bestion laughed prompting his cronies to laugh too. Adin's emotions were getting the better of him, "I'd love to race!" he said accepting his challenge. "Adin, you sure this is wise with all that's going on right now?" Lozen tried to nonchalantly discourage him. "I think he'll be alright sis, besides we're here!" Atreyu said tearing off a piece of frybread. Lozen just gave him the look, like he was an idiot. "Good, we'll start from here to Hebron mountains then back!" Bestion said snickering. Zorah hovered, "On your mark. Get set. Go!" she yelled. A Lion-Heart racing a Thunder-Horse, both were neck to neck, Adin could see he was only ahead of him by an arm's length. Bestion was flying faster gaining speed. 'Foosh' they braked, sliding on air, their wings fluttering to stop them; they both ran on the air as if it was solid ground, 'Foomp' they rocketed back neck to neck again. Adin pushing himself, the cloud skirt of a sonic boom is starting to form around his waist, sounding like the thundering of a jet engine, he whisked past Bestion, winning the race! Bestion lost control and tumbled in the air. His Lion-Heart group roared and cheered in celebration. "That's quite enough!" Cassian's voice echoed in their ears, "Return to your instructor for the last evolution of the day!" he ordered. Back on the ground, his spirits had never been higher, he beat Bestion in a fair race and he didn't get hurt at all. "Not bad Master Adin, not bad at all!" Vera said with indirect approval. "What did you think of to win?" she asked him. "I just thought, Superman!" he said with a grin. "Who is this Superman? Does he teach here?" Vera asked the group. Lozen enjoyed her piloting but her mind was triggered, the incident in Regent Alina's quarters came rushing to the forefront of her mind, she couldn't shake the look on Regent Alina's face from her mind's eye.

CHAPTER NINE

THE THERIAN CURSE

Lozen joined the rest of the group in the great hall, taking her place at the grand table, she looked worried; they could tell she was contemplating something overwhelming as she stared at her empty plate. "This marks the end of the first week! We all survived!" Atreyu said hoping she'd look up but she didn't. "Perhaps this calls for an oreo heaven?" he said thinking that might sway her. "I almost forgot, what happened with Regent Alina?" Persaeus asked with a look of great concern, "Its better if we discuss this in private. I'll see all of you in the common room", she said waving away her plate. "Guess it must have been bad", he said looking at them. "Come let's see what troubles her", Lucian motioned to the group. Arriving at the common room, they found only Lozen there, sitting by the fireplace in deep thought sipping starbrew. "What happened? Are you in trouble?" Atreyu pried. "Whatever it is we are here for you!" Adin reassured. "It's nothing like that, I'm not in any trouble. It's just, when I reported for counsel, she was thumbing through scrolls. She looked desperate to find something, she said she needed to use 'the sight' for any clues to find out what happened to Adin". "The Sight?" Atreyu said baffled. "Shhh!" Persaeus sounded with a finger to her lips. "She was able to go back and see that day in the grimoirium through my eyes". "What did she see?" Adin said leaning in. "I don't know but whatever she saw, she immediately dismissed me. I don't think that was a good sign", she professed. "I don't think she would keep anything from us if it meant Adin might be hurt", Persaeus rationalized. "Still, she must have saw something! She is proper and all business and if she saw something that made her behave like that, then something is very, very wrong!" Lozen concluded. "Tomorrow after tryouts, what is there to do?" Adin asked. "Nothing but our leisure time, to get our uniforms and assignments done before the start of the new week, why?" she asked. "We have to find out how she used 'the sight' on you, she must have discovered how in one of scrolls she had. We are going to need to get in her quarters", he devised. "That is madness! You will place yourself in a position where the temple will expel you for all time! I cannot allow you to bring dishonor to our order much less break into a Regent's quarters!" Lucian warned. "You don't have to be a part of this, none of you do! It's my life that's in danger not yours. What's the sense of being a Lion-Heart if you lack a fearless heart?" he challenged Lucian. He walked to the stairs to teleport, right before departing, he turned to the group, "I don't expect any of you to place yourselves in position to get in trouble or worse expelled. I've been on my own all my life!" he said before vanishing. "He's going to need our help!" Lozen said appealing to the group's decision. "You know that is a gross intent to break temple law and it won't just be his expulsion, it will be all of ours! We will never be Guardians!" Lucian sneered back. "Then why are we here Lucian? To become Guardians? A Guardian is supposed to protect and defend! Who are we protecting? Who are we defending? I'll tell you! Our prideful ambition to be titled a Guardian! One of our very own is in great need of our help and what do we do? We cower for fear of losing the chance at a title! I've had a fearless heart before I came here nothing will ever change that, what about you Lucian!" she stormed off in utter disgust, Persaeus trailed after her. "My sister is right brother and you are right. I will be there for my sister and for Adin", Atreyu said. "Even when it will bring dishonor on your parents, the order, your honor?" Lucian questioned him. "Helping a brother is honorable, supporting your family is honorable, my father will see that protecting life regardless of title is honorable. So, yes if it means losing everything", he said decided. "You speak folly brother, you throw away your destiny without conscious!" he said unmoved. "I understand your point brother. What would you want Adin to do if you were in his shoes?" he asked placing his hand on his shoulder. "I'll see you tomorrow big brother", he said making his way to the stairwell.

"Lozen! Please! Please stop!" Persaeus pleaded pulling on her arm. "I'm with you!" she yelled causing her to stop in shock at what she just heard. "Really? Why?" she said dumbfounded. "I know I don't seem as tough as everyone else; I know that I like looking pretty and wearing pretty clothes but that does not mean I don't know when to set all that aside to do my duty! It is as you said, one of our own is in need, plus I know you like him very much!" she confided. "You have me mistaken! I care for Adin as a friend only! Nothing more!" Lozen answered embarrassed. "Apologies for my misinterpretation", she said. "It's quite alright, thank you for being a good friend", she said smiling. Persaeus' willingness to help changed a perception she had about her. In her view, she was the 'pretty girl' that was just going through the motions, but now she understood Persaeus had resolve and a sense of duty about her. "It's late, we should get some rest", Persaeus said looking out the arched window to the dark sky. "Agreed", Lozen said draping her arm around Persaeus.

Regent Alina stood in the middle of her quarters; her arms folded with one hand resting on her chin. In her mind she kept replaying what she saw in Lozen's subconscious, she began to pace trying to fit the pieces of this mystery together. She knew this would change everything! A fledgling with no Guardian powers summons a thunder-struck and eye blaze! In all her years she had never seen or heard of a child, much less a human child, do such things. She scooped up a hand full of zilly-wood and threw it into the pontifex. "Elder Valerian please, this is Regent Alina". "Good evening Regent, is everything alright?" he asked due to the late call. "I have something I wish to discuss privately with you Elder, I'm afraid tomorrow will not do", she insisted. "I see, come to my chambers". "Yes Elder", she answered. Valerian was seated at his desk with three long scrolls reviewing each student's chosen path. Alina knocked on the door, "Come in", he called out. The heavy wooden door opened, "Thank you Elder for seeing me at this late hour", she bowed in respect. "None sense Regent, I was just looking over the scrolls Lord Hylandir brought up", looking up at her with his undivided attention, he could now see the distressed look on her face. "You asked to speak with me?" he said. "Since the incident with Master Adin in the grimoirium, I have been troubled", she said pacing the room. "As we all have, has something else happened?" he waved the scrolls away. "No, but I have seen something that I find most disconcerting. Last night, I used 'the sight' on Lady Lozen hoping to find an answer to what happened with Master Adin that day", she stammered. "And what have you discovered?" he asked with increasing anticipation. "There is no doubt that it was a thunder-struck, however; it was not a thunder-struck from some unseen enemy as speculated but from-", he cut her off. "Him!" he said finishing her sentence. "Yes, how did you know?" she said folding her arms. "Since his incident at the skychamber, I have looked into how the boy was just able to walk into a sealed room. A sealed room that had a Sentori warding spell that I put there, no less. I am convinced it was his blood as the only son of a First Knight that granted him access. I fear with the grimoirium incident, it is becoming evident the boy possesses a power he doesn't yet understand or worse how to control it and a power we don't quite understand", he said resting his elbows on the desk; his fingers interlaced. "How is that at all possible? All the children here are born of Guardians that gave up their wings, yet they cannot do any of the feats he has accidently done! I fear he is a danger to himself and the other students!" she said alarmed. "With an assassin after him, we have to keep him confined to safeguard him and keep him from potentially hurting other students!" she said. "Alina, if we keep him confined, we offer the assassin the best opportunity to strike, if we confine him what is to say that he doesn't have another incident and we turn a boy into an enemy. What then?" he said. "The boy has been discarded all his life, if we confine him all we have done is proven we are no better than his previous life. What type of Guardian would we be producing, what example to the other students?" he asked her hoping she would see the fault in her rash decision. "We must advise Lord Artorius," he said. "I have not been able to reach him!" she said. "Then we are at the mercy of fate, I'm afraid," he sighed.

Lord Artorius sat perched on a nearby peak on Mt. Hebron, overlooking the village. His cloak flailed in the wind making flopping sounds as he scanned the activity down below. The hustle and bustle of village nightlife was none of his concern, he was scanning the darkness, waiting for anything or anyone that would cue him on the plot against Adin. His eye caught the faint blue light of a campfire just outside the village on the other side of a canyon near the desolate cave of the Lamia. '*Strange for someone to be out at this time of night, let alone by a cave that once was home to the dreadful Lamia*' he thought. Stepping off his rocky perch, he dropped. Falling a few feet, he unfolded his wings, with a single flap he was thrust upwards, fully airborne.

Lord Tadrian waited inside the hut of an old fairy potion master. "How may I serve thee, mi Lord?" the potion master asked bowing. "There is a question among the healers concerning a Therian curse", he began. "Yes, mi Lord". "What can suspend its effects on the victim?" he inquired. "A Therian curse is a natural curse, surely a Guardian would know such things!" the fairy said putting up herbs. "Yes, but

Guardians do not dabble in curses, there is no need, there is no honor in dispatching an enemy by such clandestine means!" he said insulted. "I meant no disrespect mi Lord; it is strange that a Guardian would take counsel from a fairy potion master is all. I shall answer your question. The Therian curse is irreversible, it slowly kills its victims. Only the toxin of the jathma thorn can slow its power. Be warned one must never use dragon's breath, as it will quickly kill the victim". "Thank you", Tadrian said before leaving a yellow diamond on his table. "I trust your silence in this matter is sealed, for I fear what horrors may come with a reckless tongue", he warned, the fairy gulped hard nodding his head 'yes'.

Cutting through the cool crisp sky, the winds were strong, a sign the cold season would soon be upon the village soon. He flew closer to the campfire; two dark silhouettes were sitting around the fire, as he got closer, he could feel the heat of the fire near the tree top canopy. The aroma of starbrew permeated the air. He glided just overhead, soundless in his decent landing on a thick tree branch. His eyes sharpened, a Guardian can see in complete darkness as if during the day, a young fairy couple are enjoying starbrew. "This is beautiful love, thank you for taking the time to spend with me", she said. "I'm sorry but this is the best I can do for now, I know it might be a bit creepy with the Lamia cave nearby", he said. "Oh, I'm not worried my love, it has been long desolate since the Guardians defeated the Lamia", she said glancing over to the dark opening of the cavern mouth. They both stared into each other's eyes, wanting to kiss, "Strange place for romance!" Artorius' voice startled them both. "Who said that!" the boy fairy said fearing echoing in his tone, he grabbed a burning branch from the fire. Waving it around hoping to discover the origin of the voice. Artorius dropped down in front of him wings fully stretched, "AHHH!" he screamed falling backwards. The fairy girl whimpered, "Forgive us, oh Prince of the Air! We were just enjoying some starbrew", she petitioned. "Does her father know you have her here, this late?" Artorius questioned the boy fairy, picking up the flaming branch tossing it back on the fire. "No, no my lord!" he admitted. "Then I suggest you get her home before her father pulls out your wings!" he said. "Yes, yes, my lord...thank you my lord!" he said gathering their starbrew cups, wrapping up their half-eaten pastries, summoning his enchanted picnic blanket to wrap itself up together with all the other items they brought. The boy opened a fire holder, he waved his hand over the blue flame, the blue coals and embers floated into the fire holder before the two scurried away down the broken path. "Young love", Artorius reflected shaking his head. He glared into the cave opening, something dripping has caught his ear, approaching closer he saw the cave stalactites, they appeared as if the cavern had ragged teeth to devour some poor fool. A long-twisted stalactite dripped onto a growing stalagmite, running down into a pool of clear water. He stepped back; he began searching the outside of the cave mouth looking for some dragon's breath. He found some just beginning to bud. He plucked it, dropping it into the pool of water, within seconds the flower turned black; decayed. The Lamia's venom was legendary in those days of old, to protect their territory they would pollute nearby water sources. This enabled them to gather prey easier by trapping unsuspecting victims or animals who drank from their pools, it also served to defend their caverns by happenstance for anything that hunted them. It wasn't uncommon in those days, to find the remains of brave heroes in their lairs, having mistakenly drunk from a pool. Their arrowheads dipped in their venom, would pierce the flesh of their enemies, paralyzing them from within; stripping their enemies of their supernatural powers. The Lamia harvested children as their favorite food, some were kept half alive for their own diabolical plans. Their venom was of no consequence to a Guardian but to a human like Adin, instant paralysis; only to be swallowed whole. The cavern still had paintings and carvings of the Lamia; a hand painting of their queen was barely visible. He sensed movement just a few yards from the cavern. He shrunk back into the cavern's shadows; it was Lord Tadrian! He had stopped on the path to shuffle through some bushes as if he was looking for something, finding nothing he continued on the path straight to the cavern. "Lord Tadrian, fancy finding you here at this witching hour!" he announced, emerging from the dark shadows. "I could very well say the same for you Lord Artorius, above all, emerging from a malevolent cavern such as that one!" he fired back pointing his finger at the cavern behind Artorius. "You mean a once malevolent cavern, now just a cavern, an empty cavern at that", he said correcting him. "Ah, yes. You must forgive me, I still have memories when I took part in cleansing that cave from the Lamia serpents, we sealed them up behind stone walls, entombing them for all time! Pity you were not here to help us", he said with disdain. Artorius remained silent studying his face, 'The venom from the Lamia's decaying bodies have leaked all this time throughout the cavern, spilling into the cracks and nooks, making it uninhabitable' he calculated. "Have you found what you were looking for?" Tadrian asked him breaking the silence. "I'm not sure just yet", he said suspicious. "We are all working very hard! Together we will be able to save Master Adin in time!" he said with fervor placing his hand on Artorius' shoulder. "Apologies Lord Tadrian for my behavior, I meant no ill will, perhaps this mystery has overwhelmed me to the extent my manners have become barbaric", he said bowing. "Nonsense my Lord, this has been very difficult for all involved", he said. "Especially for Master Adin!" Artorius commented back. "Ah, yes, speaking of the poor boy, would you please excuse me? I have to find some dragon's breath, I believe it will help him", he said. "I am hoping that the dragon's breath will sustain him until we find his assassin", he said trying to end the conversation. "I believe I saw some at the mouth of cave, you're sure to find some there", he said. "I will, thank you", he said passing him in haste. He knelt down in front of a dragon's breath bush, "His time is close, it's almost out; I fear the worst for him!" he said aggrieved looking over his shoulder at Artorius. "As do I!" Artorius said vanishing, the sound and force of his wings blowing past him.

The next morning the chamber pontifex announced, "Glaive Star tryouts start in one hour. All interested must report in full training uniform". Lucian, Adin, and Atreyu all woke up rubbing their eyes. "I call first dibs on the shower!" Atreyu hollered out, jumping out of bed. "Oh, come on! No classes, no scroll assignments, let's go!" he motioned his hand before jumping into the shower. "It's way too early for him to be this excited!" Adin said to Lucian to break the ice between them. Lucian chuckled, "Perhaps he thinks he will be a realm champion? Let's get up before he almost drowns himself again!". Both start making their beds and laying out their training uniforms. Downstairs in the common room, Persaeus and Lozen waited for the boys. "I wonder if there will be any tension between Lucian and Adin", Persaeus said. All three boys appeared in the common room, "Are you ready to do this!" Atreyu incited the girls with radical enthusiasm. "Well if there's any tension it's between Atreyu's ears!" Lozen said causing Persaeus to burst out laughing. "What?" Atreyu said shrugging his shoulders. The dining hall was filled with students and promising gamers up early for breakfast. The smell of eggs, bacon, cinnamon rolls, pancakes, and starbrew fill the air so much that if a student wasn't hungry, they would be tempted by the unrelenting aroma to devour anything in sight. Some students were so nervous, all they could stomach were small morsels pecked from apples, bananas, and muffins. "Those who wish to tryout, the harem will be leaving in 10 minutes, report to the courtyard", a fairy valet called out. All the tryout students rushed out to the court yard. Atreyu grabbed a couple of apples and bananas for the road. Outside, Pegasus waited in three lines, all the students were eager to fly a Pegasus. "Please mount the nearest stallion or mare and strap in!" the fairy valet called out. All the Pegasus were beautiful, Taza and Gouyen were ensuring every reign and saddle was in proper order. To Adin it looked like every student except him knew how to handle themselves on a Pegasus. "Where are we going?" Adin asked Taza. "To the Isle of Avalon, where all the games are held", he said. "Is it far? What if I accidentally get lost?" Adin said worried. "Don't worry Master Adin, the Pegasus know the way, plus you have a valet. Just sit back and enjoy the flight!" he said. "I'm sorry, it's just that this is literally my second time on a horse", he confided. "I would have never guessed Master Adin", Taza teased. Taza and Gouyen gave their final pre-flight checks, "Every serial is ready for flight!" they both called out to the fairy valet. "Right! Thank you! Hah!" the fairy valet's mare galloped, jumping into the air flapping her wings. Without a command the first file Pegasus started a trot, then a gallop until jumping into the air. Lozen was in the second file, Adin right next to her in the third. "Just relax, you don't have to do anything but just enjoy the view and the flight", she tried to calm him until her Pegasus begin his trot. It was his time now, his Pegasus began to trot, he leaned down, "Please, please don't drop me!" he whispered into the Pegasus' ear, stroking her neck. His Pegasus leaped into the air, flapping his wings with vigor. The wind streaking against his face was cool and pleasant. Looking down he could see the temple was shrinking with every flap. His Pegasus climbed, she leveled off, he gazed across a sea of fluffy white clouds, tall rocky-mountains with white water falls, and dazzling seas that shimmered from the sun's rays. He confidence grew, he liked gliding through the clouds and soon thought to himself, '*I can't wait for my wings!*'. The flight path the fairy valet took gave every student the opportunity to enjoy the view. Lozen and Persaeus smiled with glee at the enjoyment of the view, Lucian looked like a mighty warrior on his Pegasus, stoic and proud. Atreyu kept failing his arms up as if he was on a roll coaster, his Pegasus did not appreciate it and would rock him to the side every now and then to make him grab hold of her reigns. "That's it!" Lozen yelled out to Adin. "That's what?" he yelled back. "The Isle of Avalon!" she yelled trying to get her voice to carry above the cutting wind. The Isle of Avalon was lush with miles of green meadows and cascading colowin trees that produced different colored leaves. Everything looked like a smorgasbord of color, the fairy valet pulled the reigns of his Pegasus, his mare dived down, wings folded back into a freefall. In the rear it looked to Adin as if the Pegasus were jumping off an invisible cliff. His turn came up, his Pegasus dived, the speed of his decent was unnerving. He felt like he would lift out of his saddle at any moment. The ground approaching faster than he anticipated, he held tighter on the reigns, his knuckles turning white from the strength of his grip. His Pegasus' wings unfolded and a soft gentle glide presumed all the way to the ground. Once on the ground, he could see everyone dismounting their Pegasus. His Pegasus, leaned down to help him slide off. "Thanks for not dropping me and thank you for the wonderful view", he said stroking her mane. The Pegasus delighted that her passenger was pleased welcomed the compliment with a nose nuzzle. "All right, everyone here?" the fairy valet called out. "Please report to Lord Gabdor in the arena to your right, thank you", he remained bowing as each student passed by him.

CHAPTER TEN

ONLY THE STRONG

Adin saw Atreyu talking to his sister about his flight with rapid hand roller coaster type gestures, Persaeus and Lucian waved him over. "This is going to be awesome!" Atreyu howled, "C'mon! Let's go!" he said jogging to the arena. They soon joined the crowd of students buzzing about all the excitement they had just experienced. "Good Morning! Welcome to the tryouts!" Lord Gabdor greeted the crowd. "First morning's agenda is Glaive Star! Let's have Lion-Heart over there, Thunder-Horse over here, Fire-Hawk right here, Iron-Bear behind me and Spirit-Wolf right over there. Chop, chop, not a moment to waste!" he said clapping his hands. All the students divided into their perspective orders. "First ten of every order step forward", he ordered. The Lion-Heart group stepped forward, "Only five? Come now! Don't be shy! We need five more!" he said. The group looked around, "I know why no one wants to step up", Adin said. Five students finally stepped up, Fujin, Bertram, Thora, Vilhelm, and Saanvi. "Good then! I see Thunder-Horse you have your team, Fire-Hawk you have yours, Spirit-Wolf, and Iron-Bear, Excellent! Now we will need three flyers, three shielders, three strikers, and one defender from each team. Decide amongst yourselves who will play each position. After you have decided we will begin instruction then a scrimmage". Lucian, Lozen, and Adin stood as strikers. Persaeus, Atreyu, and Fujin stood as flyers. Saanvi, Bertram, and Vilheim stood as shielders, and Thora stood as the defender. "Thunder-Horse have you decided?" he asked. "Yes, my Lord, ready to win!" Bestion boasted. "Lion-Heart and Thunder-Horse will be the first to scrimmage! Fire-Hawk and Iron-Bear will be second and the Spirit-Wolf will scrimmage the winner between you two! Spears!". he said lifting his arm. Two fairy attendants carrying two sets of heavy wooden chests filled with Glaive Star sticks moved onto the field. The sticks were long, carved from a wish tree with a basket netting made from Arachne silk. Enthralled, every Glaive Star hopeful grabbed a playing stick. "This is too cool", Atreyu said looking his stick over. Lucian swung his stick making a 'whooshing' sound, he was pleased. "Now gather round. Has anyone here ever played Glaive Star?" he said. The first to raise a hand was Bestion, followed by a few other students. "Good then, not too many bad habits to break. Now, this is what we call a spear. These spears are crafted from a wish tree. The basket net on the end here is made from Arachne silk, unbreakable by playing standards. The goal is to get this orbstar into your opponent's net to score one point. Your defender's job is to keep the orbstar out of the net with the assistance of the shielders, the strikers' job is offensive in nature, their job is to score. The flyers are both offensive and defensive making split decisions on 'the fly' so to speak", he chuckled at the idiom he just made. "To begin, the orbstar will pop into the air for the team captains to catch. Team captains will start with their spears on the ground", Lucian stepped up to the center as did Bestion. Thunder-Horse had Bestion, Zorah, and Ragnar as strikers. Thecla, Junsu, and Khari as flyers and Haruki, Yusuf, Nevan as shielders, and Kylan as the defender. "This will be a ten-point scrimmage!". A fairy with the game start horn stood next to Lord Gabdor. The horn blew, the orbstar popped up into the air leaving a vapor trail of sparks, Lucian and Bestion met head-on, locked in on each other; neither bending to the other's strength. Bestion with all his power managed to repel Lucian long enough to catch the orbstar, passing it to Khari. The game is now set, Khari passed to Ragnar but Fujin intercepted it passing it to Adin. Adin

162

caught it on the run, sprinting towards the Thunder-Horse defender. He saw Lozen, she was close for an easy score, just as Adin passed it, he was body-checked by Bestion. He crashed to the ground, "Only the strong shall remain my dear boy!" Lord Gabdor called out from the sidelines. "On your feet lad, that's to be expected!" he said unconcerned. Adin's vision was blurred, he was seeing double, he picked up his spear; lifting himself off the ground proved a daunting task. His body just received a full contact blow from one of the strongest students at the temple. He managed to get to his feet as he limped to run down the field to meet his team. Thecla from the Thunder-Horse passed the orbstar to Zorah, she leapt into the air, diving over Bertram and passed to Bestion as she forward rolled out of the dive. Bestion caught and flung the orbstar into the net, Thora unable to stop it. Score! All of Thunder-Horse cheered in response. Thora passed the orbstar to Vilhelm. Yusuf ran for Vilhelm, Vilhelm did a forward roll diving underneath Yusuf's spear just as he swung at his chest, to knock the orbstar loose. Coming out of the roll Vilhelm passed to Atreyu, he passed to Lucian, he swung with monstrous force as the orbstar landed into the Thunder-Horse net. Score! Lion-Heart roared in celebration but Bestion would have none of it. He will not lose a scrimmage against a team that has someone like Adin on it, in fact he refused to lose period. He charged forward targeting Adin. Kylan passed to Nevan, Nevan passed to Haruki as she passed to Junsu. Junsu passed to Ragnar but Ragnar lost the orbstar! Saanvi scooped it up, passing it to Persaeus. Persaeus passed to Adin, Bestion plowed through Vilhelm and Bertram knocking them to the ground. He intercepted Adin, cross-speared him with the shaft of his spear, the impact snapped Adin's arm like a twig. The orbstar went flying up as he smashed to the ground, "Only the strong belong here loser!" Bestion taunted standing over him before running off to finish the game. "That was certainly a good hit?" Lord Gabdor commented to one of his fairy assistants. "Yes, my lord but it appears the boy may be injured", the fairy remarked. "Nonsense, you see he's up! Attaboy boy Master Adin, just walk it off! The students are impermeable to injury you know that!" he said dismissing any silly talk about injuries. "Yes, my lord!" the fairy said realizing he would not listen. Bestion caught the orbstar, passing it to Haruki, who then passed it to Khari. Khari passed it to Bestion as he swung the orbstar for the Lion-Heart net. Thora leapt to catch it, she flung the orbstar to Vilhelm but it is intercepted by Bestion, he jumped in the air with a monstrous swing, Thora missed the orbstar by inches, the net catching it. Score! The horn blew, signaling a trade out of other students to have their try of the game. Adin refused to let one tear fall; he gritted his teeth in pain. "H-e-l-...help me up!" he petitioned Lucian with his good arm. Lucian helped him up, Lozen rushed over. "Your arm Adin! I's broken!" Lucian proclaimed. "Shush!" Lozen cautioned. "We have to get him back to the infirmary without causing alarm!" she said. Adin hobbled to sit on a stone holding his arm with Lucian and Lozen trying to conceal him to keep anyone from noticing he was injured. Persaeus ran to join them with Atreyu lagging behind, "Good game, no its alright we will be there in a minute", he told the remaining Lion-Heart players to keep Adin's injury hidden. "You okay?" Atreyu asked unaware of the seriousness of the injury. "His arm is broken!" Lucian answered. "Atreyu! Quick! Find a jathma thorn!" she said in desperation. "I'll go with him!" Persaeus offered. "Adin, pretend to laugh!" Lozen ordered. "You too Lucian! In case someone is staring, it will throw them off!" she said. Adin tried his best, gritting his teeth through pain as Lucian laughed over faking it, annoying Lozen. "I swear the both of you!" she said shaking her head. Atreyu dashed around, until he found the purple colored jathma bush with three-inch-long thorns. "How many do we need?" Persaeus asked him. "Just one but, I'm gonna grab a few more just in case", he pulled the thorns from their pods. They teleported back to the group. "Here!" he handed Lozen one thorn. Adin was now in the grip of gut-wrenching pain wreaking his arm that was spreading to the left side of his body. "Listen, this thorn contains a toxin in the husk that will mend the bone but it will cause you a considerable amount of pain on top of what you are feeling for a few seconds. I have to inject it in you", she tried to explain to him. Holding the thorn like a syringe, she jabbed Adin's arm, the toxin gushing inside his flesh, attaching itself to his bones. Adin suffered in silence, "Hold him Lucian!" she said with a tone no one had heard from her. "Atreyu, Persaeus stand behind me", said ordered. She knelt down, then grabbed Adin's arm and straightened it. Adin's eyes slammed shut, he bit down hard, but he didn't make a sound. "There! It should be fully mended by morning; you can use the rest of the thorns to manage pain!". To Adin's delight, the pain slowly lost its power over him, his body finally began to relax. "Now to just get you back to the temple without making a scene?" she said to the group. "I know!" Atreyu said, "Adin is requesting to go back to the temple early to catch up on the classes he missed!". "Brilliant!" Persaeus remarked. "That's really a very good plan!" Lozen said looking over her shoulder to compliment him. "It would be a lie!" Lucian said disapproving. "Yes, but a lie to keep him safe! Besides aren't we all lying to everyone that doesn't know his predicament?" Atreyu challenged Lucian. "Even you, big brother, have been lying this whole time!". Lucian looked perplexed and horrified. "It's settled, I'll go tell Lord Gabdor, he needs to get back to catch up on his missed classes. I'll keep him busy while the rest of you help him to his Pegasus!" Persaeus said running off to find Lord Gabdor. They waited for her to strike up a conversation with Lord Gabdor, when they saw his head nod in approval that was their signal. "Let's go quickly!" Lozen said as Lucian and Atreyu helped Adin escape unnoticed.

The Pegasus' were grazing the grounds undisturbed, the fairy valet was conducting a preflight check ensuring saddles were secure, reigns untangled, and hoof shoes still serviceable. "Pardon me Sir", Lozen said. "Yes, my Lady", the fairy valet greeted her. "My order mate must return to the temple at once!" she said. "My pleasure my Lady, but does your Lord Gabdor know he will be going back so soon?" he asked. "Yes! As a matter of fact, due to the urgency, another order mate sought permission as we speak". "Very well", he said motioning for Adin to saddle a Pegasus. His Pegasus sensed he was hurt, so she lowered her body for mount. Lucian and Atreyu helped Adin into his saddle, the sight of it looked very awkward to the fairy valet. "Its…ah…his second time on a Pegasus", she said. "Oh", the fairy valet said half believing her. "All set Sir?" the fairy valet asked Adin. "Yes Sir", he whimpered. The fairy valet whispered in the Pegasus' ear, she reared up with a loud neigh before darting forward. Adin grabbed tight to the reigns as she leapt into the air, flapping her impressive wings. "Quickly we have to return to the arena!" Lozen hurried them. The group teleported back into the arena to meet back up with Persaeus, without anyone the wiser. Adin's body was sore, bruised, and tense. He felt the urge to sleep but he kept himself awake. His broken arm was mending but still there was little use of it, for the first time he felt like maybe, just maybe this isn't right for him. All this Guardian stuff was too much and he felt as if he had given his all. The wind blowing back his hair, the flailing of his jacket against his body, he wrapped the reigns around his wrist with enough slack to reach for his necklace. He pulled it out, holding the medallion in his hand. '*What would Artorius think if I quit? What would my mother have thought?*', *she would have died for nothing!*' he declared to himself. Transfixed on his medallion, a revelation hit him! What if I can get my mother's First Knight medallion? That would get me into Regent Alina's quarters, like having a key! A new look of determination shone through his one good eye. He had a plan! A plan that would get him closer to finding his assassin. With renewed purpose he leaned towards his Pegasus' ear, "To the temple with hast!" he commanded. He straightened himself expecting the Pegasus to really take off. Nothing happened, the Pegasus continued to fly at her moderate speed. "To the temple with hast!" he repeated again expecting a different result. He remembered the old cowboy movies where the cowboy would use spurs on the back of their boots to make a horse run faster. He had no spurs on the back of his boots, so he squeezed his legs together, pressing his heels into the sides of his Pegasus. The Pegasus neighed, with a mighty flap, she rocketed like an arrow, folding her wings back like a modern attack plane just as he had seen with Lexicon. The speed was incredible, he had to lower his center of gravity or he would have been blown off by the high winds. The temple came within sight, the Pegasus started a slow decent using her wings like a parachute. She touched down gracefully, landing in the courtyard. She knelt down to help him dismount, "Thank you for the awesome ride!" he said. She responded by neighing, "Hey you understood me, didn't you? You were just messing with me!" he said amused. The horse neighed again, "Okay, okay, I admit that was clever! But now I know to watch out for you!" he said chuckling while stroking her mane. "Alright, I have to be going now, thank you again!" he said walking back to the temple dining hall. The temple seemed empty, except for the occasional temple fairy supervising enchanted cleaning supplies as he walked the corridor. '*Wonder where all the Regents are?*' he thought. "Excuse me!" he said from down the corridor. "Yes Master?" the fairy steward said. "Where are all the Regents today?" he asked. "They are in the village seeing to the Winter Solstice celebration with the village patriarchs", she said. "Right, thank you", he said continuing his way to the common room. The empty common room became alive with illumination as he stepped in, Kofka laid curled in a ball on the lounger. "Looks like you have your run of the place, aye?" he said. He thought about asking Kofka to retrieve his mother's necklace for him from the skychamber. '*Stupid*' he thought, but he remembered the conversation with the Pegasus. "Kofka", he said stroking his head. "If it's not too much trouble, would you mind terribly getting my mother's necklace from the skychamber?" he asked. "It looks a lot like this one but slightly different", he pulled out his necklace. Kofka gazed at the necklace then wagged his tail disappearing. "Wait, what?" Adin said out loud. No sooner did he say that then Kofka reappeared, holding the necklace in his mouth! "Oh, who's a good boy?" he said scratching behind Kofka's ear. Captivated he looked the medallion over, "You're my key", he whispered to himself. "What ya got there?" a familiar voice startled him, it was Atreyu and the rest of his friends, "What are you guys all doing here?" he asked confused. "Well we told Lord Gabdor that we wanted to help you catch up!" Persaeus replied with a smile as they all gathered around to see what he was holding. "It's my mother's First Knight medallion", he said holding the necklace for all to see, the medallion spinning back and forth. "Wicked!" Atreyu said captivated. "I figured if our medallions grant us access to the places we need to go, then this should be like the key for everything!". "Only one way to find out! Plus, your gonna need some help!" Atreyu said with anticipation. Adin cracked a smile, "Okay first we are going to need someone in the court yard to alert us when everyone comes back. Second, someone in the common room to alert us when everyone is actually inside the temple. Third, we are going to need someone as a lookout for the temple fairies and Regents. I'm going to need help looking for the scroll once I'm inside. Lastly, we are going to need a messenger!" he said confident with the plan he just laid out. "That's everyone little brother we don't have anyone else", Lucian said. He looked over at Kofka, "Someone? Or something?" he hinted. "Really? No way!" Lozen said in disbelief. "Have you gone mad?" she said gradually losing confidence in his insane plan. "What? He's perfect! He knows the temple layout! He understands us! He, for some weird reason, can teleport! What could go wrong with our little Lion-Heart mascot!" he said rubbing both of Kofka's ears. "Ah, first he's a Fenris! A freakin' wolf! Not a Lion! Second, what if he gets distracted?" she questioned. "What would distract him?" he smirked. "Uh, I don't know maybe a Bast!" she snapped folding her arms. "A what!" he returned with equal sarcasm. She took a deep breath, exhaling through her mouth, "A Bast is cat in your world! The primal predatory response is the same here as it is in Terra Firma, that is, a candid will chase a feline! Besides that, you only have one good arm!" she said in one breath. "S-o, your telling me that the only thing that could go wrong is a cat? A cat, that I haven't seen the whole time I've been here?" he said folding his arms. "Well, to be fair, you kinda only been 'here' for like a little over three days", Persaeus said defending her, using her fingers as air quotes. He shot her the look, 'that you're really not helping'. "Okay, well-", he stood up using his good arm, placing his hand on his chin analyzing the probability of success. "The odds are really in our favor!" he tried to rouse the rest of the group. "Listen, one of the most critical pieces to this mystery, to this craziness is in your head!" he pointed at Lozen. "And, I need to see what Regent Alina saw! Please, it's all I've got to go on! I don't know how much more I can take Lozen! Please!" his voice now desperate grasping his arm a flash of pain shot through it. "He is right little sister; his human body may not be able to take much more of this realm. Bestion seems to have a destructive obsession with him as well", Lucian heeded. "I know, I know! Maybe, if we tell the Regents about Bestion we can just hold out a little longer until Lord Artorius, Regent Alina, and Elder-", Atreyu cut her off, "Look at him Lozen! He's been tormented since he got here! He's suffering!" he said trying to get Lozen to see that Adin may not last much longer. "Where is Lord Artorius? He said he would be back in three days' time! It's been past three days! And we still have not seen him! What is Regent Alina doing? What is anyone doing but us? It's just us!" he said frustrated. "Besides, we were told to keep this secret, no one else can know and exposing Bestion, who knows what that might mean for Adin's safety", his said as his final point. "They all trust us to help keep him safe!" Lozen said, a sore lump growing in her throat. "Yes, but what good have we done? He has fared much worse under our care!" he said placing his hand on her shoulder. "Alright, I am with you", she finally conceded. "Thank you", Adin said touching her hand, she gave him a loving look. "Right, well I will post here in the common room!" Persaeus volunteered. "I will stand the courtyard", Lucian said. "That leaves me for the corridor!" Atreyu said heading to the corridor between the Regent quarters and order dormitories. "Guess that leaves me and you", Adin said to Lozen. "We don't have much time! We don't know when the Regents will return or the rest of the orders!" she provoked. "You've been there! So, can you teleport both of us?" he implied. "I'm sure I can...well this will be the first time", she said unsure of herself. "Lord Artorius would just put his...Ah!" before he could finish Lozen slapped her hand on his bad arm, teleporting them directly to Regent Alina's door. He finished his shriek of pain. "Oh, sorry!" she said with an apologetic face. "Yeah, yeah! Just-", he took a deep breath in, exhaling to settle his pain. He gathered himself, "Okay, this should do the trick!" he held his mother's medallion in front of the door. Nothing, happened, "Are you sure you're doing it right?" she whispered. "Come on! Come on!" his words turning frantic. The door began to slowly open, relieved they both stared into the room. "Let's go!" he led the way. "Do you know which scroll she used?" he whispered to her. "I don't know, when I reported she was looking over several", she said scanning the various scrolls across the table. "Great!" he gasped, "All these are written in Enochian!" he fumed. "I can read Enochian!" she said. "Okay what am I looking for?" he said. "You're looking for the word, sorry, symbol like an uncompleted circle with a di-

viding line in the middle. Like this!" she pointed. She grabbed
the scroll holding it to the wall torch light:

The sight is fair the sight is right,
The sight will show the heart's delight,
The heart's delight will show in light,
The light will show the truth in sight!

"Okay, it's a chant that has to be spoken in your
mind's eye using one or two hands", she said "That's it?"
he said unimpressed. "What more do you want?" she irked.
"No, your right! Let's go!" he grabbed her arm to leave. They
bolted out, "Ready?" she said as the door closed. "Red-a-y!"
he howled again in pain as she for a second time, mistakenly
slapped his bad arm to teleport back to the common room.
They all appeared simultaneously in the common room, Adin
flopped on the lounger. Lucian, Persaeus, and Atreyu announce in unison, "They're here!". "Oh, wait, you two are already back!" Atreyu grinned. "Jathma thorn! Jathma thorn!"
Adin squirmed in pain rocking back and forth. "What happened to him besides the obvious", Atreyu asked puzzled. "I
accidentally hit his injured arm…twice", Lozen said. "Oh, I
see. Right, well then! You're going to need a jathma thorn my
friend", Atreyu said amused handing one to him. He snatched
it, stabbing it into his injured arm. "Kofka?" he asked the
group. "Uh, I thought he was with you!" Atreyu pointed at
Persaeus. "I thought he was with you!" Persaeus pointed back
at Atreyu. "It doesn't matter; besides we found the scroll and
know what to do!" Lozen said relieved. "So, when do we…
you know…see into her mind?" Atreyu posed the question.
"Correction, when does Adin see into my mind! Not today,
any minute the rest of the order will be walking in right about
now", she predicted. Just as she said, all the Lion-Heart students came in buzzing about the tryouts. "I'm beginning to
believe she's never wrong!" Adin said leaning his head back,
totally spent for the day. "Come now little brother, you're in
need of much rest!" Lucian beckoned reaching his hand out.

He smiled and grabbed his hand, "So, what's on the agenda tomorrow?" Atreyu spouted still full of energy. "Sleeping in!" the rest of them shouted with attitude. "Geez!" Atreyu said flabbergasted before teleporting.

CHAPTER ELEVEN

THE ABYSS OF SHADOW

The heavy drapes kept their chambers dark, despite the morning sun's rays. The seductive warmth of the fireplace mixed with the chilly breeze kept Adin, Atreyu, and Lucian cocooned in their thick bedspreads. "How many jathma thorns are left?" Adin asked Atreyu from under the covers. "Uh, like two more I think". "Kofka, your super heavy!" he said to the lazy wolf. "By the way! Where were you yesterday?" he said like a concerned parent. Kofka whimpered and rolled over on his side, ignoring him. "Right", he said a little offended. He turned over, uncovering himself to pull out his mother's necklace from under his pillow. He held it over his head, the medallion spinning on its axis, he envisioned his mother wearing it. What she had to do to earn it, the battles she fought with it, the realms and dimensions it has seen. A little guilt started to fester in his heart about how he got in possession of it but he dismissed it, justifying to himself that his mother would have done the same thing. He crawled out of bed to Atreyu's bedside. On his nightstand was the last remaining jathma thorn, he stared at it. He grabbed his arm, lifting it. 'No pain' he said to himself. He checked his range of motion, his arm fully mended! She was right! A new appreciation of Lozen swelled in his heart. "Don't think I need this anymore", he told Atreyu. "No worries, I'll keep it just in case you get killed later this week!" he teased still swaddled in his blanket. Lucian started to wake up, "I'm going to get ready", he told them. "What's the plan?" Atreyu said uncovering himself with one swoop of his blanket. Adin looked to Tristan' bed, he wasn't

173

in it, "I'd thought we'd try 'the sight' today", Adin said. "This sounds like another adventure!" Atreyu bragged. "Please no! My arm just healed!" he teased back.

Down in the common room Lozen and Persaeus chatted, sipping starbrew. "So, did it hurt?" she asked Lozen. "Did what hurt?" Lozen asked. "The sight, did it hurt when Regent Alina looked into your mind?" she said between sips. "Surprisingly, no! It was like I was in a dream, then I awoke. I don't even know what she saw", she continued. "Morning!" Adin greeted them both. "How's your arm?" Lozen asked. "Why? Are you going to hit it again?" he said stepping back. "I'm just joking, it's better than new! Thanks to you!" he said smiling. "I wanted to talk to you about you know what", he said looking at Lozen. "I know, I was expecting you to inquire. Persaeus and I were just talking about that as a matter of fact", she said razzing him. "Oh, really and what may I ask were you two saying", he leaned closer. "Oh, you know, girl talk!" Persaeus answered for Lozen before they both started giggling. "I know just the place! After lunch, meet me in the temple library. No one should be there at that time of day, especially since it is our leisure time. Come Persaeus we have more *girl* talk to discuss", she said cracking a smile. "So, what do we do til then", Atreyu begged the question to Adin and Lucian. "I am going to get some practice done in the gladitorium, I have been anxious to spar with Dawn-Breaker", Lucian looked to both of them, "I'll see you in the library at the appointed time", he then teleported. "If it's all the same, I'm gonna go practice my Glaive Star swing for a bit. You wanna come?" Atreyu offered. "I think I'd like to check out the library", Adin said. "Suit yourself, see you after lunch!". "See ya!" he waved his hand, both parting ways. He didn't know where the library was so he had no choice but to walk. Leaving the common room, he ventured out into the Hall of Lords, passing other order students. "Excuse me, where can I find the library?" he asked a temple steward. "The repository? Go straight from here then take your first left to the dragon door. Go through there, the repository is on the third level", he said resuming his moping supervision. "Thank you!" he said heading towards the dragon door. "My pleasure Master!" the steward said. He followed the directions until he came to the dragon door, what a door it was! The double door had two large dragons facing each other, '*A dragon sometimes symbolizes wisdom*'; interesting he thought. The door opened, stepping through the threshold, he felt a trembling in the ground beneath him, suddenly the whole room started to move up to the third level, like an elevator! The scraping of stone against stone was nearly nonexistent due to the numerous times the stone elevator has been used during the temple's lifetime. The stone floor stopped at the third level, resulting in a deep thud. The repository was a magnificent sight! Shelves floor to ceiling lined the walls filled with scrolls in varying sizes. There were wrap around walkways connecting each floor. In the center was a large stone water fountain filled with fiery water. In the center of the fountain was an elaborate sword carved from stone, with half of the blade's body and handle sticking out of the water. The ceiling had a mural of the cosmos. "Hello?" he announced creating a lasting echo, forgetting he was in a library he quickly covered his mouth, embarrassed. He walked closer to the fire fountain, in front of the fountain was a pontifex along with a bowl of zilly-wood. He didn't know what to do, the pontifex in his experience was used to communicate, like a telephone of sorts. He grabbed the usual handful and cast it into the pontifex's small green flame. The green flame was something new, he had never seen a green flame in the pontifex, all the ones he used had a blue flame. The green flame grew larger and brighter waiting for him to say something. "I would like to see the First Knight history, please?" he said quite unsure if he was even supposed to ask for such things through the pontifex. Baffled, he looked around the room. '*Maybe there's another way?*', he began looking around. Some shelves had crystal panes that

175

had to be slide to retrieve the desired scroll. He studied the tapestries for a clue nothing, growing frustrated he looked up at the mural again consequently. One small green flicker caught his eye high on one of the shelves. "How on earth do I get up to you?" he grumbled, seeing no way to reach that height. He walked to the shelf with the green flickering light, staring up trying to figure out a way to get to it, when the stone tile he was standing on began to lift with him. This took him by complete surprise! The stone took him within arm's reach of the flickering light. The scroll's silver cap was glowing, he grabbed it and unrolled it, feeling the stone starting to descend, he looked it over. "Enochian!" he said agitated, "I can't read Enochian!". The stone tile returned back into its slot. He found a reading spot on a marble table podium with what appeared to be a large ink flagon labeled 'Seshatry' in bold black letters with a quill inside. Rolling out the scroll he hoped there may be some symbol or word he might recognize. The scroll contained only symbols that were completely foreign to him, wishing the symbols would somehow magically translate, he knew it might be possible but not at his level. The thought of finding someone to translate it was also on his mind but he quickly dismissed that idea, that would certainly spoil the plans he had for the using 'the sight' and he would definitely lose the privacy he needed to conduct it. He glanced at the quill, he lifted it out of the flagon only he didn't know the quill was abnormally long, longer than the flagon; tipping it over. The golden glittery powder poured all over the scroll. Mortified, he quickly wiped it off. Staring at the scroll he knew he was done for! The remaining powder was scattered all over the scroll, he carefully picked up the scroll to funnel the remaining golden glitter back into the flagon. Setting the scroll down the golden glitter stuck to each symbol, "Great!" he groaned with looming anxiety. Looking around for anything to wipe the golden glitter, nothing was useable. He grabbed the quill again, only this time he lifted it out of flagon carefully. The quill's feathery head at the end gave him an idea, 'Perfect!', he thought, '*I can try to brush this stuff off the symbols*'. With renewed fire he started to gently brush the first symbol, as he did the symbol changed with each brush stoke to a letter in English, he stopped. He continued on the second then third symbols, brushing more and more until he ran the feather the length of the sentence revealing an English translation. "This quill is freakin' awesome, like an old school magic maker!" he uttered brushing line after line of symbols until the first page was legible. The first line read: '*The First Knights*'.

> *The history of the First Knights was powerful, yet brief. The First Knights have led the way in every major campaign since their inception. Born out of dire need for the last realm, Terra Firma, to be completely liberated from the last remnants of the zoon infestation. The most sinister, most hellish, blood thirsty, spirits and creatures hid in in the shadows of Terra Firma. Some found refuge in the forests, preying on any who crossed their paths. Some found shelter in dwellings preying on the unsuspecting. Some sealed themselves deep within the labyrinths of dark caverns hoping to wait out their celestial warrants. Others fled to the mountains; certain they would remain secluded until evil once again reigned. Others retreated into the darkest, coldest depths of the seas hoping they would be forgotten. Many found asylum within the bodies of man. The horror of being slaughtered by the First Knights created desperate attempts of the remaining zoon on to build an alliance with evil hearted mankind. Some fell under their spell with promises of power, wealth, and immortality only to suffered their zoon constituents' fate. Never had there been such a terror from winged avengers in all the realms since the beginning as the First Knights. The zoon shivered, groaned, and laid in sheer trepidation waiting for their time to come to an end at the hands of a First Knight. The very words that became synonymous with the First Knights' wraith struck eternal fear deep into the heart of the most vile and vicious wretch became legend– 'I have come for you!'. The First Knights hunted all of them until corruption destroyed them from within...*

"We're here!" Lozen called out from the stone elevator. Adin jumped at the sound of her voice; he was so focused on reading the scroll he didn't even hear them arrive. "What ya reading?" Atreyu asked. "History of the First Knights, it's incredible. These guys were not to be messed with!" he said impressed with what he had read so far, rolling up the scroll. This brought his mother and Artorius into a whole new light. "Hey where's Lucian", he asked the three of them. "Don't know, we thought he was already here with you!" Persaeus answered. "I've been here the whole time alone", he said. "Something must've come up, he wouldn't stand us up, especially when we're getting so close!" Atreyu asserted. "We will have to fill him in later tonight", Lozen said. "Okay, how do we start?" Adin asked. "First we need a chair, I was sitting down when Regent Alina did it". Atreyu and Persaeus each grabbed a chair from a nearby reading table. "First you have to put your hands on either side of my head, then say the words", she instructed. "Alright, here goes", he said placing his hands on either side of her head. "Close your eyes now repeat after me. The sight is fair the sight is right! The sight will show the heart's delight! The heart's delight will show in light! The light will show the truth in sight!". Nothing happened. "Try again", she said but concentrate, clear your mind. He readied himself again and spoke the words once more. Suddenly, he was transported back to that day in the grimoirium. Everyone suspended in mid fall or on the ground. He looked around at their faces frozen in shock and fear. He saw himself, surrounded by bluish-purple tinted flames, '*How could anyone survive this*' he thought walking carefully to himself. He remembered shielding his eyes upon hearing the thunder-struck in a flinch reaction not because his eyes were affected. The light radiating between his fingers and his cupped hands was an amazing shade of blue. He drew closer to himself, walking like he was on a bed of ice. He got within inches of his own face; he couldn't believe what he was witnessing with his very own eyes! His eyes weren't his eyes! They were illuminated in fiery blue flames! Blazing Eyes! "A-d-i-n", a soft drawn out whisper called to him. He looked around for some-one, finally glancing in Lozen's direction. "A-d-i-n!" the voice called out again a little louder, it seemed to be somehow com-ing from Lozen. "A-d-i-n", it said louder, peaking his attention he started to walk towards Lozen. "Adin!" Lozen's voice said calmly only this time Adin could see her mouth didn't move at all. He inched closer to her, looking intently at her mouth to see if it really was her calling him. "Lozen, are you calling me?" he asked placing his hand on her shoulder. "ADIN!" Lozen's voice screamed. He was pulled back from her subcon-scious back into the repository. "You guys won't believe what I saw!" he said as excited as ever until he saw the expression on her face. "What? What's the mat-", he didn't get to finish. "Master Adin Elijah! You have been reported for intentionally, knowingly, recklessly, and with lawbreaker negligence to com-mit the crimes of: trespassing in a Regent's quarters, obtaining a restricted scroll of enlightenment, unauthorized use of said restricted scroll of enlightenment, and conspiracy to involve order students in illegal activity of personal design!" Regent Alina fumed with Lucian next to her. "Seize them!" she or-dered the Gatekeepers. "Secure their medallions!" she barked. "With pleasure, Regent!" Pateon said with a smirk. "Why Lu-cian!" Adin demanded. "We were lying little brother; I was lying! I helped you commit these crimes against the temple out of respect for your cause. Now please extend your respect for my cause, I could not live with the guilt of lying!" he said with resolve. Persaeus whimpered in the background as she was be-ing placed in magical restraints along with Atreyu and Lozen. "Will we be expelled?" Lozen asked her. "It has yet to be de-cided, Elder Valerian will judge, but I'm afraid Master Adin's fate rests with the Council of Light!" she said looking out-raged at him as he was restrained. "Regent, this one has two medallions! Looks like this one is Lion-Heart and this other... well, well, well! Lookie here! This, this is a First Knight's me-dallion!" Pateon boasted. "That's how you did it!" she boiled,

"That's how you got into my quarters! How did you come by this medallion!" she urged angrier. Adin would not say a word; he would not give up Kofka! Sensing he would not answer her, "Take them to the tower!" she commanded. "The towers of Suratrat?" a Gatekeeper questioned. "Yes", she said looking away from the group in disgust. "You heard her Gatekeepers! Secure the prisoners in the tower to await trial! Looks like you really are special boy, special enough for the tower!" Pateon jeered at Adin. Lucian stood with his head held high, his honor and his integrity sustained. "Captain!" she said halting the criminal escort. "Place Master Lucian in restraints as well, he was still a party to this criminal endeavor!" she commanded. "It is only right that I be held accountable too!" Lucian retorted. "Did you think that you would find mercy for exposing this plot, for your involvement with these crimes?" she rebuffed. "No, my Regent. I sought atonement for my honor, for my heart, I know I have sealed my own fate as well; my honor is now restored", he said joining the prisoners. The stone elevator ride was silent. "I know why you did it. Thank you for helping me find what I needed to find", Adin said to Lucian. He was stunned, he thought for sure he would hate him along with all the others. Lucian began to feel conflicted; he was sure this feeling was attributed to all the lying but now it was because he was the catalyst to his friends being imprisoned in the tower. "What of Lord Artorius?" Adin asked the guards. "He has no power here, lawbreaker!" Pateon snarled. "He should be imprisoned along with the lot of you!" he sneered. They marched the group in front of all the other order students, this was especially hard for them when other Lion-Hearts were present. "Glad I'm not a Lion-Heart!" Vito's voice bellowed out from the growing crowd of spectators. Adin questioned why they would be paraded around for the other order students to see; they could have just teleported them but he guessed it was because they were the poster example of what happens when you violate temple laws. They teleported outside the temple walls to the tower. It stood massive in height, concealed by a thick mist of fog. They all stood shaking, staring from the ground, the height of the tower exceeded their sight. Unlike some ancient prison tower's weaknesses, being attached to the primary castle or temple with an entrance at the bottom, the Suratrat resolved those weaknesses. It was separate from the temple and there was no entrance at the bottom, each section reserved for the weight of the accused crime, with the very bottom for the most severe. A true dungeon that reached into the limitless depths they called the abyss of shadow. "Take them to the holding cells, leave the abyss of shadow for the abomination!" Pateon ordered his men. "Abomination!" Lozen said glaring at the hateful Captain. "Forgive my manners lassie, I meant to say this fraudulent Guardian!" he mocked. Fearing for his friends, Adin struggled in his mind. He knew none of them would be imprisoned if it were not for him, his selfish plan! Instead of waiting for Artorius, Elder Valerian, Regent Alina, and Lord Tadrian to help him; he took it upon himself causing nothing but his friends' freedom. He could take the guilt no longer, "It was me!" he shouted, "It was all me! I forced them to help me using order loyalty! I am the guilty one, the designer of this plot to violate the temple laws! I'm sorry, truly sorry to all of you! You have been nothing but the most loyal and best friends I have ever had, forgive me!" he begged. If he had to be imprisoned in a scary sounding place like the abyss of shadow, he at least wanted to go knowing he tried to atone for his selfishness and find forgiveness with the only true friends he had ever had in his entire life! Elder Valerian and Regent Alina both arrived in time to hear his admission of guilt. "Is this true?" Regent Alina asked all four. All four stared at Adin for an answer, he nodded his head 'yes' for them to say. "Yes, it is true! We all did what we felt was right for Adin", Persaeus said surprising everyone. "Is it true, you followed this plot out of order loyalty to a fellow comrade?" Elder Valerian asked her in a way that made Persaeus feel he did not enjoy seeing them in chains. "Yes, Elder", she said. "Release these four, they are to be detained in their chambers until their punishment has been decided. They will not be expelled today!" he ruled. "What about Adin?" Atreyu appealed. "His fate as Regent Alina has said, is now in the hands of the council, I'm afraid". "How can that be?" Lozen challenged. "He's one of us!" she said trying to sound diplomatic. "He is the son of a First Knight, the only son of a First Knight. The council still burns with the sting of betrayal from the First Knights order. It is out of my hands Lady Lozen", he explained with displeasure. Adin stood facing his friends in restraints, he thought back to home, to Sister Lizzie before he was teleported to the top of the Suratrat. Standing on the soul stone triggered the tower's crown peaks to fold in until each point met in the center like the top of a teepee. The peaks burst into blazing flames of bluish-purple fire. "You know what that is boy? That's angel fire! One touch and you'll burn off of those little digits of yours! Or an ear!" Pateon laughed as the soul stone descended. The sound of grinding stone against stone etched itself in Adin's mind, he looked up at the fleeting light. The shadow soon gave way, with only the angel fire's light left. The floor stopped with a crunching sound; the darkness was unlike any darkness he had experienced. Pateon pushed him into the void, the hungry shadow of the abyss. The only light casted from the angel fire was ascending, until nothing but the void of blackness. "Elder Valerian will see to you shortly!" Pateon said. "When?" he yelled, fear reeking from his voice. "When he feels like it boy!" he mocked. Adin prepared himself, his mind ran wild with ghastly creatures, monsters, haunting phantoms that all awaited him in the darkness. He stood silent, he could feel his heart pounding within his chest, his knees were shaky, his hands clammy. He had never felt this afraid before in all his life. Aside from everything he felt, the despair was what overwhelmed every inch of his being. The loneliness crept all around him as if it were alive.

Elder Valerian stood stoic in the Court of Lords. Every Regent and Lord stood awaiting his word. "The Lion-Heart Order has suffered a most grievous of violator, a lawbreaker. Master Adin Elijah awaits judgement in the Suratrat at this very moment. Because of his angelic blood line, he must be judged by the Council of Light before any sentence can be instituted. His chamber mates and order comrades are prohibited from any and all communication with him, if he so desires, he may have one starbrew cup a day. Once the Council is ready, we will escort him to trial for judgement. All matters concerning Master Adin Elijah or mentioning of his name are strictly prohibited. That is all", he said. "What of Lord Artorius? He brought the boy and dare I say is quite fond of him", Cassian blared out. "The Gatekeepers have been instructed to escort Lord Artorius to me once he has returned", he said concluding the meeting. Lord Tadrian stood among the crowd, allowing everyone to leave until he was the last person. "Elder, the boy is still in need of medical care", he said concerned. "Yes, Lord Tadrian but what ails him?" "I found a counter agent to what may help him". "Oh?" Valerian said intrigued. "Dragon's breath has a property within it that can halt the curse's saturation!" he said. "I don't think it will be necessary now Lord Tadrian, he will soon be banished from this realm, I imagine, once the Council has passed their judgement. We must now focus on the assassin! Thank you for working so diligently in his case, I know this must have been quite difficult for you to treat a human boy versus the normal maladies you encounter", he said attempting to solicit a particular response from Tadrian. "Yes, Elder it has been quite difficult dealing with the boy", he said with a look of uneasiness shaping his face.

Atreyu sat on his bed; his head hung low. Lucian sat by the arched shaped window peering out at the tower, "You know when I first came here, I swelled with pride! I was ready to take my place as a Guardian, there was nothing that would stand in my way. When I met all of you, I felt the same feeling, now all I feel is emptiness. All I've ever wanted is to take my place as a Guardian, to honor my parents who gave up their wings so that I could be. All Adin wanted was to discover who his mother was and I only added to his tragedy and pain. Yet he still stayed", Lucian in deep revelation. "You did what you thought was right, like Adin", Atreyu said.

Persaeus and Lozen sat on the stone window seal peering out towards the tower. "I hope he's alright", Lozen said. "He's survived this far, I'm sure he will find a way", Persaeus said trying to offer her some comfort. Adin sat down in the darkness, scared of what he couldn't see. He crossed his legs; the darkness was unbelievable! He lifted his hand in front of him but he could not see it. His only sense was touch, the cold wet stone he sat on was all he could feel. He sat for hours, dosing off only to wake again to darkness. He concentrated on images of his friends, the first time he met Artorius, life back home. Every image that ran through his mind somehow became more defined because of the darkness but would just as quickly fade, he grew colder with the darkness. The next morning Atreyu, Lucian, Lozen, and Persaeus were all summoned to the Court of Lords. They met in the common room. "Do you think they will expel us?" Persaeus asked. "No, Elder Valerian said we would not be expelled, remember?" Lozen said trying to comfort her now. "Yes! But what if he changes his mind?" she said. "If we get expelled, we will get expelled together!" Lucian said. Lozen and Persaeus sensed a change in Lucian, "Together", Lozen said in agreement. One by one they entered the Court of Lords. "Sit", Elder Valerian commanded. "It pains me to go through these proceedings, it pains me; that before me is Atreyu son of Asatini, Lozen daughter of Asatini. Lucian son of Zuberi, Persaeus daughter of Dione! Before me are the offspring of respected Guardians and friends that I still love and care about!" he paced back and forth like an angry lion. '*I must be an Elder first in these matters*', he said to himself. He cleared his throat, "Master Adin took all the blame upon himself, however; all of you were willing participants! That my dear children cannot go unpunished. I have decided to forty-five days of temple confinement assisting in the stables, kitchen, and temple stewardship! Any appeal can be made with your Regent. Regent return their medallions if you will", he said. Alina returned each of their medallions. "Report to the stables at once, Taza and Gouyen are expecting you", she said. They all left as instructed, "What of Master Adin?" she asked Valerian. "I'm on the way to see him; would you care to join me?" he said. "Yes". They teleported to the tower then to the top, the soul stone activated the crown peaks, angel fire engulfing them. Adin felt the tremble, then heard the unmistakable sound of grinding stone. His could see in the darkness the glow of angel fire; the brightness grew too much for his human eyes that had grown accustomed to the black void. He shielded his eyes, "Adin". "I am here Elder!" he said, recognizing his voice, walking to the bright beacon of light unsure if he was hallucinating. "Come child", Alina said; her voice soft and gentle. She could see he was shivering, cold, and damp. She took her cloak, wrapping it around him. She rubbed his cheeks trying to warm them. "Here", she gave him a cup of hot starbrew. "T-h-a-n-k you", he said shivering, warming his face with the steam. Valerian had not seen this side of her before, that is; like a surrogate mother. The warmth of the angel fire was welcoming to him as they stood at the opening threshold. "The Council of Light will convene on your matter after this week", he said. "I have to stay down there for a whole week!" he gasped. "The council is busy with the village Winter Solstice; they do not wish to jeopardize political affiliations", Valerian said. Adin paused, letting the heat of the cup warm his hands, "I know I will be expelled and banished. I have not heard or seen Lord Artorius for more than a few days now, if I am sent back before he returns will you please tell him I'm sorry", he said taking a long sip of his starbrew. "Of course, you have my word!" Alina said. "I'm afraid its time", Valerian said; his eyes struggled to mask his sorrow. He stepped off the soul stone, watching Elder Valerian and Regent Alina until the last shade of light succumbed to complete darkness. On cue, the darkness wrapped itself around him tightly with its cold embrace; the complete opposite of how Regent Alina's cloak had first felt. The crown peaks crackled in flame as they ascended back to the height of the tower, "You know Artorius will not stand for this!" she said. "He knows the code, even he must abide by temple law. The Sovereign help us!" he said.

Standing in the flood of darkness around him, he decided if he was going to spend a week in the bowels of the tower, he would find out just how large of a room or cavern he was in. He began counting his steps until he slammed right into a rockface wall. *"Okay that's forty-one paces from the center"*, he said rubbing the pain on his face, trying to keep his mind centered. He felt around the wall, its texture a combination of smooth and jagged edges hoping to find something that might be useful to start a fire; after all he had a cloak to burn if need be. It was impossible, how could he find anything to start a fire, giving up he turned around in despair leaning his back against the wall, he let out a sigh. His legs gradually begin to flex, his back sunk against the rock face; his enthusiasm drooped in unison with each inch of his body until his full weight finally collapsed to the rock floor, he buried his head between his legs, "I wish you were here mother!" his voice squeaked. The stone grinding sound radiated in his ears, could it be? Was the darkness now fully manipulating his senses? The light of angel fire simmered. He rose, could this be a hallucination? He readied himself, making his way through the black void in the direction of the angel fire. Its simmer turned brighter as if each of his steps fueled its illumination. The soul stone crept in his view, who could be coming down he thought. Maybe, it was

Artorius! Then panic struck him, what if it was his assassin! If it was, he had enough of the darkness, enough of surviving this realm; enough with all of it! He assumed his fighting stance, thinking back to the grimoirium, he focused his mind; his only thought was summoning a thunder struck. He didn't quite know how he did it but he knew his angered fueled it and his anger was at its peak! The soul stone, breached the tower opening, he could see a foot into the breach. It slowly continued, now a two-foot opening became visible, his breathing increasing with each passing second. Four furry shadowy legs silhouetted by the angel fire light became visible, "What the-", it was Kofka! He leapt on top of him knocking him backwards. Wagging his tail, licking his face, excited to see him! He could barely get a word out! "I'm happy to see you too boy!" he said ruffling his ears. "How'd you get down here huh? Did Lozen send you, did one of the guys? No matter! I'm so glad you're here!" he rejoiced. Since he had been trapped here, the despair was overwhelming but now with Kofka present, a spark of hope ignited in him. The thought of escaping with him was tempting. "Alright boy! Let's go!" he said waving his hand to him as he dashed to the soul stone, Kofka barked in agreement right on his heels. Adin stood in the center of the soul stone, Kofka sat down beside him. "Come on already!" he said. The soul stone would not move, the angel fire above him continued its steady burn. He looked around, pushing against the tower walls, hoping he would push against some secret stone that would start the soul stone up. So close to escape, he was still trapped! He paced, struggling to think of another way out. The reality of his predicament was undeniable, as a Suratrat prisoner nothing could escape. The tower was not just a prison, not just enchanted, it was designed for much more than that. It was designed to imprison one's mind, body, and soul. He had wondered why there were no chains, why he was not bound; the chains were the darkness! The chains of darkness that wraps around your body, the chains of darkness that constrict your mind, the chains of darkness that weigh down your soul! Kneeling down on one knee, "I need you to do one last thing for me boy!" he said. "Find Lord Artorius, find and tell him all that has happened, tell him I am down here!" Kofka barked. He stepped off the soul stone, just as he suspected, it began to lift with Kofka as its only passenger.

CHAPTER TWELVE

THE LADY IN WHITE

The dining hall was louder than usual with the excitement of the Winter Solstice shortly approaching. The festivities on schedule to kick off the start of next week. This was a chance for the students to truly experience Erindol's weeklong celebration. The Winter Solstice symbolized the appreciation between the interdependency of all the inhabitants. This was also the first time; all the students would see their parents as customary after the first week of the temple indoctrination. Lozen picked at her plate, worried about Adin. Unable to sit still in her thoughts, she teleported to the common room from her dining chair. Atreyu looked at Lucian then at Persaeus with a look that said, '*Lets go too!*', they all nodded; teleporting.

Lozen stood staring in front of the fire place in deep contemplation, the blue flame coloring half of her face. "You okay Sis?" She looked at Atreyu with defeated eyes, "I don't understand why they would do that to him! To place him in that place! Knowing he's not like us!" she said tears forming in her tortured eyes. Atreyu hugged his sister, Lucian and Persaeus stood in silence behind Atreyu with their heads down. "You know he's tough right? You know he comes from a place called Texas in Terra Firma, right? They're like the toughest human warriors around over there! That and they talk like dis", Atreyu said trying to mimic what believed was a true Texas accent. This broke Lozen's despair a little forcing her to giggle at Atreyu's horrible attempt. "They don't all talk like that", she said struggling to contain her laughter, "Tay chur do!" he said. Lucian and Persaeus cracked smiles. "Adin doesn't talk

189

like that!" she said. Thora suddenly appeared, "Come quick! Lord Artorius is here! The Gatekeepers are escorting him to Elder Valerian in the Court of Lords!" Everyone teleported outside to the Court of Lords, a crowd had gathered, everyone trying to hear through the walls at the proceedings. "This is preposterous! Release the boy!" they could hear. "The boy stands accused as a lawbreaker of multiple temple laws and you demand his release? A disgraced First Knight? By what authority do you claim?" Pateon said. "Shall I show you!" Artorius said making a bee-line for Pateon, his subordinate troops stepped forward their hands on their weapons. "Artorius, stop!" Valerian said. "Captain Pateon speaks the truth, Master Adin has broken temple law and by temple law he must answer!" he argued. Artorius looked around, he was surrounded by Gatekeepers and Regents. There was only one choice he had that would guarantee Adin's freedom and the charges dismissed. He lowered his head, steading his breath, "I confess!" he said his eyes bursting into electric blue as he opened them. "I've bewitched him to commit those crimes!" he said. "Not good enough boyo, the little mongrel already confessed to everything!" Pateon said. "Then I shall have to sweeten the pot! I've come for you Elder!" he charged towards Elder Valerian, the Gatekeepers drew their weapons. They were no match for this skilled and deadly warrior, he crushed them with little trouble, blazing a path through them to his target. All five Regents sprang into action; Regent Cassian stood little chance as Artorius wrecked him. Regent Serene and Tiberius tried to overpower him but they too soon joined Cassian on the floor. Regent Marius with all his brawn was smashed with great ferocity. Regent Alina remained the only Guardian left to stand in his way, she paused, "Stop this madness please!" she begged. He advanced detached from her plea, with no choice she attacked, she was defeated with ease. She laid on the stone floor watching in horror as he stood in front of Elder Valerian with both of his swords at the ready! "Don't do this!" Valerian said. Artorius twirled his swords and drove them into the stone stage floor. He grabbed Valerian with one hand, drawing his other hand back to deliver a deadly blow. Alina climbed to her feet, her breathing forceful, she sprinted, holding her hand out for her sword. Her sword jumped into her hand as she ran past, she leaped into the air. Valerian blocked his telegraphed strike, flipping him head over heels to the ground, Alina's blade barely missing Artorius' head as she came swooping down for a death blow. The gatekeepers were upon him, placing magical restraints. Two Gatekeepers tried pulling his swords from the stone floor. "Are you alright?" she said. Valerian was quiet for a moment, scanning the aftermath of the mayhem, he brought his gaze back to her, "Meet me in my chambers for counsel", he said. "As you wish, my Elder", she said sheathing her sword, then bowed. "Those swords cannot be pulled from the stone", he said passing the two Gatekeepers on his way out. "That's why he doesn't belong back here!" Cassian said wiping the blood from his mouth, the other Regents just looked at him. Artorius was shoved out of the Court of Lords, the door opened so violently that the students had to jump back just in time to avoid being smashed in the face by the heavy wooden door. Lord Tadrian appeared, bolting into the room, "I heard what happened, is anyone hurt?" he said. "Don't know how bad, might want to check on the Regents. He gave us all a good thrashing!" a Gatekeeper said readjusting his armor before joining the prisoner escort. He walked past the other Regents, "Is everyone alright?" "Yes, Lord Tadrian, thank you. Other than our pride, I believe we are all fine", Tiberius said. "Very well", he said, a glint of light off of one of the swords caught his peripheral vision. Intrigued he walked over to the two swords embedded in the stone floor. It was strange to see a Guardian's weapons in such a state, he walked onto the stage, placing each hands on either sword handles. He began to step away when under his right foot, on the stone floor it was slick.

191

He lifted his boot, to his surprise was a small puddle of blood. He bent down, placing his fingers in the puddle to check. He inspected the substance, rubbing his fingers together, he knew without a doubt it was blood, but who's?.

The students were shocked watching Lord Artorius being led away in restraints. "What's the charge?" a voice called out; Lozen, Atreyu, Lucian, and Persaeus pushed their way through the crowd of students, emerging in front of the prisoner escort. Pateon stopped, "The charge?" Pateon raised his voice for all to hear, "Lord Artorius is charged with conspiracy and forceful attempt to assassinate The Chief Elder!". Pateon's declaration stunned every student present, their faces dropped. Lozen stood shocked in complete disbelief of what she just heard, placing her hand on Artorius hands, *'Please say it isn't so'* she said in her mind'. *'It was the only way!'*, he said without saying a word. "Move on!" Pateon said pushing the escort along forcing her out of the way. "It's to the Suratrat for you my failed friend! But then again, you've been there, before haven't you?" he sneered. Hearing Pateon's last remark gave Lozen and Adin's friends another shock of their lives, like a triple punch to the stomach. Pateon read the look on her face. "What? You didn't know dearie?" he said to her as the escort marched on. "Oh yeah, that one there, he's been in the tower before. Looks like we should have kept him there, aye?" he nudged her. From the Court of Lords to the Hall of Lords the students followed gawking at the once respected, Noble Wolf of the Spirit-Wolf order that rose to the rank of Captain in the First Knights.

The tower's foggy mist parted revealing its stone edifice, Artorius stood silent. Pateon stood gazing at the tower's height, "Don't know what all the fuss is about you anyway! I thought Elder Valerian wiser than that, to let a mongrel like you back in the temple", he said looking to Artorius. Artorius would not give him the satisfaction and remained silent. "Well, now we get to trade one mongrel for another! But don't you worry boyo! Your little mongrel pup in there will mess things up again and I'll be there to give him a right proper fix!" he said pointing at the tower base. They teleported to the soul stone, "Remember this?" he said looking down at the soul stone. "Yeah, you remember! I know, so old, we ain't changed it a bit. You know how we Guardians love our traditions!" he mocked. The soul stone began to sink, grinding past the inner walls of the tower. Artorius looked up at the folded peaks consumed in angel fire. "Not to worry, everything is just like you left it last time, right down to the abyss!" he smirked. The soul stone finally stopped with a crushing sound, "Last stop! Hades!" he taunted. Artorius focused his eyes, even in the shadow of the abyss the power of a Guardian's eyes did not work so well. It was part of the enchanted meant to hold the most powerful. He caught sight of a dirty stained cloak heaped up on the damp floor. He realized the cloak had a partial Lion-Heart Regent seal, '*Thank you Alina*' he said himself. "Adin!" he said running to it. His hands still in magical restraints, he pulled the hood away revealing Adin's face stained with dirt and debris. He tried to stir him by shaking him, "How long has he been here!" he demanded. "Not long, why? The mongrel can't be hurt!" Pateon snarled. Adin wasn't responding, "Adin, my boy, wake up", he said again, scooping him up. "Ar-Artorius?" He let out a sigh of relieve. "Is it really you? You've come back?" he whispered. "Yes, I am here my boy. I'm so sorry, I've should have never left you", he said while carrying Adin to the soul stone. "I-I messed up bad, that's why they put me here", he said with fading strength. This crushed him to his core, the boy was fighting to survive in a place he had brought him to as a human against impossible odds. An old locked away feeling of searing guilt manifested itself, resting its weight on his conscious. "I'm sorry I brought you here Adin. I'm sorry this happened to you but it's going to be okay now, everything is going to be okay now". He knelt down holding Adin readjusting the cloak. "Please?" Artorius said looking at his cloak clasp then to a Gatekeeper. "Ah, go ahead!" Pateon said authorizing his guard to unclasp the cloak. "Please wrap him carefully", he said. This guard respected Artorius, "I will Cap-I will Sir", the guard said correcting himself before making a serious mistake in front of Pateon. "Almost forgot!" Pateon said placing a spell restraint mouth guard on Artorius. "Don't want you calling any of your pals or conjuring any mischief", he said before kicking Artorius in the chest off the soul stone. He went crashing to the ground, the darkness welcoming him again. He didn't care, Adin was safe and cleared of all charges, that was enough for him. To spend all of eternity in darkness as punishment was more merciful that his guilt.

Regent Alina knocked on the door, "Come in". She stormed in confused, angry, unable to make sense of what just happened. "He could have killed us all!" she said pacing the length of the room. "He didn't", Valerian said. "Precisely! He didn't, but why? That's the question!" she said pointing her finger. "Perhaps we should ask him tomorrow?" he said. "I have made the council aware of the new developments, they seem more content that they finally have the very last of the First Knights". "What turned their sights from Master Adin to Artorius?" she said. "That my dear, that is the question indeed! I can only surmise Master Adin is just a memory of the past, Artorius is the past still alive", he said. The chamber pontifex burned bright, signaling a summons. A voice announced, "A thousand apologies Elder, Master Adin has just been admitted to the infirmary". "Thank you, I shall see to him shortly, what of his condition?" "Forgive me Elder, Lord Tadrian would not divulge his assessment. He stated he would reserve that information for you alone". "He is acting under my orders, advise Lord Tadrian that I will be there to hear his assessment!" he commanded. "Yes, my Elder!". "Before we go, we need to pick up a few students", Valerian said. Regent Alina knew exactly who he was talking about. "I'll summon the girls, you the boys", she said rushing. "Why, yes Regent!"

he said at her order. "Forgive me, I don't know what came over me", she said downcast. "It's quite alright. I was using that Terra Firma sarcasm again!" he said chuckling at how she had lost her composure for a brief second.

Regent Alina waited for Lozen and Persaeus, how she would be received played on her conscious. No matter how they felt about her, she wanted to be the one who told them Adin was free. The image of his suffering was relentless in her mind, never had she felt so conflicted. She had done the right thing; she had upheld the temple laws against a lawbreaker. Perhaps she should have left his punishment into the hands of Elder Valerian but what would he have thought of her inability to govern her own order. Her thoughts were interrupted by Lozen's voice. "Regent you summoned us?" she said. "He's here", Alina said. "Where!" she said her face flushed wish joy. "Come, let's go together!" she said. "Attention!" you have been summoned to the common room by Elder Valerian. Lucian and Atreyu sat up startled, they looked at each other and jumped out of bed, grabbing what proper clothes were laying around to throw on. "What do you think is going on?" Atreyu said. "Don't know brother but if the Elder is summoning, we mustn't waste any time.", Lucian said putting on his boots. They appeared in the common room; Valerian was inspecting the tapestries. "Elder", they both said bowing in respect. "It's been so long since I've been in the common rooms, we are going to need new tapestries", he said. Both stood expecting the worse, Atreyu couldn't take the suspense anymore, "You wanted to see us Elder?" "Yes, come with me", he reached out and touched both their shoulders, teleporting to the infirmary door; it opened. Lozen, Persaeus, and Regent Alina were there, gathered around a bed with someone in it. Atreyu and Lucian rushed in, Adin lay unconscious. "He is in pretty bad shape, he's stable for now. He's going to need a lot of rest", Tadrian said. "How long will he be like this?" Lucian asked. "That depends heavily on his will, his human body has endured more than it can bear, he is passing I'm afraid!" he said writing in his scroll. Everyone understood what the he was saying, Alina cupped her hand around Adin's head, "I must go, all of you may stay until his time comes. I shall return shortly", she said walking out the infirmary trying to hide the forming tears in her eyes. She arrived in her quarters, she looked at all the scrolls scattered all around. *'All Adin wanted was information and I made him pay with his life for it'* she said to herself, tears running her face.

"I am going to retire to my quarters, you may use the empty beds to rest tonight, I hope tomorrow will be better", Tadrian said. "Thank you, my Lord", Persaeus said answering for the whole group. The night was dark now, Lucian stared out the window beside Adin's bed. Lozen sat on Adin's bed holding his hand. Atreyu sat on the floor, his back against his bed. Persaeus sat on the bed next to him, her head hung low. "Do you think, he will", Lucian said trying to clear the lump in his throat. "Don't think like that!" Lozen said the tone in her voice struggling to remain strong. "Jathma thorn", Atreyu said. "What?" Persaeus asked. "Jathma thorn! There's one left back in our chambers!" he said capturing everyone's attention, standing up. Lozen looked at Lucian, "Its worth a try". Persaeus stood up, "What could it hurt!" she said. Atreyu ran out the infirmary in a blaze, "You know you can just teleport, right?" Persaeus yelled at him. Adin felt himself falling without end, his body striking black water, sinking. No strength in him he let himself sink; the cold water froze every inch of his body but he didn't care; he was too tired to fight. He let the depths swallow him until he saw a blurry ball of burning white light from his murky decent. It struck the black water racing to him, it burned under water never losing its energy, leaving a long boiling trail behind it, he closed his eyes waiting for the inevitable. The burning light was upon him, a hand reached out to him; somehow, he sensed the hand. He opened his eyes to the blinding light. He took hold of the hand, it pulled him inside it. He found himself sitting on the snow-white sand of a beautiful beach that he had always dreamt of. The waves rolling and crashing to shore, the bright sunlight and cool breeze felt loving for some reason; he sensed someone sitting next to him. He looked over, the presence was feminine but he couldn't see the details of her face, the light emanating from her was too much for his eyes. He tried to shield his eyes for a better look but it was no use, he looked back down. What he could see was a long white flowing dress draping the same slender figure, the lady in white. He looked back at her face, shielding his eyes, "Where am I? Who are you?" he asked. She answered him for the first time in all his life, "Where you are is who you are. I am what you have always been", she said her voice echoed with each word, he couldn't tell if he was hearing her words in his head or in his ears. This racked his mind; it made no sense. He thought he should start again by introducing himself, "I'm sorry, my name is Adin. I'm not quite sure what I'm doing here", he said hoping to elicit some type of answer. "The decision has always been yours", she said. "What decision? I don't know what you mean!" he said frustrated. "The fight is here, Lion-Heart", she said placing her hand over her heart. "What fight? How do you know I am Lion-Heart? Who are you?" he said frightened, crawling backwards to gain distance. He blinked, she now towered over him. "It's time", she said touching her hand to his heart, a flash of light struck. He found himself in the dark water again only he was being propelled to the surface at great speed, he launched from the water into the void, his speed increasing. "Woah!" he yelled as his body shot up, he gasped from his bed drawing in a deep breath waking Lozen-who had fallen asleep sitting by his side. His gasp startled the rest, waking all of them up. "Wha-what happened?" he said. "Your free!" Lozen said. "How?" he said confused. "Lord Artorius took your place," she said. "Why? He had nothing to do with it! I did all those things, not him!" he protested. "It's what he wanted", she said. "How do you know?" he argued, he didn't want Artorius paying for his crimes. "He told, me with 'the sight'", she said, "Just before they took him away". He studied her face; she was telling the truth; not just trying to make him feel better. "I guess the jathma thorn worked!" Atreyu said. "I'll let Lord Tadrian know!" Persaeus said throwing zilly-wood in the pontifex.

Lord Tadrian arrived first, "Oh, my boy you've come back from the brink of certain death!" he said. "I must admit, I'm at a loss, not hours before you were moving into Sheol," he said. "Maybe this helped", Atreyu said handing him the used jathma thorn husk. "We've been using it to help him with some of the injuries", he said with pride. "Have you now", Tadrian said examining the thorn. "Yup, Lozen thought of it, we've used like three of them so far, that one being the last", Atreyu said. "Clever girl", he said under his breath. Elder Valerian arrived with Regent Alina. "Master Adin, I see you've returned to us", he said pleased. "Only because Lord Artorius took my place", he said sinking back into his pillow, hating what he just learned. "I know you care for him; we-you mustn't dwell on such troubles, you must rest", Alina said. "I believe this is yours", she said placing his Lion-Heart necklace around his neck. He was happy to have it back, "We will discuss your mother's medallion when the time is right, for now it is safe", Valerian said.

Artorius rose back to his feet, he manifested his wings. He began to lean back using his wings to brace his body's weight. He looked like he was laying completely flat, like on an invisible table. He rested his arms across his chest, this was an old way in which Guardians mediated, he closed his eyes allowing himself to drift. He hadn't meditated in centuries, meditation was a way for a Guardian to stay dormitive in his mind, body, and soul. It could also be used to relive events in order to find revelation. His time as a Terra Firma Guardian gave him unique insight into mankind's nature, culture, and society. He learned to disconnect himself to 'ride the dragon's breath' as it was referred to. This practice was highly frowned upon by Guardians after his time at the temple, it was little understood or appreciated. He felt his spirit separating itself from his mind and body, causing him to lose all his physical senses of the realm. His vision narrowed, he found himself in a dark war-torn world. The sky was painted blood red, the earth under his feet was black sand mixed with ash. A warrior in black panoplian armor fought against many, thousands of combatants lay before him defeated. Those that were left attacked him to no avail, he conquered them all, crushing each foe that dared to challenge him. His weapon, prana, and randori skills were unmatched for the doomed warriors. Guardians flying to meet him in battle only suffer the fate of the brave dead. Artorius felt fear permeating the air, the dark knight threw his arms up in victory. Hundreds of thousands of Guardians and zoon lay dead, this dark knight isn't a hero! He was a monster; a conqueror! Among the dead lay all the order Regents and Elder Valerian! He was horrified, he found Alina laying lifeless. He fell to his knees, the look in her eyes was empty, he was too late; closing them he glared toward the dark knight. His eye blaze ignited to avenge his brothers and sisters, he reached for his swords but they are not there! He ran to the dark knight jumping into the air to 'Superman' punch him. His strike landed with no effect; the dark knight seized him by the throat. Lifting him with one arm he tossed Artorius behind him like a rag doll. He toppled, his body burying in the ground left a long trench, ash floated to the ground, debris fell in all directions; the dark knight turned to face him. Picking his head up out of the ground his vision was blurred, his smeared silver blood is caked with debris and ash. His vision slowly came back into focus except for two blurry objects sticking out the ground in front of him, the dark knight stood defiant in the distance. He focused on the blurry objects only to find they are his swords that were impaled in the ground in front of him. He rose to his feet with new confidence, pulling them from the earth. He twirled them into a fighting stance, the dark knight still stood there undeterred, he was daring him to attack. He ran towards him with full speed, deploying his wings with both blades in hand, the dark knight did not move or react. He tightened his left-handed grip on the sword handle, he lunged, stabbing into the dark knight's chest; the blade broke upon impact. He compensated, leaping into the air for a death blow spinning around striking the dark knight's helmet with a reverse right-handed slash, the sword's blade broke upon impact. The dark knight seized him, grabbing hold of both his hands that still held tight to what was left of his two star-ore swords. The strength of the dark knight was overwhelming, He gave a thundering war cry trying to break free with all his might, he was no match for this monster's power. The dark knight forced the broken blades into his body, Artorius valiantly resisted until the blades pierced his flesh. He lost, the life draining from his face, his eyes reflected helplessness and hopelessness, he slumped to his knees. The dark knight removed his helmet, tossing it to the ground; his face was hidden behind his long brown hair. He could feel the breath of life slipping out of him. He must know who this dark knight was, he looked up at him. The hot wind blew the hair out of his face, Artorius' eyes widened, it was Adin! His body sunk into his knees, brokenhearted not believing what he saw, never looking away from Adin's face. He sat back on his heels, struggling to draw his last breath; the wheezing rasps until there is no life in him. His head drooped to the side, his body hunched slightly over, his hands fell limp to the ground then a burst of light.

His eyes jerked open; he was back in the shadow of the abyss. He didn't move, his mind trying to process what he had just seen and felt. Was this Adin's fate? He would never let that happen to him even if it meant losing his own life; that old guilt crept back up upon him again.

Elder Valerian and Regent Alina waited for Lord Tadrian to meet them at the base of the tower, its fog parting, waiting for them to enter. Tadrian arrived late, "Forgive me, Elder. I was seeing to Adin", he said. "Oh, not at all, how is he?" "He is well, gaining strength at the speed his human body will allow" he said optimistic. "I am glad to hear that. I see you brought your treatment kit", he said. "Oh, yes Elder, during the altercation, I believe Lord Artorius may have been injured. I found blood on the stage floor by his swords", he said. "I see, Captain Pateon never reported the prisoner suffered any injuries", he said reflecting. "The injury must be of a cosmetic nature. Those kinds of injuries are frequently missed", Alina said. "Right you are Regent but in the interest of righteousness, I believe we have an obligation to ensure the prisoner is without injury", Tadrian said. "I couldn't agree more Lord Tadrian. Everyone ready?" Valerian said, they all nodded 'yes'. The sound of the soul stone grinding against the tower's interior wall stirred Artorius. He stood to his feet; he began walking to the arched shaped exit to greet his visitors. Standing before him were two visitors that he expected but not the third. "Before any questioning, may I examine the prisoner?" Tadrian said. "Yes, of course", Valerian said. "Lord Artorius, forgive me but I fear you may have been injured in the incident, may I examine you?" Artorius could not speak, he could only nod his head 'yes'. He began his examination, "Ah, here we are!" he said behind him, lifting up the back of his damp hair. "He has a small laceration just below the hair line. Doesn't look bad but in here, it may not heal. The enchantments hinder anyone imprisoned down here". What he pulled from his treatment kit, no one could quite see. Suddenly Artorius pulled his head away as if something stung him. "Quite sorry my Lord but the wound needed to be cleaned", he said dabbing the back of his neck. Artorius stared at him with threatening intensity. "Right, well I think you will be fine now. I've completed the examination; I'm all done here!" he darted back to the safety of the soul stone. Regent Alina and Elder Valerian approached Artorius, "He's awake Artorius!" she said, her smile was uplifting. He could only nod that he understood. "I don't agree with what you did but I think I know why you did it. The council will demand your execution. I don't want to lose yo-forgive me, I must go", she sputtered returning to the soul stone. "She says the truth, the council will execute you Artorius there is no question of that. Are you sure this is what you want or what you need, to be free?" he probed. Artorius looked at him, his eyes told that he struck a nerve in him. "I know your guilt is all that drives you, it's also what has stripped you! If this boy is to make it through, then he is going to need you. If you are executed, you will have robbed him of a chance at life in his own world!" he said angered. Artorius reached out his bounded hands to him, a polite interruption, he didn't have much time to warn him. Taking hold of his hands with his, '*A friend's wounds you can always trust but an enemy will multiply kisses. I have scoured the village, the mountains, the skies, and waters; there is no greater threat than that what lies within the temple*' he imparted to him using 'the sight'. This unsettled Valerian, he paused for a moment, "Your trial begins the first moon after the Winter Solstice, the Sovereign help you", he said coldhearted before joining Regent Alina and Lord Tadrian. They departed, using the last of the angel fire's ambient light, he checked the back of his neck, lightly touching his wound. He looked his fingers over, they were stained is his blood but not in a way he expected. His eyes widened, looking up at the bottom of the soul stone, unable to yell or speak to get Valerian's attention he could do nothing; panic began to fill his heart. He struck the side of the tower wall as a desperate attempt to get their attention. The thud vibrated throughout the tower to the soul stone, "Tortured soul, he can't take the torment of the abyss", Lord Tadrian said.

CHAPTER THIRTEEN

THE FAIRY WITH NO WINGS

"Forgive me, I've just returned from the tower", Lord Tadrian said entering the infirmary. Adin was up, everyone sitting around his bed, Kofka curled up at his feet. "The tower! Is he alright?" Adin said. "He, is doing just fine, not to worry. You, however; need to rest. Your still cursed boy!" he pointed at him, checking a scroll. "I'm fine, I'm ready to go back to training!" he said removing his bedsheets. "Lord Tadrian is right, little brother you must rest", Lucian said. Adin looked around the room, he knew he should rest but knowing Artorius is locked up because of him, birthed a foreign feeling within him, guilt. "The celebration starts tonight. There won't be any training, perhaps music, food, games, and fireworks will help keep him from any harm?" Lozen suggested. "Great idea, Sis!" Atreyu said. "He can't surely be in any trouble at a celebration", Persaeus said. Lord Tadrian knew that he would not win the debate, "This goes against my better judgement. Very well, I will leave him to your care but only with your Regent's permission!" he said. "Of course, I'll advise her now!" Lozen said darting to the pontifex, "Excuse me, Lady Lozen, I believe that is my responsibility?" he said. "Right my Lord! Forgive me!" she sat back down. "Are you hungry?" she said to Adin while Lord Tadrian contacted Regent Alina. "Starving!" he said. "I think I have some frybread somewhere", Atreyu said patting his jacket and pants pockets. "That's so gross!" Persaeus said watching him look for old frybread with a disgusted look on her face. "It's a magic world, magic food! Duh!" he said. "Yes Regent, I will inform them now. Wonderful news! Your Regent has allowed him into your care under one condition, all of you are with him at all times", he said. Adin stepped out of bed, "Well let's go then", he said to the group. "By the way, magic doesn't keep food from spoiling no more than it can make you smart!" Lozen said. Lucian roared in laughter as they teleported to the common room. A knock on the infirmary door, "Come in", Tadrian said. Two fairy temple wards bowed and entered the room, "Yes, thank you", he said. They began changing the bedsheets, throwing away dressings, one grabbed the jathma thorn. "Wait! Not that, I will dispose of it, thank you", he said grabbing the fairy's arm; the fairy surrendered the thorn. He walked to the large arch window at the end of the infirmary, he looked out the window in the direction of the Lamia cave, he tightly gripped the thorn forcing it to crumble in his hand.

The dining hall was louder than usual with students going to the court yard and back. "What's going on?" Atreyu said to Thora. "Fairy, Elven, and Dwarf vendors are here!" she said. "What for?". "The Winter Solstice! You're not going in temple uniform, are you?" she said looking to each of them. They all looked embarrassed, "No, of course not", Atreyu said trying to play it off. "Rig-h-t! Okay then, you all should get a move on before all the good stuff is bought up!" she said half believing them. Lozen and Persaeus darted off to go see what they could find, "Well what are we waiting for?" Lucian said. In the courtyard were vendor stands selling perfumes, jewelry, boots, fine Elven jackets, Fairy gowns, Dwarf regal shirts, and of course starbrew along with the customary pastries. Even some of the Regents were there too, browsing around at all that was being offered for sale. Alina found a beautiful purple and white fairy gown, "Only three ruby shekels Regent!" the vendor said. Fairy gowns were very exquisite even for informal wear, this price was more than fair. Persaeus was more inclined with clothing and fashion trends, Lozen felt overwhelmed with all the choices. Persaeus purchased an

Elven gown in a white to fading pink print. "Why haven't any of you gotten anything?" she said to the group, they looked at her as if they didn't quite know how to ask her something. "We need help!" Atreyu said sheepish. Persaeus smiled and chuckled, "Of course but first we have to start with Lozen, all the boy clothing doesn't run out as fast as the girls!" she said pulling Lozen by the arm. Soon Lozen found a maroon fairy houppelande dress with gold trim. "Now that is a dress!" she said looking over Lozen's shoulder. Lozen smiled, proud of herself for choosing well, all her life she was raised with her brother to be a warrior, fashion was not on the forefront of her father's upbringing. Anything that had nothing to do with the Guardian way of life was inconsequential to her father. Lucian found a Dwarf regal shirt in black with silver lining with matching pants. Atreyu found an Elven mandarin collared jacket in light tan with brown trim. Adin found a fairy dark blue short waist jacket with gold trim. "So, how does this work?" Adin asked. "Well Master, you pick the fabric and style you like, then we receive your measurement record, we design the clothing, then deliver to your chambers", the vendor said. "How long will that take? Will it be ready in time for the celebration?" he said doubtful. The fairy vendor looked at him strange, "Why yes Master, in some cases it will be done as soon as you return to your chambers, it has always been that way", he said. "Right, forgive me! How much?" he asked, the fairy smiled, "For you young Lion-Heart only one blue diamond!" he said holding his smile. "A blue diamond! A bit much for a fairy jacket!" Atreyu said coming to Adin's aid. "Why yes Master, this jacket isn't just for show, it has enchanted protection against many weapons", he said. "Why would I need a jacket like that?" he questioned. "The fabric is an old jaculus dragon hide inventory. 'The Great Javelin Snake' many called it, very rare and special, the jaculus' skin is resistant to most weapons. "We'll take it!" Atreyu said. "What?" Adin said displeased. "Think about it!" he whispered to Adin. Adin handed the vendor a quarter size blue diamond, "Thank you for your purchase, please see us again!" he said flicking the diamond up in the air, "We here at the 'Crooked Arrow, aim to please!" he said with a wink. They all gathered at the center of the court-yard. "We have a few hours before the celebration, so we best get a move on to get ready!" Persaeus said.

"You certainly clean up well", Lozen said to Adin. He along with Atreyu and Lucian appeared in the common room all dressed in their new clothes. "You too!" he said. "So, what's this celebration all about?" he asked the group. "I'll tell you on the way", she said. "You mean we are actually going to walk?" he said in disbelief. "Why not?" she asked. "Well we are always teleporting from here to there, I just figured that's what we will always do", he said. Lozen laughed, "We aren't training so we can take our leisure", she said. The Moirai bridge was erected, fairy vendors pulling their carts traveling back across to the village. There were some people going to the temple, "I thought no one could go to the temple", Adin said. "During the celebration, former Guardians are invited to visit the temple to see their old orders and comrades, like my father", she said. He was lost, he didn't understand what she was telling him. As he understood it, he was half human, half angel, he thought Lozen, and all the other students were just like him. "Aren't you like me?" he said. "No, there hasn't been anyone like you for almost three thousand years. My father and my mother were Guardians, when they had my broth-er and I, they gave up their wings just like your mother gave up hers; for you. Our mom died after she had us", she said. "My mother died too after she had me", he said, he never knew Lozen and Atreyu had lost their mom. "My father was a Spirit-Wolf and my mother was a Lion-Heart. Lord Artorius and my father were in the same order", she said. My father and Lord Artorius were part of the Noble Wolf , a club that provided humanitarian efforts to Terra Firma", she said. "Ar-torius never told me any of that", he said a little taken back.

"Well, from what my father said he was a big advocate for Terra Firma, sometimes getting into trouble but after his promotion to the First Knights and then their disbandment; he was never the same. My father mentions him quite often in all their adventures together and I even remember seeing him when we were young, he was always so kind to us", she said reflecting back. His perception of Artorius had always been that of a warrior through and through, no time for friends or love or anything that didn't require a battle. "So, I just got done talking with Tristan", Atreyu said. "Who?" Adin asked. "Tristan! The other boy that bunks with us", he said looking at him strange. He had forgotten all about Tristan, the only time he ever saw him was when he was sleeping. "Anyway, Tristan said that there is this new Terra Firma delicacy called a 'funnel cake'! Its topped with strawberries, this stuff called ice cream, whip cream, and nuts", he said excited. "I've had a funnel cake before, they are quite good!" Adin said. "Oh, now I am for sure going to try one or maybe two!" Atreyu said. Adin was enjoying the walk, he had almost forgotten how a simple walk can lead to so much; except for the occasional ache in his body, he was in pretty good spirits. All the talk about Artorius started to bring him down, "I wonder if he will be okay", he said looking back towards the temple. "You underestimate him, he has been there before and he had good reason", Lozen said, they came to the cliff face of the village. The village looked completely different than what he remembered, as they entered, the beat of drums could be felt. The village was truly alive touching each of his senses at once, the smell of pastries was the first thing that hit him. The sweet aroma of vanilla mixed with chocolate and waffle cone sent his stomach into a frenzy. The upbeat sound of fairy music, the flutes and drums stirring everyone to dance and sing. The vibrant colors of string-fire wrapped around trees, strung across vendor shops painted a smorgasbord of color that livened feelings of tranquility. "So, what do we do first?" Persaeus said. "Maybe we should all figure out what we want to do that way we don't split up leaving Adin", Lozen said. "All I want to do is get my hands on a funnel cake, maybe a few games, maybe a few rides", Atreyu said. "I want to hear the poems of valor", Lucian said. "I want to dance", said Persaeus. "I want to visit with father", Lozen said. "All I want is to visit the Nineveh", Adin said. "The Nineveh it is!", Lozen said.

"Terra Firma's newest delicacy! Funnel Cake! Yes, I know it sounds strange but let your taste buds decide! Only one emerald shekel!" a fairy vendor with a wooden cart yelled out to passersby. They all bought a funnel cake from him; each tore small pieces of their funnel cake to snack on while walking to the Nineveh. His second time at the Nineveh was just like the first, students stood around the statues, reading their inscriptions; the doors of the Nineveh were open for anyone interested. "Ah, my boy!" a voice called from the second floor. "Who's that?" Atreyu said. "That's Davalin", Adin said. "So good to see you, my boy! I am sorry to hear about Lord Artorius", he said. "Yes, it is good to see you as well Sir, how did you know?" Adin asked. "It's extremely difficult to keep a secret such as that, especially one that involves one of the last of the First Knights. Who are these finely dressed companions of yours?" he said. "Forgive my manners, this is Atreyu, Lozen, Persaeus, and Lucian. They are in Lion-Heart with me". "Please to meet you all, is there anything I can show you?" he asked the group. "Can you show us the history of the First Knights? I read a brief history in the temple library but didn't get a chance to finish", Adin said. "Come with me young Lion-Hearts!" he motioned for them. Walking through the halls, they were able to see ancient weapons in glass cases, ancient clothing on stone statues, old scrolls written in the most ancient of languages from the realms. Finally, they came to a hall, that bore the First Knights crest. Entering the hall, stood life size statues of the First Knights' members in solid gold. This was the first time Adin saw his mother's face, the craftmanship was astounding. Her face was so young, so confident, so powerful. Her hair pulled back into a single braid, with the length resting on her shoulder. Her armor molded to her frame; her longsword slung cross shoulder made her look intense. Adin couldn't help but touch her face, he had longed to see her beyond the confines of his imagination. He stepped back to see her in all her glory until he saw a face next to hers. The pleasure of the moment, now fled. Dagon stood to the right of her; this was now the first time he laid his eyes on the one responsible for his mother's murder. "You can't imagine the political objections to this hall, the Council of Light was furious that it was erected", Davalin said seeing the look on Adin's face. "The only ones that belong are my mother and Lord Artorius", he said. "Yes, but history can never be filtered or incomplete, we must tell all of history no matter how painful or how wonderous it once was. I'll leave you to your thoughts". Adin walked around the image of Dagon, studying it, the features of his face the determined look in his eyes, burning everything it into his mind, '*I will never forget this face*' he thought. To her right was Artorius, he looked the same but different. He looked without the weight of tragedy upon him. He wished that Artorius looked this way all the time. The other two knights, he didn't care to give a second thought, the only two he loved were next to each other surrounded by traitors and enemies of the realms. To the left and right were scrolls ceiling to floor like tapestries giving accounts of battles, virtues, thrones, rescues, and citations. The scrolls were written in Enochian, "Lozen! Can you help with this?" he said. Lozen was with Atreyu reading a scroll on the other side, Lucian and Persaeus were further down the hall. "Need you to translate this?" he said pointing to the scroll behind the glass. Looking over the scroll, Lozen translated, "It says, 'The Battle of the Lamia Caverns'. That happened right here just outside the village! Looks like your mother lead a contingent of Guardians to expel the Lamia. The Lamia were responsible for the village's missing children, they feed upon them". "Feed upon them?" Adin said. "The Lamia are humanoid serpent people; they caused much harm to Terra Firma in the old days. They can appear as a human, fairy, or elf from the waist up; from the waist down is the rest of their body, a long thick serpent's tail. They would attack their victims in the night, biting their necks injecting their venom. The venom would temporarily paralyze the victim, making them unable to use any magical or physical defense. The victim was then swallowed whole!" she said. "You don't think?" Adin said. "That can't be, you have no bite marks", she said. "If the venom was milked or taken from one, then an assassin could practically use it anywhere or on anything!" he said. "That may explain your cell suppression!" she said. "Keep reading for any other clues!" he said. "You guys come over here", he yelled. Atreyu, Persaeus, and Lucian ran up to them, "What's matter?" Lucian said. "I think we found what I was cursed with. The venom of a Lamia!" Adin said. "Are we dealing with a Lamia? They're extinct", Lucian said. "Hard to say but if we are dealing with the venom of a Lamia and where there's venom-". Lozen said, "There's a Lamia!" Lucian said. "You see here?" she said pointing to the list of names of Guardians that participated in the mission. "This is your mother's name and here is-". "What?" Adin said. "Lord Tadrian's name, he was there too!" she said tapping on the glass. "We've got to tell Elder Valerian!" Persaeus said. "Quick! Find a pontifex!" Atreyu said. They all searched for a pontifex until they found one in the Bistro Court. Lozen threw in the zilly-wood. "Regent Alina please", she said. "One moment please. I'm sorry Regent Alina isn't answering", the temple steward said. "Okay, how about Elder Valerian or a Regent?" "I'm sorry they are all out for the celebration and the temple couriers have been reassigned to the village assisting with the celebration". "We will have to find them in the village! Come on!" Adin said. They ran out of the Nineveh, "Thank you for coming!" Davalin said as they ran past. "Why are we running?" Atreyu said, "Let's just teleport!". "How are we going to teleport to somewhere we haven't seen Atreyu?" Lozen said, "They could be anywhere!" Persaeus said. "All we have to do is find one of them, shouldn't be too hard!" Adin said. "That and we don't know if the assassin is out in the village!" Lucian said. "Stupid place to try and kill someone with a village overflowing with fairies, elves, dwarfs, and Guardians!" Atreyu said. "No! It's perfect, too many people not suspecting a thing all caught up in the celebration, it the perfect cover!" Adin said. They got to the center of the village, there were so many people, one could not keep track of where everyone was going. The light of the day faded into evening; the fireworks would soon start. The village was now near impossible to move through, the fairies, elves, and dwarves from all over the realms were there, even the night sky was littered with fairies looking for the perfect view to watch the fireworks. "I hate to say this, but we have to split up!" Adin said scanning the crowd. "He's right", Lucian said. Lozen was not at all happy about the decision but she knew under the given circumstances it would make better sense to split up, covering more ground; thereby increasing the probability that they would find someone that could help them. "Here's the plan! We split in five directions, north, south, east, west, and central; look around each area until half way through the fireworks then back here!" Adin said. They all agreed, Atreyu went north, Lozen went south, Lucian went east, Persaeus went west, and Adin stayed central. Adin could see all the crowds gathering, left the alleys along with some of the out-laying streets empty. A fairy pushing a peddler's cart walked down the dark alley towards him, her cloak dragged on the ground behind her. "Happy Winter Solstice Lad!" she said, "Would you care for some of the best starbrew?" she said handing him an empty cup. Her face was hidden in the shadow of her cloak hood, her blonde hair a dull shade of yellow, "No, thank you, I'm actually a little busy right now", he said looking around at all the faces not really paying her much mind. "That's quite alright my boy, an old fairy like me can't even give a cup of my best starbrew away much less sell a cup, enjoy the celebration dear!" she said depressed as pushed her cart. "Wait, wait, I'm sorry. I'll have a cup, how much?" he asked feeling sorry for her. "For you young Lion-Heart its free if you only grace me with your name", she said. "Come sit here and I will pour you a cup of the best starbrew like you've ever had, it's a real knockout", she said patting the wooden bed of her cart. He sat down, her trembling hands shaking as she held an old kettle. "So, lad may I have the pleasure of your name?" she said again pouring his cup. "Yes, its Adin, Adin Elijah", he said. She smiled, her cheeks lifting unnaturally high, she steadied her hand using her other hand as she poured the piping hot brew into his cup. He took a sip, the flavor washed over his taste buds. "This is really, really good!" he said, the fireworks began shooting into the air with thunder-like explosions alighting the night sky with an array of colors. "Oh, my boy you've made me the happiest Lamia in Erindol!" she said right as a huge explosion erupted. Adin began to lose feeling in his legs, a numbing sensation felt like it was crawling on him, "I'm sorry, I didn't hear you, what was that?" the loss of feeling started to rise in his stomach, then to his chest. "Where are my manners? My name is Nyah, I'm a Lamia!" she said putting away her kettle. By this time, he had lost the feeling in both arms, they dropped, his hands numb couldn't hold his cup; dropping it. Her tail sprang out from under her cloak, catching the cup, raising it to her hand. The numbing sensation spread further to his throat and mouth rendering him unable to scream or draw attention. His eyes began to fixate, her smile reached from ear to ear. He fell backwards into the bed of her cart; another firework explosion masked the sound of his body hitting the wooden bed. She quickly folded his legs, then pulled a worn dragon's hide tarp to conceal her prize. "Happy Winter Solstice", Lozen said startling her. "Oh, my dear child you gave this old fairy quite a scare", she said grabbing her chest. "Forgive me Fair-Lady but have you seen a young boy around my age wearing a blue jacket with golden stitching?" she asked. "No, my dear, I'm afraid not. Is everything okay?" she said concerned. "Yes, it is, thank you. I see you are a starbrew vendor", she said. "Yes, dear but I've run out unfortunately", she said holding the kettle upside down. "I see, pity. If by chance you happen to see or run into him, can you tell him Lozen is looking for him? He was supposed to meet me and our friends here. It's very important like life and death!" she said. "Oh, dear, of course, if I see…I'm sorry, what's his name?" she said. "Adin", Lozen answered. "Adin. If I see him, I will most certainly let him know a beautiful girl is looking for him", she said. "Thanks, but we are just friends", Lozen said. "I see, well good luck my dear", she said turning her cart to push back up the alley. Lozen watched her push her cart all the way up the alley, '*Strange*' she thought, '*I don't think I saw any wings*'.

Nyah pushed her cart unchallenged, all the way to the outskirts of the village. The light from the fireworks splashed the woods with reds, greens, blues, and yellows. The cheers, music, and singing coupled with the loud explosions let her slip away unnoticed. Her plan had almost run afoul, who would have thought something as simple as a cup of the 'best starbrew' would reward all her years of planning and partnership. Her partner soon proved unreliable from the beginning, so she took matters into her own hands when she spied Adin and his murdering Guardian mentor on top of Mt. Hebron, her revenge was finally at hand. She had him as quick and as easy as her kind were known for catching their prey, she took him without a single person knowing! No sneaking into children's bedroom windows or babies' cribs, oh no; just a drop or two of venom in her 'best starbrew' was all it took. There was no one to save the boy now, his fate would be that of so many children that fell victim to her kind. She was only a serpentlet when her mother's glory and power as the Queen of the La-mia was destroyed at the hands of a First Knight named Tess-la. Her mother's screams and cries still echoed in her mind, but vengeance burned deep in her heart and now she had her prize! She stopped at the headway of the hidden path to the cavern. She tilted the cart, dropping him to the forest floor, "Whew, the cold season is coming, time for me to change into something more comfortable", she hissed. Her skin was itchy, cracking, and dry; she grabbed at her face tearing off her old skin. Her new face was young now, spotless, and bright. Her hair was a thick mop of reddish-blonde strands that fell past her shoulders, she finished peeling the old skin from her arms; dropping it to the floor with little regard. She slithered over to him, his eyes still fixated, his body still catatonic. She bent down, "How did you like the Therian curse I used? I would have never anticipated its effect on you. You see for a Therian curse to work at full potential the victim has to curse themselves, so you can imagine my joy when my mad scien-tist moment produced a result causing your cells to repress! I thoroughly enjoyed watching you suffer trying to survive in a place that doesn't even want you!" she said with a soft tap on the end of his nose. She reached into the bed of her cart, pulling out braided horse hair rope. She tied his legs togeth-er, bounding them so tight, his boot heels clacked together. "Ready my young Lion-Heart", she said dragging him at an incredible speed, until she reached the mouth of the cavern. "I've worked so hard on this cavern, making it uninhabitable, I was going for an enter at your own risk theme. Oh, I have to warn you, it's quite slippery; your head might get bumped along the way. No matter your bruised skull will be easier to digest", she taunted dragging him into the mouth of cavern.

Atreyu, Lucian, and Persaeus all met back up with Lozen. "Hey where is he?" Atreyu said. "I was the first one back and he wasn't here when I got here", she said. "They're gonna expel us for this for sure, we lost him!" Atreyu panicked.

"He knows how to teleport back, something isn't right!" Lozen said. "Assassin!" Lucian said. "Did you see anything? Hear anything, was anyone here when you got back?" Lucian said. "Just an old fairy vendor selling starbrew", she said thinking back to her conversation. "But she didn't have any wings, oh my Sovereign!" she heaved. "Which way did she go?" Lucian said. She pointed down the dark alley. "Let's go!" Atreyu said. Following the trail, they found the abandoned cart. "That's the cart, I'm sure of it!" Lozen said. "Are you sure?" Lucian said. "Yeah, she's sure", Atreyu said picking up the shedded skin of Nyah. "Super gross!" Persaeus said. Lozen picked up Nyah's trail following the smashed-down grass and foliage leading to the mouth of the cavern. "The trail ends here!" she said looking at the enormous dark opening. "Let's go, there's still time!" Lucian said. "We are not prepared to fight a Lamia!" Lozen said stopping him. "She's right!" Persaeus said. "Who are we gonna find in time?" Atreyu cried. "Quick to the common room!" Lozen said. In a flash, they all arrived in the common room. "What are we doing here? Adin's in trouble!" Atreyu exclaimed. "Quick everyone! Look for Kofka! "What do you mean, look where?" Persaeus said. "Just look, everywhere! The chambers, the infirmary, everywhere we have seen him!" she said. They each teleported to all the places they remember seeing Kofka, checking over and under beds calling out his name. They all arrived back in the common room, "Nowhere, we can't find him!" Atreyu panted. "Kofka! Where could you be!" Lozen said, her fear beginning to grow. "The skychamber!" she said. "How are we going to get to the skychamber, its off limits!" Atreyu said. "No, it's not! The temple is open for visitors and former Guardians, remember?" Persaeus said. A look of hope came across each face.

Nyah dragged Adin down the slick winding stone path deeper into the cavern. Stalactites hung down the cavern ceiling, each looking as if they could fall at any moment. Stalagmites cluttered the cavern floor, some towering in the middle of dark pools of water. Giant pieces of limestone rock weighing thousands of pounds lay all around like icebergs. The air was moist, the stench of moldy rock was sickening. Adin's head bumped into several make shift stone steps carved out of the solid rock. "This cavern was once a thriving home to the clan of the Manastir. We were worshipped in Terra Firma's Greece, mankind believed us to bring wisdom and prosperity, that is; until the Guardians banished my kind to this realm. We had grown accustomed to feeding on children you see, the Terra Firmians sustained us, but the fairy, elf, and dwarf children, they were such a delicacy!". She dragged him across a bridge all the way down to the Queen's Room some 1,600 feet at the very bottom of the cavern. The room was divided by two raised pools of dark water each with a tall stalagmite in the middle lit by yellow flame, the ground was littered with the bones of her prey. Adin's body remained stiff as a board; his heart pounded. He tried to move but it was no use, his muscles would not respond, even his eyelids were unable to shut. "I watched your mother destroy my mother in this very room!" she said bitter. "Fate has smiled upon me young Lion-Heart", she smirked. Her tail slithered to him, coiling itself around him; she lifted him with ease, her tail muscles flexing, squeezing, and wringing his body. She was constricting him, each breath he took, she squeezed.

They stared at the door of the skychamber, "So what do we do now?" Atreyu whispered. Lozen gave him a strange look, "Why are you whispering, no one is here other than the Gatekeepers and they are outside patrolling the temple walls!" she said aggravated. "Right, sorry", he said. She studied the door, she leaned her ear against it, then knocked, "Kofka! Kofka, hey boy! Its Lozen are you in there?" she said. "This is a waste of time, he isn't in there!" Lucian said. She ignored him and called to Kofka again knocking on the door, "Kofka, Adin's in trouble and we really need your help!". A bark came from the room, "Kofka!" she said overjoyed. Kofka appeared behind them and barked. "Kofka, come here boy!" she said. He went to her, expecting the customary scratch behind his ears, she obliged him, she touched her forehead to his, "Kofka, Adin is in trouble and we need Artorius' help! He's locked away in the Suratrat. There might be a way for him to get out with his First Knights medallion. Can you get it and take it to him?" she pleaded. Kofka barked and vanished within a few seconds he appeared with Artorius' First Knights medallion. "Good boy! Now get it to Artorius! Hurry Kofka!" she said. "Now what?" Persaeus said, "Now, we find a Gatekeeper, quick everyone!" she said pounding on the skychamber's door. "Did she just say a Gatekeeper?" Lucian said.

The sound of the soul stone stopping echoed in the abyss, Kofka stepped out cautiously, scanning for his old master. His mouth holding Artorius' necklace, he huffed into the darkness, the sound of his huff bounced off the unseen walls hidden away in the abyss. His nose caught his sent, he began trailing the sent until he found him down on both knees. Kofka sniffed around his old friend, nuzzling his hands and face trying to rouse him. "Kofka," Artorius' eyes said with his strength rapidly diminishing. Kofka whined for him to get up but the abyss had taken so much of his vitality. Kofka dropped the necklace from his mouth into his hands. Artorius struggled with the last of his strength to lift his hands over his head only to fall face first on the stone floor, depleting him of all his strength. Kofka began licking his face trying to keep him conscious, he moved around to his hands, still holding the necklace. He grabbed at the necklace with his teeth and pulled it free from his grasp. Then Kofka did something amazing, he placed the necklace around Artorius' head, pulling the necklace gently down with stunning precision. He sat waiting for the necklace to rejuvenate his friend. Artorius remained unconscious, Kofka barked, but still nothing. He whimpered crawling on all fours to Artorius, he began digging and pushing his muzzle under his body to roll him over causing the necklace to finally lay around his neck. Artorius' eyes burst in electric blue blazing light, he broke the magical hand restraints, and ripped out the magical mouth restraint. The shadow of the abyss seemed to flee in terror as the power of the last of the First Knights stood in its midst! Artorius rose up, he breathed a deep breath feeling the power radiate inside him. Kofka wasting no time jumped on him, Artorius ruffled his ears in praise, Kofka bowed his head. Artorius bowed his head to meet Kofka's, suddenly he saw the skychamber and heard Lozen's plea. "Thank you, my old friend!" he said before shattering through the tower wall, crashing through the ground to the surface, sending a ripple that was felt all the way to the village. Everything stopped for a brief moment, the dancing, music, and cheers. Everyone looked at each other perplexed, silence falling over the celebration. The members of the Council of Light looked to the temple, Elder Valerian and all the Regents knew something was wrong, "The temple!" he said ordering every Regent back. Artorius appeared at the skychamber just as Captain Pateon and his men were about to take Lozen, Atreyu, Lucian, and Persaeus into custody to be brought before Elder Valerian. "What in the name of the Sovereign are you doing here!" Pateon shrieked. The First Knights medallion glowed bright as the sun, suddenly his armor burst through door latching onto his chest, arms, and legs; he outstretched his arms. "I'd move if I were you", he said to Pateon right as his swords tore through the stone wall landing in his hands. The sight of him brought the whole garrison to their knees, "P-P-Please Lord Artorius...Captain; I was just doing my duty!" Pateon cried on his knees with both hands in a praying manner. "Where is he!" Artorius demanded, "He's in the Lamia cavern!" Lozen said. A titanic flap and he was gone knocking everyone backwards, dust and debris filled the air, "P-P-Pretty t-terrifying fellow, everyone to the citadel!" Pateon stammered trying to gather himself. A glimmer of gold shot through the sky with a blue lightning trail.

Valerian and all the Regents arrived at the citadel, "What has happened!" he said outraged. "Lord Artorius has escaped!" Pateon whined. "How? Impossible!" he said. "These rascals are to blame my Elder, they helped him!" he said pointing at the group. "If this is true, you will answer to the council!" Alina threatened. "Yes, Regent but you don't understand we had to do it! For Adin", Persaeus said. "Adin's been taken by a Lamia, she's going to kill him in the cavern!" Lozen screamed. "It is true Elder, we tried to find you all but couldn't so we did what we thought was right and helped Lord Artorius escape to save Adin!" Lucian said. "Endowed as a First Knight no less! Gather every Gatekeeper! Regents, arm yourselves! You four remain here! To the caverns now?" he stressed. "Are we going to battle my Elder?" Pateon trembled. "With a First Knight, one does not go to battle but to his death!" he asserted.

Artorius arrived at the mouth of the cavern, "Stop!" Valerian said with a force of fifty Gatekeepers and all five Regents. "Brother, we don't have time for this! Adin is in the very hands of death!" Artorius seethed. "Captain Pateon! You are the only legitimate authority here take your finest warriors and rescue the boy! The rest of you take Lord Artorius into custody", he commanded. "You heard him, move out!" Pateon said marching his men into the mouth of the cave, the rest circling around Artorius.

All the commotion could be heard down in the queen's room, "You hear that young Lion-Heart? That's the sound of your rescuers! Not to worry, I've thought of that! There is so much danger in a cavern like this!" Nyah cooed as she squeezed Adin tighter, laughing with each twist of her coils. The venom began to wear off on him, he could wiggle his toes and fingers. "Feels like my venom is wearing off on you! You got some life left in you still! I do love my meals fresh with some fight in them!" she hissed.

CHAPTER FOURTEEN

THE BOY WITH FIERY EYES

"Your kind chose to do those awful things! The Guardians were bringing justice!" Adin grunted. "You speak of justice! Your mother destroyed a mother in front of her only daughter and you speak of justice!" Nyah shrilled with such anger, her eyes blinked to their true form, yellow slit reptilian eyes. She slithered to the queen's room entrance with Adin in tow, she drew a metal flask with an emblem of feathered wings on it. She uncapped it, tilting its contents with one hand on the pad of her finger, she drew a line from the floor up along the threshold of then entry; re-dabbing her finger until she traced all the way around the entrance using her tail to reach the top. Adin could hear the clacking sounds of boot heels and the metal clanking of armor. "I suppose you think you will be rescued? Listen! They are but a breath away but I have such wonderful games for them!" she said.

Lozen, Atreyu, Lucian, and Persaeus appeared behind Artorius. "Go!" he said motioning with his head into the cavern. Lucian nodded his head, "Come on!" he said running inside the cavern. "I'm sorry Elder!" Artorius said drawing his swords, he jumped into the air summoning red lightning, his blade glowed red with red lightning wrapped around it. "Brace yourselves!" Valerian wailed, he knew this tactic and it was for multiple attackers with devastating effectiveness. He came down like a hurricane striking the ground with both swords causing lightning strikes to blast everyone off their feet. Valerian summoned an Eleloh shield spell, the shield absorbed some of the impact, he still was pushed backwards; his heels dragging into the ground. Lord Hylandir appeared, drawing his sword laying the spine in the crease of his elbow, "Evening Artorius!" he said. "Lord Hylandir, I would have thought you retired your sword by now!" he taunted. "You know us sword fighting immortals! Always running around believing there can be only one!" he said taunting back "I don't want to fight you Artorius!" he said dejected. "Then don't! I don't want to hurt you my old friend, my old teacher!" Artorius said hoping to discourage the building confrontation. "You know I can't let you go; you will have your day at court!" he said circling him. "So be it!" Artorius said. "Remember you wanted this brother!" Hylandir said summoning his eye blaze with a twirl of his sword into an attack position. Artorius had faced the sword master countless times when he was training at the temple, he was Hylandir's greatest student. Mastering the sword then the two-handed sword, he knew despite his First Knight power, Lord Hylandir could hold him off long enough for them to mount one coordinated attack. Artorius looked around, everyone's eyes were in full blaze, the Gatekeepers and Regents had encircled him closing the distance in and around him. "Now!" Valerian ordered, at once everyone swooped in on him! Artorius summoned his eye blaze. Spells were cast, arrows soared, swords swung, javelins flew, maces smashed; he fought them all. He repelled Hylandir and Alina away, "Hey I thought you were the only sword master that won 'the game'!" she said panting. "You know he is a First Knight Captain!" he said with sarcasm. They both looked at each other and charged back in.

Pateon's men descended halfway through the cavern, one stepped on a stone that sunk down, a tide of arrows fell upon them. His men kept walking through the unyielding tide of arrows striking them, "Foolish Lamia!" one said. "Doesn't this serpent know that Guardians are impermeable to such reckless attempts!" one boasted. Their decent slowed, Nyah knew the arrows would do nothing more than be a nagging annoyance to a Guardian but that wasn't her plan. Further down another stepped on a trap stone that sunk down, a massive multi ton rock from the ceiling fell, crashing into the walls, shredding more rock until a landslide of stone laid in front of them. "Cursed half snake abomination!" Pateon shouted at the top of his lungs. "Destroy the rock, I don't care if you have to use angel-fire!" he ordered. His men began conjuring fire spells to melt the rock and others began smashing it. "Captain, can we use star-fire?" one shouted up at him. He took a minute to think, "No! It may endanger the boy with that amount of power, it could collapse the whole cavern!" he said, the soldier nodded his head. The massive land slide of rock was finally cleared, they trekked faster through low ceiling, twisted pathways, until they came to a bridge connecting one land mass to another. One Gatekeeper stepped across, triggering an abyss of shadow to fall upon them leaving everything in a black void. "Blasted reptilian scum!" Pateon howled from the darkness. "No one move! The abyss will cause you to lose direction! I want everyone to summon the star-light charm!" he shouted. One by one each Gatekeeper had a halo of dim blue light crowned above their heads. "Deploy your wings, move in a wedge formation, 50-meter spread!" he ordered. "Now listen up lads! I want the flanks to get airborne, we need to know our depth! Everyone else move forward of the light in front of you, if anyone gets misdirected, we will come back for you!" he promised.

Artorius fought nonstop, as soon as he would knock someone away two more would be back at him from another direction. He took his battle to the air, knocking all who challenged back to the ground, he realized all this battling was in vain and he knew it was just a matter of time before someone was gravely injured or destroyed. He lifted both swords, pointing them to the sky above, "Imperimo-Astra", two long bolts of gold colored lightning struck his swords illuminating them.

"Take cover!" Valerian yelled at the top of his lungs. This was Heavens-Fire he was summoning! Heaven's Fire could be used to destroy a whole planet in full conjuration. Artorius swooped down, flailing his swords to the ground causing a massive blast of cosmic energy blasting everyone away. Those in the air were sent into the sides of mountains, some knocked all the way back to the temple, and some knocked into the village tumbling across roof tops. The Guardians on the ground were blown into tress and boulders, some were impressed in the ground several feet. From the air it looked like a mini nuclear blast, he conjured only enough to dispel his comrades, not hurt them. This gave him enough time to descend the cavern to rescue Adin if he wasn't already late, a streak of gold shot into the cavern.

Pateon along with his men emerged from the abyss, no one left behind, he may not be the most liked Captain but he knew how to lead and knew how to get his men to an objective. The queen's room entrance lay before him, he took a knee drawing his bow string back, the rest of his men collapsed around him drawing their bows. Pateon had Nyah in his sights, "Take her!" he commanded to his men, Nyah held Adin in front of her as a shield, "Ateh!" he said, his men lowering their bows to rush her. She recited the Enochian angel fire chant, "Fotia-Storum," behind a human shield, the entrance sparked to life in a wall of angel fire, engulfing the entrance in the inextinguishable flame. Pateon's men slammed into each other, unable to get past the fire. Angel-fire can only be extinguished by the Guardian's blood used to conjure it. "Find another way!" Pateon ordered, the force of his desperate yell can be heard at the cavern's entrance. His men began melting rock as fast as they could.

Lozen, Atreyu, Persaeus, and Lucian found Pateon and his men at the queen's room entrance, tearing through the rock face wall to get to the other side. "Angel fire!" Lozen said, they could see Adin helpless against the Lamia. "We are too late!" Lucian said. "Looks like we have an audience! They will get an unprecedented view of a Lamia's feeding habits! Nyah said unfolding her fangs, she lifted him up with her tail proclaiming, "Mother! This day your daughter avenges you!"". Her mouth began to open unnaturally wide; Adin didn't want to see her wicked twisted face, he couldn't believe his life would come to this end, the voice of the woman in white whispered in his ear, '*The fight is here, Lion-Heart*', feeling the medallion press into his chest. Nyah took great pleasure watching him cower as his final defeat, she delighted in her last opportunity to mock him before his death, "Your death won't be the end, after I've finished with you, I'll will take your precious friends! I leave you with that last thought my dear Lion-Heart!" she swore to him as she pulled him close. The threat of all his friends being eaten, ignited a deep fire within his heart. "I won't let you!" he said ripping open his eyes, they began to change color at he slowly lifted his head to face her. She shut her mouth, pulling him closer towards her, she recoiled frozen in fear; terrified by what she was witnessing. "What's this! It can't be!" she cried, her face in sheer terror. His eyes started to burn bright blue, the fear paralyzed her, running through her veins like venom. Never has she seen a human exhibit the trade mark eye blaze of a Guardian! "I won't let you take them!" he shouted, his eyes in full burn. She could feel him breaking free, raising his hands; forcing his arms out from between her coils. She was losing her suffocating grip, "How can this be! You're saturated with my venom and my Therian curse, enough to kill one hundred men!" she whimpered. Her panicked reptilian eyes quivered, her voice shrieking with every inch of control she was losing around his body. Her coils slipped off of him unable to contain him, the muscles in her reticulated tail strained at their max trying to keep her failing grip.   His arms and hands were free now, his hands glowed a reddish-blue. "I won't let you!" he shouted again striking her in the chest with both fists, a thermo-punch, sending her soaring backwards into the cavern wall. Her body slamming in the jagged rock crushed her vertebrate, her bones splintering and breaking; piercing her internal organs. Her upper body blackened, burnt to a crisp, sizzled with the smell of her burnt flesh. He stood over her, his eyes still burning bright blue, his glowing hands slowly started to fade to normal color. No life was in her, she was destroyed, his eyes slowly returned to normal, looking at her he felt sorry for her, sorry that her obsession for revenge led to her death but he wasn't about to let anyone hurt his friends. He turned to the burning entrance; every eye was upon him. He tried walking to the ring of fire, he felt his legs giving out, his strength drained. He collapsed to his knees, he needed help. Artorius wasted no time, he ran through the flames knowing he would be burnt to a cinder but not before he reached him. Just as his body gave way, falling face first, Artorius burst thorough the fire ring, sliding on his knees, he caught him just in time. Cradling his head to his shoulder, "I've got you my boy, I've got you", he said holding him tight. The sizzle of his armor from the angel-fire cooled. Adin was unconscious but safe, the angel-fire had done its worst on him with little effect. How the Lamia got a Guardian's blood would remain a mystery to be solved at another time, for now Adin's health was his utmost concern. Pateon's men were finally able to break through the layered rock. Lozen, Persaeus, Lucian, and Atreyu all rushed inside to their friend, relieved he was safe and the Lamia destroyed. Valerian entered the room followed by all the Regents, "I'm sorry brother", he said looking down at Adin. "Summon Lord Tadrian, Master Adin in injured as well as Captain Artorius!" he said to Pateon. "Let's get you to the infirmary!" Artorius said.

Outside the mouth of the cavern everyone gathered, "After, I take him to the infirmary, I surrender to you Elder", Artorius said. "I don't believe imprisoning an injured Captain or anyone is honorable at this time. You and Master Adin are in need of healing, stay with him until he awakes", he said placing his hand on his shoulder. "Can we stay with him too?" Atreyu said. "We?" Valerian said with one eyebrow lifted. "Yes Elder, all of us. You see Elder we are a team, all of us are his family", he said pointing to Lozen, Lucian, Persaeus, and Artorius. "I guess that kind of makes you like his almost real dad", Atreyu said to Artorius not sure how to say he is a father figure to Adin. "Very well. Captain Pateon seal the entrance to these caverns!" Valerian ordered. A week passed; Adin awoke on the day of Artorius' trial. "Good morning mighty serpent slayer!" he said. "How are you feeling?" Lozen said. "I feel like Kofka weighs a ton!" he said sending everyone into a chuckle. "I'm glad your awake, I wanted you to have this before I left", he said grabbing Adin's hand placing a balled-up necklace in his palm. Adin looked it over, it was his Spirit-Wolf medallion. "What, why?" he said confused. "Today's my trial, I don't know what will be decided, what my fate will be. No matter what, it does my heart good to know it's in a Lion-Heart's safe keeping, he said standing up. "I'll go with you!" Adin pleaded. He smiled down at him, "You've been asleep for almost a week; you need to rest. Elder Valerian and Regent Alina will take very good care of you!" he said giving Adin a hug, "I promised your mother I would always watch over you, I hope I have fulfilled my promise to her!" he said, looking to the group. "Thank you! You will all make extraordinary Guardians, I'm sure of it!" he said shaking each of their hands. "Ahem! Pardon me Captain, its time," Pateon said standing with his prisoner escort. Artorius nodded his head, and walked to his prisoner escort, he outstretched his hands to be restrained. "No, need for that Captain", Pateon said. Before being escorted to the High Court, Artorius turned to face Adin, "The ones we love are always here", he said placing his hand on his heart.

The sky mountain was home to the High Court where the members of the council known as Law Lords, resided, governing the affairs of all the realms. It is also where the most serious of crimes were judged and sentenced. The mountain's height reached beyond the clouds, lending to its appropriate name. Artorius peered out at the sea of white fluffy clouds awaiting his appointed time. "I was wrong about you, all the things I've heard, nothing could be further from the truth! What you did for the boy proved you're not a coward or a sluggard" Pateon said. "No need to apologize Captain", he said. "Captain Pateon, Sir! They are ready for him!" a guard called out. "Good luck Captain", Pateon said to Artorius. "Thank you, Captain!" he said shaking his hand. Artorius was marched under heavy guard to the High Court to Judgement Flat. In front of him was a semicircle table with five members of the High Court. The Law Lords: Cein, Joran, Uvon, and Despa sat to the left and right of the table, in the middle was The Guardian Chieftain, Puriel. The court spectators sat behind the council in stadium styled seating. "Is the accused prepared for judgement?" Puriel said. "I am Chieftain", he said. "The charges before you are of celestial violations, the forbidden use of a First Knight's medallion, conspiracy to assassinate the Temple Elder, escape from the Temple Suratrat, the forceful attack on the temple's Regent class, and the forceful attack on the temple's Gatekeepers", she thundered. The sounds from the court spectators were mixed, among them were Artemis, Finnobar, and Davalin. "How does thoust plead?" she said.

"Not guilty my Chieftain!" Adin said, the spectator's voices erupted with oohs and gasps. "Who is this fledgling", she demanded. "Forgive me Chieftain, I am Adin Elijah of the Lion-Heart and I have come to share in my Lord Artorius' fate!" he said. "We all have!" Atreyu said with Lucian, Persaeus, and Lozen by his side. Puriel sat back to consult with her fellow Law Lords, "We shall hear your testament!" she said. "My Chieftain, I am the son of Tessla of the First Knights Order. I was brought here as my inheritable right like my mother before me. A plot was discovered soon after I arrived in which, I was cursed by a Lamia, my body could not evolve to its Guardian state. During this time, I suffered greatly and was detained in the tower of chains for violating temple laws", he said hoping to sway their judgement. "I'm well aware of your temple violations?" she said tapping a scroll she had next to her. "I used my mother's First Knights necklace to gain access to Regent Alina's quarters in search of a scroll that contained the chant for 'the sight'. One of my order mates saw an anomaly during a training evolution", Adin said looking to Lozen. "You are referring to the thunder-struck?" she said. Adin nodded yes, "Whom was this order mate?" she asked. "It was me Chieftain!" Lozen said. "What was seen?" Puriel said to Adin. "I saw myself with eye blaze my Chieftain," he said. The spectators gasping became increasing louder, "Do you have a witness that can collaborate this", Cein said. Regent Alina raised her hand, "I can, I used 'the sight' on Lady Lozen. It is as Master Adin says", she said. "Go on", Uvon said to Adin. "For my violation, I was sent to the Suratrat, Lord Artorius took all the blame and I was freed. Shortly after I was abducted by the Lamia during the village Winter Solstice, Lord Artorius escaped to save me", he said looking to Artorius. "How did Lord Artorius come about the forbidden First Knights armor?" Joran said. "That was us, Sir", Lucian said. "We just thought what we did was right to save a life", Persaeus said. "You see, we are all family and he's like his dad", Atreyu said pointing to Artorius. "If there is any punishment that must be dealt, let it be against me. I am the reason all this happened", Adin said to the council. The council deliberated amongst themselves for a short period.

"Your history as a First Knight Lord Artorius is not an honorable one, once again we find you disobeying our laws. You broke temple laws to save a boy, a boy whom has demonstrated extraordinary apt to break temple laws as yourself. I can only surmise that these willful law violations were for a purpose much greater than yourself, to save a boy, a human boy trying to manage in a realm that was not made for his kind. The council has unanimously declared you free of all charges!" she said, the crowd roared in delight. "Defeating a Lamian princess is no easy feat for a young Lion-Heart", she said. "It was going to hurt my family", he said looking to Artorius and his order mates. "Surviving in this realm as a human is no small feat as well, truly remarkable", she said looking to her left then to her right at each Law Lord. They all nodded their heads, "Elder Valerian, prepare this young Lion-Heart for his wings!" she commanded. Valerian presented Adin before the council, all the Regents stood behind him at attention, Artorius to his right and his order mates his left. Puriel stood up from her seat prompting the rest of the Law Lords to do the same. "Kneel!" she commanded, she and the rest of the Law Lords drew their swords, "By the power entrusted to me by the Sovereign, Adin Elijah of the Lion-Heart you are hereby awarded your wings in accordance with 'The great feats of heroes' scroll", she said placing her sword on his head, the Law Lords placed two swords on his shoulders and two on his either side of his arm, the gleam of the sun on their blades left him looking like he was silhouetted in light. "Arise, Adin Elijah for your wings are bound to you for all time until death or passage. Good luck as you earn your place as a member of the 'Thin Gold Line'", she said.   Adin stood spreading his wings, everyone burst into cheers; clapping as hard as they could. He looked over the span of his wings, they were eggshell white with golden-red tips. A deep sense of pride swelled in him. "You can stop staring Sis, it's getting a little uncomfortable", Atreyu whispered in Lozen's ear making her blush instantly. Valerian walked over to Artorius, "Sorry about the tower brother", Artorius said. "It was old anyway, plus I think we can find better use for it or we could always use your quarters", he said unable to contain his laughter. "My quarters?" he said with a raised eyebrow. "Yes, your quarters, the skychamber is now your permanent quarters", he said. Artorius laughed, "Very well, I submit to good counsel!" "So, what do you want to do?" Atreyu said to Adin and the group. "For starters, let's get an oreo heaven!" Adin said. "Well, what are we waiting for?" Atreyu said. "I'll meet you there!" Adin said, spreading his wings, you guys try to keep up!" he said, diving off the edge of Judgement Flat, with one flap he was gone. "You know he's going to be doing that all year!" Atreyu said chuckling to the rest of the group, they all just shook their heads.

A knock on the door, "Come in," Lord Tadrian said. "Evening my Lord, we have come to turn over the sheets", two temple stewards said. "Of course, please come in. I will be taking my leave, please lock up after, I'm sure I will be receiving no patients with formidable injuries for the remainder of the year", he said. "Yes, my Lord", the stewards said bowing. The pontifex announced, "Lord Tadrian, Fair-Lady Artemis wishes to speak with you". "Yes, put her through please to my private quarters", he said. "My Lord, forgive the lateness of my calling but I'm afraid I have news that would have benefited you much earlier", she said. "Yes, go on", he said. "Your inquiry into the village questioning starbrew vendors had me thinking. My fairies usually have vendors they work with exclusively for our needs, namely food and drink. When Lord Artorius and Master Adin arrived here, I held a dinner in their honor. I dismissed my fairies and purchased from vendors we do not normally do business with, one in particular that claimed to have the 'best starbrew'. As I am sure everyone is aware by now of the sinister plot the Lamian princess put into motion was perpetuated by my hand. You see, I purchased the starbrew from her that was given to Master Adin when he and Artorius came to dinner", she said remorseful. "I see, well that is of no consequence now thank goodness, have you spoken about this to anyone else?" he asked. "No, my Lord. May I ask why you ask?" she said concerned. "I would let old things die as they were, such as this, you see your sprawling business enterprise may come under scrutiny if this information were to fall on ears less understanding than myself", he said. "I see my Lord, will that be all", she said hastened. "Yes, my Fair-Lady", he said smirking.

The defeat of Nyah, the Lamian Princess and the cavern sealed by tons of rock posed no more shadowy threat to village. Adin's archeus burned out the Lamia curse in his body, giving him a small glimpse of the power, he had within all along. His destiny is slowly unfolding, he has suffered, he has made friends, he has found a mentor, and he has found purpose. All these things he will need in the coming year, his destiny is not one that can be taken lightly, his destiny is one that will change the balance of all the realms. How the journey of his destiny will shape his heart has yet to be seen.

The Hehleon realm holds all the defeated evil and death in one place, no light is ever upon it, it was created to house the sinister plague that once ravaged the realms. A cloaked figure limped cautiously through the darkness; lighting cracked overhead in the gray dreary sky. The landscape is filled with dead rotted trees, streams of black water, and burnt ash as soil. Howls of supernatural ferocious beasts pierce the air, the shadow of dark phantoms stalking; running from shadow to shadow, the growling of monstrous creatures warns of an agonizing death. The cloaked figure stood before the Hill of Evil, a monstrous mountain of black jagged rock, with only one good arm, it carefully scaled down into the black mist in search of the ruins to the Temple of Sedah. It wheezed with each step, its skin was burnt and cracked, each twitch of its muscles sent currents of pain throughout its body. Down the broken stone stairs, it crept until it came to the entrance carved out of the mountain, a large boulder blocked the entry. Its eyes flared a faint red, rolling red lightning in its hands until a ball of unstable energy is formed. It flung the energy ball at the stone boulder incinerating it on impact, dust

and debris shot in all directions, crumbling rock debris fell, the cloaked figure was knocked backwards. It scampered to its knees, heaving with exhaustion, gazing at the entry's inscription −*The Forsaken Dragon*, is revealed; the cloaked figure recited the chant in a raspy choking voice,
"Awaken He, ole Lord of Night.
Awaken He, with dragon's might.
Awaken He the darkest knight.
Awaken He who slays the light!".

      The inscription glowed a pale-white, it unlocked, the cloaked figure pushed the door open with all its strength; stepping inside the shadow of an abyss. Within the abyss, appeared a ring of angel fire surrounding a tall stone sarcophagus, a fiery prison. The cloaked figure removed a flask from under its dingy black tattered cloak, emptying its contents all the way around the angel fire. The angel fire flickered, then slowly extinguished. It placed its claw-like hand upon the lid caressing the curves, shapes, and recesses of an engraved dragon. With one single push, it sent the lid sliding off, the sounds of the lid breaking apart as it struck the floor echoed all around; the sides of the sarcophagus fell away with deafening thuds. Inside the sarcophagus lay a body wrapped in dragon wings. The lifeless body lay supported by the wing tips, suspended in midair meditation. Its face was covered except for its eyes, the cloaked figure whispered, "He is here, my Lord!" suddenly its eyes flung open in pale glowing ivory-white light! The cloaked figure knelt in a genuflection pose, screeching with delight, extending its damaged half torn bat wings.